# DARK MOON OVER BROOKLYN

M. J. Van Buren

**Kaw Valley Spring**

*To Lynn, my sine qua non, always*

# CHAPTER 1

Kitty Toulkes woke with a start. After a moment's confusion, she realized the hammering she heard was not the dwarves at the forge but someone (probably not a dwarf) at her apartment door. Shaking off the dream, she stepped into her slippers and stiffly made her way to the door.

"Who's there?" she asked, trying to peer through the peephole.

"It's me! Gretchen from across the hall! Open the door! Please!" A soprano voice ended with a wail.

Kitty flipped the bolt and opened the gray-painted steel door.

"Have you seen Annie?" The face surrounded by strawberry blonde ringlets looked strained. "She's gone!"

"No, I haven't seen her for a day or so. What do you mean 'gone'?"

"I mean, she left, with that...man! Yesterday sometime. She didn't come home. She isn't home! He's not a safe person. I'm so worried." Clutching her pink-flowered wrap, Gretchen started forward, stumbled, and fell against Kitty. "I'm so scared!"

Staggering backward—more with surprise than with the weight of the slender woman she was now holding up—Kitty tried to calm her neighbor. "I'm sure she's okay. Probably they just went somewhere and she forgot the time, forgot to let you know, something like that. She'll be back any time now."

"You don't know Annie. She's meticulous about things like that. She doesn't just go off. This guy has her under some kind of spell. Did you know he was her boyfriend in college? That's bad enough. And to show up after all these decades? There's something wrong, I know it!" Gretchen backed away, tears welling up, her pretty face quivering.

"Here, sit down." Kitty led her across the floor of the open loft to a chair by a small oak drop-leaf table. "Let me get you something to drink—and here are the tissues.

"I'll fix you a cup of tea, okay?" Kitty hefted the electric kettle on the kitchen counter to be sure it had water and flipped the switch. "And you can tell me why you think something is wrong." *Other than, your girlfriend has been off overnight with her old beau.*

"Well, to start with, she's been weird ever since he showed up. She gets all moony-eyed when he talks. And it's like I'm not even there. When I came home Monday night and he was there...well, she'd told me he was coming—he called her up in the middle of the night!—anyway, when I came in, she introduced him: 'This is Donald Forthright,' and that was it! No small talk to put me at ease with him, no explanation beyond what she'd already told me. Just, 'This is Donald Forthright,' and then they went back to talking as if I wasn't even in the room!"

"Will you have regular tea? Or some chamomile?" Kitty wanted to hear more, but Gretchen was so keyed up, it seemed useful to try to introduce a different subject. Kitty set out two brightly-glazed porcelain mugs. "These are my brother's cups. He's a potter. In Santa Fe."

Even to Kitty, this sounded like a clunky *non sequitur*, but it did take Gretchen's attention briefly away from her distress. "They're lovely," she said, lifting one of the brown and green cups. "Does he do this professionally?"

"Yes, he's been doing ceramics for, I guess, close to 40 years. I feel lucky to have so much of his stuff."

Gretchen sat silent, chewing her lower lip.

"Chamomile?" Kitty held up the box.

"Ok, sure. Thanks." Gretchen wiped her eyes. "You have to help me. Should I call the police?"

"You could, I guess," Kitty ventured. "But maybe you should wait a little while. Surely she'll be coming back real soon, and it could be awkward if you've gotten the police all worked up for nothing."

"But it's not like her!" Gretchen was adamant. "She never goes off without telling me, at least how long she expects to be gone. And usually she texts me every few hours when she's away. I've texted her I don't know how many times. Her phone is off, I just know it. Maybe he's killed her. Or kidnapped her. Or...." She broke off, put her hands over her face, and wailed.

Kitty poured the tea.

# CHAPTER 2

Oddly enough, Kitty had already heard about the 2:00 a.m. phone call. On the previous Sunday afternoon, she and Annie had both been waiting at the bus stop in front of the seven-story red-brick warehouse-turned-apartment building everyone fondly called The Cocoa Factory.

"I would have hung up," Annie had said, without preamble. Kitty might have thought the squarely-built woman with short-cropped gray hair was talking to herself, except she glanced Kitty's way as she continued: "Probably should have hung up. He must have been drunk, calling like that at two o'clock. But Goddess help me, I recognized his voice after all these years!" She paused, seeming to expect a response.

"At two in the morning?" Kitty shook her head sympathetically. "It's a wonder you could even understand anything he said, much less recognize his voice. That's an awful time to be woken up."

"Tell me about it!" Annie stared up at the still bright September sky and frowned. "He said he'd explain when he came by."

"So he's actually coming here?" Kitty had asked, curiosity aroused in spite of herself.

"He said he would. Tomorrow. I don't know when, exactly. I gave him my cell number."

"Did you tell Gretchen?"

"That he's coming, not that he's an old boyfriend. She'd freak out. That was a long, long time ago, anyway."

"What's his name, did you say?"

"Dan. Daniel Oponuno. He's from Hawaii. Back when being born in Hawaii wasn't political."

"Is he good-looking?" Kitty wondered aloud.

"Well, he was then. Why? Are you interested?"

"Always interested," Kitty said, lifting one shoulder.

"Well, I can't say for sure you're welcome to him." Annie smiled coyly. "I'll have to let you know."

"Did he say what he had been doing?"

"No. He had to be drunk, calling at that time of night. He said he needed a place to stay. He was drunk, I'm sure." Annie raised her eyebrows, shrugged, and then sighed heavily. "He may not even show up. I'll probably be sorry if he does."

"He's going to stay with you?" Kitty was astonished.

"I said he could. I'm almost sorry already, but you know—well, I've always wondered. What might have happened, what he did after, you know."

"Where are you going to put him?"

"On the couch. It isn't too bad to sleep on."

"So he's not very tall?" Kitty looked quizzically at the other woman.

"Hmm! Well, he'll just have to cope. I remember him as being tall."

\*\*\*

That had been Sunday, and Kitty hadn't had any real conversation with Annie since. In point of fact, it was unusual to have had any real conversation with her at all. Gretchen was right; Kitty didn't really know Annie. Most of their interactions had been limited to brief exchanges in the elevator, about the weather or someone's pet dog. They had certainly never before gotten to the point of sharing personal life or feelings, so Kitty surmised Annie must have been more agitated about the situation than she was willing to admit.

And Kitty had also seen the man in question. Monday evening, arriving home after her 6-hour shift at the City Tech counseling center, she'd stopped at the Food Friend on the corner to pick up some roasted cauliflower and a couple of chicken fingers from the deli. As she was paying at the small front counter of the natural food store, she had seen Annie come in with a tall, mocha-skinned man. Good-looking, I guess so! Slightly grey at the temples, but with a face mostly unlined. Big guy, but muscular, not fat. He has to be over 60, if he's Annie's age, she thought. Not bad for a near-geezer!

Making a point of going out the front way, Kitty had caught Annie's eye and smiled broadly. She'd have to introduce him.

But Annie hadn't. A curt nod of acknowledgement was all Kitty got.

Later—it must have been Tuesday morning—Kitty had seen the two again, very briefly, in the elevator. That time, she had gotten an introduction, but only first names, and no more.

***

Now, thinking over what she knew, she recognized an anomaly. She was sure Annie had originally mentioned a Hawaiian surname. And the name Gretchen had just used was definitely European, even British-sounding.

"What did you say this fellow's name was?" she asked Gretchen, as the latter delicately sipped her tea.

"Don. Donald Forthright, or Four-something," Gretchen said. "It didn't really register with me.

"Hey, Kitty, I'm really sorry for busting in on you like this," she continued after a brief pause. "But I'm really freaking! I assumed she would come home overnight, and when I woke up and she wasn't there...."

"It's okay," Kitty said soothingly. "I'm sure everything's okay, but I understand how upsetting it must be for you." She paused, then continued. "So what do you want to do now?"

"Can I just sit here awhile? You go ahead and do whatever you need to do. I just don't want to go back to 5F right away."

"Sure. It's fine." Kitty looked down at her blue cotton nightgown, cocking her head and frowning in mock disapproval. "I suppose I should probably get dressed."

"What time is it?" Gretchen asked.

Kitty glanced at the digital readout on the microwave. "6:35. Do you have to go in to work today?"

"I think I have to. I'll have to get going soon, but if I'm a little late it won't be the end of the world. I wonder, is there any way you can let me know if Annie comes home?" Gretchen started bravely. And then, "Oh, I don't see how I can leave, not knowing if she is okay. I'll call in sick. I'll...I don't know what I'll do." And she began to cry in earnest—deep, choking sobs.

Kitty pulled a second oak chair out from the table and sat with a silent sigh and a grimace. What could she say? She reached for Gretchen's hand and squeezed it gently. "It's okay, it's going to be okay," she murmured. "Just let it come. You'll feel better."

After a few moments, when it seemed the sobs were unlikely to subside quickly, she scooted her chair closer and awkwardly tried to put an arm around the other woman. Gretchen turned and threw herself into Kitty's arms, leaning into Kitty's shoulder. Her crying became even more dramatic before gradually subsiding.

Finally, she raised her head. Kitty lifted one arm from Gretchen's shoulder and offered her a tissue, patting the other shoulder in what she hoped was a soothing but not patronizing manner. "Want another cup of tea?"

"No, thanks. I'm okay now." Gretchen straightened. "I'll go to work and hope I hear from her soon. Thank you. I'm sorry, I'm afraid I've soaked your nightgown." She tried to smile.

"No problem," said Kitty, feeling the fabric on her shoulder, which was, actually, quite damp. "Okay, you go on to work, and let me know when you hear from Annie. Or if I see her here first, I'll call you. If you want me to, that is."

"Oh, yes, for sure. Please! Here, I'll give you my number." Gretchen took the notepad and pen Kitty proffered and wrote down her number. She stood, and then waited while Kitty wrote her own number on the bottom of the page and tore it off. She started toward the door, then stopped. "And, Kitty, thank you so much for listening. I'm sorry I'm such a mess. But Annie and I have been so happy." She paused, then turned back to the door and left, closing it softly behind her.

Kitty sat down, looking blankly at the notepad with Gretchen's neat printing. "Whew!" She took a deep breath and blew it out again. Then she got up, and retrieved her mobile from her bedside to enter the number. I could go back to bed, she thought. But that would be pointless after all this. Better to just go ahead and get dressed and start the day.

She walked back into the bedroom, which, other than the bathroom, was the only actual room-with-a-door in her loft apartment, converted like the rest of the building from warehousing to manufacturing and finally into living space. Heading for the closet, she caught a glimpse of herself in the mirror, and sighed. The nightgown was a little too form-fitting for her liking, showing every bulge and sag of her 70-year-old form. Not that she was altogether unhappy with her looks. She knew she looked better than many her age, mostly due to good genes. Even though her face looked more like her Swedish grandmother's every day, it was relatively unwrinkled. And her hair, like her dad's before he died, was still more brown than silver. Getting old was no treat, but as everybody said, better than the alternative.

# CHAPTER 3

Later that day, Kitty waited for the 62B bus to take her to City Tech in downtown Brooklyn. When the bus arrived, a few minutes late as usual, she stepped on board, dipped her senior discount METROcard, and lurched into the disabled seating nearest the door as the bus took off with a jerk into the traffic. If someone got on who was disabled or truly elderly, she'd have to move, she knew. She glanced down the aisle to be sure there were seats available, just in case.

The bus stopped next in front of a smoke shop plastered with gaudy posters. A slim dark-skinned young man got on, followed by a frail-looking man with a few days growth of white beard. Kitty rose and moved several rows back to an empty seat on the side away from the six elevated lanes of the Brooklyn-Queens Expressway that shadowed Park Avenue. "That's Park Ave, Brooklyn," you had to always tell the cab driver. "Not Park Ave, Manhattan."

When the bus turned away from the BQE to follow the edge of the old Brooklyn Navy Yard, Kitty thought for the hundredth time how sad it was that nobody had succeeded in saving the beautiful and historic officers' row. The house next to the fence had been taken down over the summer. Of course, that one was long since way past saving, with trees growing through the roof. Yet, it did seem sad.

At the next stop, by the Navy Yard's historic front gate with its pair of brick and white marble gatehouses, several young people who were probably City Tech students got on, as well as an Asian grandma with a preschooler in tow. Kitty always wondered where her fellow passengers were going. It was a safe bet most on this bus were headed to the Jay Street-MetroTech subway station. But where after that? Manhattan, of course, on any one of several trains, but also other points in Brooklyn. Or Queens, if you took the 62 in the other direction. You could go anywhere in the world from here.

As she rode, Kitty considered the curious situation her neighbors had going. Gretchen was frantic with worry. And it seemed Annie was acting at least uncharacteristically, if not erratically. Annie had always seemed very private, not given to personal revelations. Yet on Sunday she had chattered on about this old boyfriend as though she and Kitty were intimate friends.

And even allowing for understandable jealousy on Gretchen's part, Annie's failure to check in was apparently extremely unusual. Well, there was nothing she could do about any of it, Kitty decided. So might as well not dwell on the subject.

At the next stop, a broad-hipped young woman with bronze skin and improbably apple-red hair squeezed into the seat next to Kitty. Across from them a wrinkled grandmother in white blouse and slim blue skirt tried unsuccessfully to get her grandson to stop kicking the seatback in front of him, while a tall man with skin the color of dark chocolate stood near the front of the bus, dignified in a suit and tie, swaying with the movement of the bus.

A Hasidic man with ringlets and hat got on at the next stop, as did a tired-looking white guy with pointed black beard, dressed in wrinkled khakis.

Noting the usual variety of colors and ethnicities of the New Yorkers getting on and off the bus, Kitty wondered idly whether Annie's friend was one of those rare "pure" Hawaiians. He could be, she supposed. She didn't know precisely what the typical Hawaiian looked like, though she thought this Don had actually looked more African than Pacific Islander. Maybe he was a mixture, like most Americans. We are a mongrel nation, she reminded herself, cousins of everyone in the world. Of all the countries that should not be having racial problems, we would surely qualify. Her own family heritage, albeit only from Europe so far as she knew, was made up of at least four different nationalities, each coming to the New World at a different time.

When Kitty got out at the Jay Street-MetroTech stop, a group of Asian teenagers, laughing together, came rambling up from the subway. It was clear they were all as American as could be.

Kitty crossed the street and popped into the Starbucks. "A large soy latte," she told the barista. She'd at least be caffeinated enough to get through her office hours this afternoon. Heading back up the street, she worked to recall the face of this Don Whatever-His-Name-Is. Now that she considered it, "whatever his name is" remained an open question. She was sure Annie had called him Opu-something, because it had reminded her at the time of Opus in Bloom County.

He was brownish, but not really dark. He'd look strikingly exotic in any American setting other than New York City—or Hawaii, of course. Close-cropped hair, dark eyes, broad shoulders. And tall, certainly over 6'. For someone at least in his mid-60's or even early 70's, which he must be, Annie's mystery man carried himself like an athlete who had not let himself get out of shape.

Holding her coffee, Kitty walked up Jay Street and crossed the street at the light. In front of the banners reading "New York City College of Technology," she dodged a pair of students studying each other's faces so intensely as to be oblivious to what was going on around them. Arriving at the front doors of 300 Jay Street, Namm Hall, she deliberately closed her mental book on the Annie questions and turned her thoughts to work.

The glassed-in entry hall was full of sound and hurry, with uniformed guards checking ID's of students and faculty as fast as they could. Ages of the students varied from 18 to 78, Kitty figured, with modes at around 23 and 38, if she recalled the stats correctly. City Tech students, apart from those coming fresh from high school, tended to be trying college as a way to progress in a current career or as a step toward midlife career change. Either way, they were mostly intensely focused on how their course work could help them get ahead.

Once through the security check-in, Kitty made her way

against the tide of students headed toward the exit. Once she reached the Counseling Services Center, she wound her way through the reception area crowded with mostly young people, studying at desks, or sprawled in chairs around the perimeter as they waited to see one of the counselors on duty. Her office was half-way down a narrow, institutional-beige hallway. She unlocked the door and caught a pale blue envelope stuck between door and frame before it fell—all without dropping her latte.

The old Army-green metal desk facing the door was flanked by two metal filing cabinets, both securely locked. Setting the coffee on her desk, Kitty unlocked the left cabinet, and then flipped on the desktop computer. Her waist pack went into the bottom drawer of the desk. When the computer came up, she quickly checked her schedule to see what Alicia, the receptionist and all-around good gal, had in store for her.

Four appointments, each in its own fifty-minute slot. None of the student names seemed familiar, but Kitty consulted her paper files just to confirm that they were all new clients. This time of year, that was quite typical. And the issues they were dealing with could be anything at all, from an unexpected pregnancy to a course that really was or at least was perceived to be "too effing hard" for a student's limited background knowledge.

The first client wasn't due for about ten minutes, and the envelope turned out to contain merely a message from a colleague about an upcoming office social event. So after laying out fresh file folders, Kitty sat down to do a little relaxation breathing. By the time a young man appeared at her door, yellow "Initial Interview" form in hand, she was feeling relaxed and focused, ready to give the client her full attention.

# CHAPTER 4

In the bus on the way home that evening, Kitty heard her phone tinkle. It was a text from Gretchen: "Pls come over as soon as u get home."

Kitty dumped her purse in 5G, relocked the door, and stepped across the narrow hall to knock on her neighbors' door.

Gretchen opened the door at once and motioned Kitty inside. "Oh, Kitty! I'm so glad you're here!" she said. "I'm worried sick. I've called Joe, Annie's ex-husband, and he'll be along any minute. I'm hoping he might have some idea where she could have gone. And I think he knew this guy in college, too." She paused for a breath and then rushed on. "Can I fix you a drink? Or a beer?"

"I'll take just a glass of water," Kitty said. And then the doorbell rang.

"That will be Joe. Would you get it?" Gretchen said from the kitchen, which had an extra wall, making it a little more separate from the living room than in Kitty's place.

Kitty opened the door. A tall balding man in blue jeans looked quizzically at Kitty. "Joe?" she asked. As he started to nod, she hurried to add, "I'm Kitty, the neighbor from across the hall."

"Joe Treacher." His voice was deep and the handshake he offered was firm but not painfully so. Kitty thought he looked a little like a taller Bruce Willis.

"Come on in, Joe," called Gretchen from the kitchen. "Can I get you a beer?"

"Not right now, Gretchen. Thanks."

"Joe was telling me he knows this Don fellow, from when they were all in college together," Gretchen said, coming back into the living room space with a glass of ice water in one hand and a Heineken in the other. "I think he's scary. What can you tell us about him, Joe?" She handed the water to Kitty and snapped the top on the beer. "Have a seat, both of you." She gestured toward the dark brown corduroy-upholstered couch, but didn't sit down herself.

"I played football with him." Joe sat forward on the edge of the sofa, his hands on his thighs. "Didn't really know him well, but he didn't have a very good rep with the other players. I mean, as a person. He was a helluva tight end."

"What do you mean he 'didn't have a good rep'?" Kitty asked.

"Generally speaking, people didn't trust him. He was a swinger with the ladies. A real charmer, evidently, and he'd have several girls on the string at once. He almost got beat up once in the locker room after he'd tried his moves on the first-string Center's girlfriend."

"Were you and Annie dating at that time?" Kitty sat down at the other end of the sofa and took a sip of water.

"We were friends." Joe glanced up and away from Gretchen. "Good friends was all."

"Look, Joe. Here's what's happening," Gretchen said. "Annie has gone somewhere, presumably with this Don Whoever."

"His name was Dan back then. Daniel Oponuno, if I remember correctly."

"Well, whatever his name is. I think he's taken Annie somewhere, and goodness knows whether he's bewitched her or worse."

"Strange word choice—'be-witched.'" Joe's lip twisted wryly.

"You didn't see her, Joe. She was like a different person when he was here. Attention all glued to him, and completely ignoring me, as though I wasn't even here. I'm scared!"

"I think anything you can tell Gretchen that might give her reason not to worry would be helpful," said Kitty, turning toward Joe. "This guy was probably a good-looking football hero, who had all the girls in a tizzy back then. But now...well, is there any reason to think he'd be dangerous?"

"Can't really say. He wasn't square with the women back then. That's what the other guys thought. He'd be dating girls from different dorms, and each one seemed to think she was Number One." Joe frowned. "Gretchen, did you hear anything that would have suggested he was trying to get something from Annie? Money, or some kind of business deal?"

"No, they were mostly talking about old times when I was in the room. Once, I came in from the kitchen, and whatever they were saying, they shut up suddenly. So, no, I didn't hear anything."

Gretchen set her beer on a table that looked genuinely old and battered, rather than stylishly distressed, then walked to the coat closet and took out a turquoise hoodie, which she pulled on over her emerald green v-neck tee. "Will you both have a bite to eat so we can talk some more? I'll run down to the store and pick up something. Some sliced ham and salad, if that's okay," she went on without waiting for an answer.

"Sure," Kitty said, "but you don't really have to feed me."

"No, I want you here. We need to figure out what to do."

"I'm fine with whatever you bring," Joe said. "We'll stay here, in case Annie comes home."

As soon as Gretchen was out the door, Joe turned to Kitty. "I don't know how well you know Annie and Gretchen," he said.

"Annie hardly at all," Kitty acknowledged. "Gretchen and I talk sometimes in the elevator, or we've had coffee downstairs at the Food Friend a couple of times. I wouldn't say we were close friends, but I like Gretchen."

"Well, somebody else probably needs to know the 'rest of the story' before I get very involved in any expanded hunt. I don't want to tell this to Gretchen unless it becomes relevant. I think it would be painful to her." Joe laid a big hand on his chest. He lowered his chin, sighing heavily.

"Annie and I were, as I said, very good friends at college. I would have called her my girlfriend, except that I knew she was dating other men, including Daniel. This was when we were seniors. One night she called me and said she had to see me. I came over to the dorm and picked her up. We drove around and she told me she was pregnant."

"By...?" Kitty couldn't stop herself.

"Not by me, for sure," Joe said, smiling. "No, by Daniel, though I got the impression she couldn't be absolutely certain. She hadn't told anyone else. She was sure she wanted an abortion, which was totally illegal in Missouri at the time. So, long story short, I drove her to Colorado, two states away, where you could get an abortion with two doctors' signatures. We got one doc to sign off, but couldn't get a second.

"I thought she was going to go ahead and have the baby. I wanted to marry her. We'd pretend it was mine, I thought. But she didn't want a baby, and she didn't want to marry me. She wanted a life with Dan. I tried to warn her that wasn't in the cards, but she went ahead and talked to him. He must have let her down gently, because she was never angry with him afterward. Just desperate."

"So... you went ahead and got married?" Kitty was having trouble taking it all in.

"Not right then. That came later. You're old enough to know about coat hangers?"

Kitty nodded, holding her breath.

"Well, one night, a few days after we got back from our useless trip, Annie used a coat hanger. Her roommate and I took her to the hospital. She almost died. The baby had certainly been Daniel's. When she had to drop out of school, I left, too. I wanted to be near her, but she wouldn't have me then, so I went into the Army and eventually went to Vietnam."

"And Dan. Or Don?"

"I never saw or heard of him again. And as far as I know, neither did Annie. He was a couple of years younger than us. I always supposed he graduated with his class, but where he went from there I have no idea."

"Nor, probably, did you want to ever see him again, right?" Kitty said.

Just then they heard Gretchen at the door. Joe put his finger to his lips in warning, and Kitty nodded her acceptance of his wish for discretion.

# CHAPTER 5

Gretchen spread the food she had bought on the heavy old-fashioned table. "Please help yourselves," she said, setting a carton of Newman's Own Pink Lemonade on a pad in the middle of the table.

"Can I help with anything?" Kitty asked belatedly.

"No, just bring your glass, if you want to." Gretchen set two more glasses out from the small sideboard. "Want that beer now, Joe?" she asked.

"Sure," Joe said. He came to the table, and began spreading brown mustard on a slice of rye. "Looks like good ham," he said.

"They have a good deli downstairs," Kitty commented. "Except for the fish. Don't order the cooked fish."

"I agree," Gretchen chimed in. "The fresh fish, on the other hand, is usually very good."

"Well, I probably won't be shopping there anyway," Joe said. "Since I live in Williamsburg."

"Right," Gretchen agreed.

"What do you do in Williamsburg?" Kitty asked.

"I'm retired," Joe said. "Long since retired from the Army, more recently from one of those agencies where if I told you anything about it I'd have to kill you." He smiled, looking more relaxed than Kitty had seen him since he came in. "And you?"

"I'm retired from teaching at CUNY. Now I work a few hours a week at City Tech, just helping out doing counseling," Kitty said.

"And Gretchen? I know you work in Manhattan, but what do you do?" Joe took a big bite of his sandwich.

"I do ordering for The Strand," Gretchen said. "I always wanted to work in publishing. It isn't exactly what I had in mind, but at least I'm around books." She too looked more relaxed for the moment. "Why don't we go back to the living room? I don't really want to sit at the table, for some reason."

When they were settled in the "living room" area of the open loft, everyone attended to food for a little while, without saying anything.

Finally, Gretchen broke the silence. "So, Joe, I asked you over to help me figure out what to do." She looked into Joe's face as though hoping to pull some magic out of his dark eyes.

Joe finished chewing and returned Gretchen's intent gaze. "So when did Annie leave? As far as you know?"

"Sometime on Tuesday. They were here when I left for work, and gone when I got back."

"And you haven't heard anything from her since then?"

"Nothing. And I usually have a text or call from her every few hours, even when I'm at work." Gretchen's blue eyes filled with tears. "I can't imagine she wouldn't have called if she were able to."

"Okay, that's at least 24 hours, more likely 30 or more. It can be a challenge to get the police to take it seriously, but we could file a missing person report. You'll need to think hard about how to present it, and be sure to take a photo and description with us."

"Isn't there anything else we can do?" Gretchen looked ready to cry.

"You've tried calling her, texting her, emailing, I suppose?" Kitty said. "Have you put out an inquiry on Facebook? I mean, to your mutual friends? Maybe she would have contacted someone else."

"I hadn't thought of that," Gretchen said. "I don't really think she would, but it's something to try."

"I don't mean to scare you, but we can also try phoning hospitals," Joe said. "That's really one of the first things to do, actually."

"Okay, let's divide up the work," Kitty suggested. "Joe, would you be willing to call hospitals? Gretchen, if you trust me to do it, you could set me up on your Facebook page and let me post an inquiry, while you find a photo and write a description of Annie to give to the police."

"Are you sure you have time for this, you guys?" Gretchen asked.

"I'm okay," Kitty said.

"I am fine with the time," Joe said. "I'm not sure the hospitals will talk to me since I'm not next of kin, but I can try. Gretchen, not meaning to pry, but do you and Annie have an officially registered domestic partnership agreement? Or have you gotten married and I just haven't heard?"

"Domestic partnership," Gretchen replied with a slight duck of her head. "If you run into trouble, you can hand the phone to me. Thanks so much, both of you. Here, Kitty, I'll get you set up on my Facebook. You could send a personal note to my 'close friends' and then post something in my status for everyone else."

Joe was already on the phone. As Kitty waited for Gretchen to pull up her Facebook page, she heard Joe explaining gravely to a hospital receptionist that "my children's mother is missing."

By the time Gretchen had found a photo and finished writing up a description—a task that was interrupted by two bouts of crying and one phone conversation with a hospital official who was not persuaded by Joe's rich baritone voice—Kitty had finished on Facebook, and Joe had called all the nearby hospitals.

"I can call the further-out ones if you like, Gretchen. There are 16 hospitals in Brooklyn. I didn't go on to Manhattan or Queens."

"No, you've done enough for now, Joe. Thank you very, very much."

"Do you want to go to the police station tonight?" Joe asked. "I'll drive you. It's over by the Pratt Institute."

"I don't want to, but...yes, let's get it over with."

"I'll say goodnight, then," Kitty said. "It's good to have met you, Joe, and, Gretchen, don't hesitate to call me later if anything comes up. Will I see you in the morning?"

"Maybe. If you don't mind," Gretchen said. "Thank you so

much, Kitty." She came to Kitty for a hug, which Kitty willingly accepted.

# CHAPTER 6

"I think I could use a drink," Kitty said aloud to herself, once back in her own apartment. She opened a kitchen cabinet door and pulled out a bottle of Cabernet. No use saving it for a special occasion, she guessed. Or maybe this was a special occasion. Just not the kind you usually celebrated with a good wine!

Glass in hand, she sat down at her desk and opened her Mac-Book. She hadn't wanted to mention it to Gretchen, but maybe cyberspace would know something about this Daniel/Donald Oponuno/Forthright. At least she could see what turned up.

Donald seemed to be the name he was going by now, so she decided to try that first. "Donald Forthright" turned up nothing, as did also "Fourthright" and a couple of other alternate spellings. But when she typed in "Daniel Oponuno," all hell broke loose, digitally speaking. Maybe Gretchen was right to be worried. The first listing under "Daniel Oponuno" was a federal court indictment for armed bank robbery. Another site had a grainy picture, purported to be from the bank camera, of a man who certainly could have been a younger version of the one she'd met on the elevator.

There were several stories of arrests in the 70's for political activist protests of various kinds and in various places. None of those seemed to have led to prison, but the federal indictment from 1981 was still open, at least from what Kitty could glean.

In any case, this seemed to ramp up the situation considerably. No longer could Kitty reassure herself that this fellow—Daniel Oponuno, aka Donald Forthright—had looked Annie up merely to sell her some life insurance. His motives here could still be benign, but it appeared likely that he himself was not.

Now Kitty wished she had asked Joe for his phone number. She needed to talk this over with someone before telling Gretchen what she'd found. Maybe she was overreacting, or misinterpreting what she was seeing on the screen. She sincerely hoped she was.

She couldn't very well ask Gretchen for Joe's number, or to have him call—not without an explanation which she was unprepared to give. She'd just have to hope he showed up again, and soon. She sipped her wine and let her mind wander.

What did this Dan guy want with Annie, anyway? Kitty didn't know enough about Annie to make any guesses based on the woman herself. But if her old boyfriend was hiding from the law —which could explain the two different names—was he expecting Annie to help him in some way? And how had he located Annie? Kitty didn't even know whether Annie now used her maiden name or Joe's last name, or some other name altogether.

She wasn't scheduled at City Tech tomorrow, so there was no urgent need to get to bed. Besides, even though she felt tired, she was more keyed up than sleepy. Was there anything more she could learn from the internet? She signed into Facebook and searched Gretchen Morten. On that now-familiar page, she looked for and found photos of Annie posted by Gretchen and mutual friends, eventually finding her name: Annie Wellington.

Now she had two possible ways to go. To Annie's FB page, to see what she could find there, or to Google, to search the entire web. But suddenly, Kitty felt sleep about to overtake her. The decision of which road to explore first seemed too much. It could wait till morning, she thought, as she finished off the last few drops of wine in her glass. Bed was calling. And she would answer.

# CHAPTER 7

The next morning, Kitty woke to her familiar alarm, not to pounding on the door. The dream that faded as she woke had been some kind of anxiety dream, one of those where she was supposed to have been teaching a class and had forgotten to meet with the students for the first three weeks of the semester. Even though she had retired from teaching four years earlier, she found this was still the most common dream-story through which excess anxiety surfaced. If she had dreamed explicitly about the situation with Annie and Gretchen, those dreams had been earlier in the night, and she didn't recall any.

Stretching to get rid of the worst of the kinks before she tried to get out of bed, Kitty thought about the previous evening. More clearly than the night before, she now understood that she needed to talk out what she'd found online. Assuming she couldn't locate Joe without alarming Gretchen—which seemed almost certain—she had to find someone else with whom to share the concern and on whom to test the suppositions she was mulling over.

Then she realized that any one of several colleagues at the counseling center could serve as the confidante she needed. So even though she didn't have to go in to work at City Tech today, a trip to downtown Brooklyn was in order. She'd look at the Center schedule and then give one of her friends a call and make a coffee date.

After a quick check of the online schedule, Kitty phoned the Center and asked for Janice Medwick. "Hi, Jan," she said, when her colleague answered. "This is Kitty Toulkes. I notice you have a couple of open hours around midday. Could I buy you lunch in exchange for a confidential discussion about something I've run across?"

Jan quickly agreed, assuring Kitty that she didn't require payment in the form of lunch. "I'll look forward to seeing you, Kitty. Just come on to my office any time after 11:00, and we'll take off," she said.

Well, that's good, Kitty thought. And I'll have time before I leave to look up and see what more I can find out about Annie.

After a quick breakfast of yogurt and a banana, Kitty took her coffee to the dark blue recliner in the area of her loft apartment that she considered her living room. She set the "I got mugged in Brooklyn" cup on the little end table and re-opened her laptop. "Annie Wellington" in the Facebook search line quickly brought her to the desired page. But as she had partially anticipated, almost nothing was open to "public" view. Just Annie's name, a generic cover photo, and the name of her Missouri college.

"Annie Wellington" in Google also turned up very little. A story about her recent retirement from a job as a horticultural therapist at a small mental health clinic in Queens, and a reference back to her Facebook page. So, if Kitty were going to learn anything more about Annie, it would have to come from Gretchen, or perhaps from Joe.

With that thought in mind, Kitty realized she hadn't heard anything from Gretchen that morning. Maybe that was good. Either perhaps Gretchen was sleeping in, or best of all, maybe Annie had come home.

Kitty considered phoning, and decided that could be done during the bus ride downtown. If Gretchen was working today, she'd be gone now, and it wouldn't make any difference whether a call came sooner or later. She'd either answer or not, but at least Kitty would have made the effort to reach out. And while it seemed inappropriate to ask personal questions about Gretchen's partner on the phone, maybe Kitty could find a way to bring up the question of Joe's phone number.

Time to get going, then, if she was to make the bus in time to get to City Tech by 11:00. Kitty selected a pair of black cotton slacks she knew showed off the buns she worked so hard to keep shapely, a black cotton sweater, and substantial black (was there any other color in NY?) shoes. Grabbed her (black, of course) waist pack, switched off the coffee pot, and hurried out the door. Just before she locked up, she hesitated, then opened the door again and packed her laptop into its carrying case. Swinging the stout leather strap over her shoulder, she left the apartment again and dashed for the elevator.

A middle-aged woman with a Shih Tzu, from a few doors past Kitty's, and a young man from down the other hall with a beautiful Doberman on a leash were already waiting. So the elevator came quickly. But negotiating three people, the toy dog, and the Doberman all on board took a bit of doing. (Why anyone would want to keep a dog that big confined in a city apartment Kitty couldn't fathom!)

As the elevator door opened on the small, undecorated lobby of the Cocoa Factory, Kitty remembered she hadn't picked up her mail from the day before. But there wasn't time for that now. She dashed past James at the desk with a bare nod, hurried through the open door and across the courtyard, and reached the pavement in front of the building just in time to catch the 62B.

# CHAPTER 8

As the bus moved down Park Avenue and the Cocoa Factory faded in the distance, Kitty settled back and thought about what she knew. Whether he was calling himself Daniel Oponuno or Donald Forthright, Annie's old college boyfriend had called her at ungodly 2:00 a. m. Sunday morning. Annie either invited him or agreed to his request to visit and stay overnight on Monday. Known or unknown to Annie (but almost certainly unknown to Gretchen), Daniel Oponuno was wanted for armed bank robbery, and perhaps for other crimes. He and Annie were both gone from Apartment 5F, presumably (but not certainly) together, and Gretchen was extremely concerned that Annie had not communicated with her for what had now stretched into two days. Calls to area hospitals had turned up no trace of Annie.

Of course, she didn't actually know for certain that Annie still had not contacted Gretchen. Surely Gretchen would have let her know—but there could be many reasons she would not have done so, including that Annie was in some kind of trouble and didn't want anyone else to know about it.

Kitty also didn't know whether the Facebook alerts she'd sent from Gretchen's page had turned up any information, nor what had happened when Joe and Gretchen went to the police.

She really needed to know these things before trying to think through what to do next—including when or whether to tell Gretchen what she'd learned about Daniel Oponuno online. Of course, if they had given the police that name, Gretchen and Joe might already know they were dealing with a federal fugitive, not merely an annoyance from the past. She needed to call Gretchen.

The call went through, and rang multiple times before going to voicemail. "Gretchen, this is Kitty. Please give me a call when you have time. I'm hoping you have good news and Annie is home. But if not, I'd just like a status update."

Kitty looked out at the scene rolling by. If Gretchen hadn't heard from Annie yet, she must be getting absolutely desperate. And Kitty couldn't see any way she really could help. As the bus turned onto Jay Street, she gathered herself, ready to face the crowds getting off and the bustle of the sidewalk in front of City Tech.

The sandy brown brick facade of the eleven-story Namm Hall building always seemed deceptively peaceful, in contrast with either the surrounding downtown streets or the halls and class-rooms. Once inside, Kitty began threading her way through the mass of students changing classes.

"Mrs. Toulkes!" A slight young woman with dark hair in an at-tractive shingle cut called out.

"Oh, hello, Serena." Kitty recognized the girl as a student who had been in her office a couple of times already in the semester. "How are you doing?"

"I was just coming to see you. I didn't have an appointment, but I was hoping you could see me."

"Well, actually, I'm not working today. I'm just here to have lunch with a friend," Kitty said. "Can you make an appointment for later or come in when I'll be having open office hours?"

The girl's face fell. "I don't know," she said. "I...I was really hop-ing to see you now." She twisted a corner of her dark blue skirt between her fingers.

"Tell you what, Serena," Kitty relented. "It's a little while be-fore I am supposed to meet my friend. Why don't we go into my office and we can talk for at least a few minutes, and then make an appointment for sometime later."

She knew only too well the pressures some of these young people were under. Many of them worked full time, in addition to going to school. A big percentage were the first in their fam-ilies to go beyond high school, and a lot of them had complications at home—either children of their own or parents and/or sibs who sometimes (deliberately or otherwise) ended up being something less than supportive of the student's educational and career goals.

Serena, as Kitty remembered it, was from a big Hispanic family. Her parents were first-generation, and Serena herself was the first of the children born in the US. Her mother had some kind of heart problem, and two older brothers worked with her father in some type of merchandising.

Kitty led the way through the reception room, past Alicia's desk, and down the hallway to her office.

"Have a chair, Serena," she invited. "Just let me get my things off and your file out."

"Thanks so much for seeing me," Serena began.

"It's okay," Kitty said. She quickly unlocked the file cabinet, pulled a folder, and then seated herself behind the desk. "So what's happening with you?"

"I know I'm getting behind on my work. I have tried talking to my teachers, but of course everybody thinks their class is the most important. I don't know what to do." Serena looked ready to cry.

"Can you tell me why you are getting behind? I thought when we talked earlier you weren't finding the work too hard." Kitty searched her memory of what the complications had been before.

"Oh, I don't know." Serena tried to sound off-hand. "Just lots of things. I was hoping you could talk to my teachers and maybe get them to cut me some slack."

"That's usually not my role, Serena," Kitty said. "But tell me a little more and maybe we can find a way for me to help, or a way to plan so that you do get caught up."

"Well, for one thing, my brother—well, my mother is worried about him, and I'm worried she will be having a heart attack from worry. And—well, I'm worried, too."

"What is it that's so worrying?" Kitty was used to this kind of hesitancy to reveal family problems. "Remember, Serena, anything you say here is confidential," she coaxed. "I won't tell your teachers or anyone else unless you give me permission."

Serena hesitated. "Mama thinks he is using drugs. He probably is, and I think he is also selling. If he is, he could bring the whole thing down on us."

"Which brother is it?" Kitty asked, consulting a family chart from the file.

"Manuel," the girl muttered, twisting her fingers.

"He works with your dad and Julio in the business?" Kitty found the names on the chart. Serena was the third eldest child, and the oldest girl, of seven.

"Yes, and the little boys all look up to him. They all want to be like him and Julio."

"Is Julio aware that Manuel might be into drugs?" Kitty knew she was pushing it, asking a lot of questions, but it seemed best to get a clearer picture of just what Serena was up against before suggesting any action.

"I'm pretty sure not, or he would have had it out with Manuel. Juli is dead straight." Serena looked at her lap. "That's probably why Manny is doing it. He can't compete with Juli in Papa's view. He's always second. Not as fast, not as smart, not as obedient. You know."

"So you are worried about your brother and also about your mother. Does that mean that some of your mother's work is falling to you? Is she feeling too ill to be up and about?" Kitty was guessing now, something she knew was risky. But she was also watching the clock as it moved past 11:00 and on toward 11:30.

"Oh, not so much that. It's just hard to concentrate. I'm the only one Mama talks to. It's always been that way. I'm her *niña especial*, her *preciosa niña*—-her precious, her special little girl. And I can't seem to do anything to help. If I tell Papa, he'll only make things worse. If I tell Julio, the sky is falling! Manny will leave, if Julio doesn't kill him first."

"Would it help if you had a place to do your homework away from the house, Serena? I mean, I know it wouldn't help the situation with your brother, but I'm trying to think, short-term, how you could get through the semester. And then we can try to work out a plan for what to do about the home situation."

Serena sat staring at the floor.

"Do you think that might help?" Kitty nudged.

"Maybe. But I'll still be worrying."

"Of course. But if you can concentrate on your work for even a few hours every day, that might make it easier. And we can also tell each of your professors that you are having some family complications that make it hard to get the work in on time, but that you'll be doing all you can to catch up and complete everything by the end of the semester."

Serena set her mouth and nodded. "Without saying anything about what I've told you, right?"

"Right. Of course!" Kitty assured her. "What are you taking, again?" She looked in the file, but didn't find a course list right away. Serena listed off her three courses and Kitty wrote them down, along with the professors.

"I'll draft up a note that you can look over and when you okay it, I'll send it to each teacher. This is something I do once in a while when circumstances seem to call for it. And do you think you can work in the library, or do you need access to any special tools for your web design class?"

"I think if I just stay in the library with my laptop, I'll be able to work there. I'll have to explain to Mama that I am working on special projects, and have to stay after class. Some days that won't work, but I can try it, anyway." Serena looked determined. "And can I come in again to talk some more? I really want to help Manuel if I can, and Mama has to stop worrying."

"Yes, of course, Serena. You should stop by the front desk and get an appointment for the earliest date that is convenient for you. I'll be looking forward to talking with you some more, and we'll see what we can come up with." Kitty wasn't all that confident they could help unless Manuel wanted help, but she didn't feel a need to tell Serena that, not just yet, anyway.

Serena rose from the chair with a firm air, and stood looking at Kitty, who had also stood up, and was starting to reach out for a handshake. "I'd like a hug, not a handshake, if you don't mind," Serena said.

"Of course not," Kitty said, smiling. She came around the desk and opened her arms. The girl was hardly an armful, but she squeezed so hard Kitty had to suppress an involuntary groan just from the pressure on her ribs. "I wish you good studying, and I'll look forward to seeing you again as soon as you want. Just check with the scheduling desk on your way out. Okay?"

"Okay." Serena sounded brighter than when they started, at least. Kitty walked her to the door and stood silently as the girl headed toward Alicia's desk.

# CHAPTER 9

Kitty glanced at the clock. It was nearly noon. She'd used up half of her own time with Jan. Well, it couldn't be helped. She grabbed her bags and jacket and headed down the hall to Jan's office.

"I'm really sorry to be so late," she told her friend a few moments later. "A client caught me just as I was coming in the door, and it seemed to be a near-emergency. I really appreciate your waiting for me. Do you still have time to go out for lunch, or do we need to grab a bite in the caf?"

"I can go out, if we go someplace close. I imagine you don't want to be in the cafeteria if you have something you want to talk about." Jan was a short, slender woman of about 45, with sandy hair that seemed to have a mind of its own. Her brisk walk matched her temperament. Kitty always felt she was running to keep up—physically, and mentally as well. But, she reminded herself as they hurried out the door, that very quickness made Jan ideally suited to the current situation.

As they made their way to the Starbucks, Kitty outlined what she knew about Annie, her once-upon-a-time boyfriend, and the general situation.

"So, if I understand," Jan said, when they had ordered and were waiting for their food, "Annie's in a committed relationship with Gretchen, but now seems to have gone off with a man who was her boyfriend all the way back in college. And her ex-husband tells you she aborted a baby during the time she was dating this guy. Even more concerning is the information you just picked up from the internet about the man being possibly a fugitive from justice."

"Yes, and Gretchen—I know her slightly and I feel like—well, I like her. I feel for her. She's almost beside herself. I haven't talked to her today. I was really expecting her to call."

They picked up their sandwiches and moved to a table, where they squeezed into wooden chairs and sat almost elbow-to-elbow with a purple-haired young woman and her hunky, heavily-tattooed male companion.

Kitty continued in a lowered voice: "I don't know whether the police have become involved, but I'm not thinking they'll do much unless they know about the federal charges. And I don't really want to spring that on Gretchen when she is so upset already."

Jan took a couple bites of her grilled cheese before commenting. "I gather that you're wanting to help, but you don't know how to proceed?" She looked sympathetically at Kitty.

"I feel absolutely stymied, and that's the truth!" Kitty admitted, while smiling inwardly at the classic counseling style her friend was adopting. "I simply don't see anything I can do. And I feel like somebody has to do something!"

"Do you think it's your place to tell the police what you learned about the robbery charges?"

"Or at least that he is using an alias? I don't know. Someone needs to be sure they know about it. It seems like he could be dangerous to Annie, or even to the rest of us, assuming they come back, and I have to suppose she doesn't know it. But I'm not sure how much I want to get involved with the police angle at this point."

"Well, I wonder whether finding out what the police have been told might be the next step." Jan took a long sip of the iced tea she had ordered. "If you don't want to ask Gretchen, then you need to talk with the ex-husband. Right?"

"Yes, I believe so. And I can only find him through Gretchen."

"But you know his name? Have you tried Googling him?"

"I know his first name; I'm not sure about his last name. But wait. He might be a Facebook friend of Gretchen's. It's worth a try, anyway." She cleared a space on the table and opened her laptop. The cafe's WiFi came up immediately. Logging in to Facebook, Kitty went straight to Gretchen's profile page and and began skimming through her "friends," looking for Joe. She didn't see anyone who resembled the man she had met in Gretchen's apartment, although there were several Joes, two of them apparently women.

"Ok, that was a wash-out," Kitty acknowledged. She closed the MacBook. "I can try some more later."

"Hey, sorry," Jan said, glancing at her phone. "I have to go or I'll be late for my next client. Let me know what you find out, and if I can be of any help, don't hesitate to call. Do you have my cell number?"

"I think I do. Let me check," Kitty said. She searched for and found Jan's name in her phone contacts and read off the 718 number. "That right for your cell?"

"Right," Jan said, gathering herself to go.

"I'll come with you," Kitty said. "It won't make any difference whether I reach Joe now or later this afternoon." She scooted back from the table and stood up, her chair scraping on the tile floor.

As the two walked back toward the Namm Building, Jan said thoughtfully, "I don't know that I was of any help. I wish I had some magic wand that would get things moving and everyone back safely."

"I know," Kitty said. "I think that's what I'm looking for. A magic wand! I ought to be able to make things right, and I just can't." They reached the door, which a heavy-set young Black man was holding open for a group of young ladies. "I'm going to leave you now," Kitty said.

Still holding the door open, the man gestured and raised his eyebrows, cocking his head in an "are you coming?" sort of way. Jan nodded to him and slipped through the doorway.

"Thanks, and I'll see you soon," Kitty said.

"Okay, don't hesitate to call if I can help, and be sure to phone or text me when she comes home," Jan called over her shoulder.

As Kitty waited for her bus back home, she pondered what seemed to be the major question before her. Was it her place to make sure the police knew about the federal charges? Or at least about the fact that Dan/Don was using an alias, probably to hide from his indictment?

The fact of that charge, even if you gave the man the legal benefit of the doubt, made the situation seem much more precarious. She really hadn't had a chance to explore this with Jan as fully as she'd hoped. They'd spent most of their short time just reviewing the basics, and now Kitty found herself still feeling a strong urge to "do something," without any clear sense of what needed doing.

As she was fretting over this, Kitty's phone rang. She snatched it out of her bag, and noted the call was from Gretchen. "Yes, Gretchen," she said anxiously.

"Oh, Kitty. I'm so glad I caught you. Are you on your way home? Because Annie called. She's okay. She's coming home!"

"Oh, I'm so glad to hear that!" Kitty felt a load lift from her shoulders.

"And I hope you'll come on over as soon as you get home."

"I'm just about to catch the bus at Jay Street," Kitty said. "Should be home in about 20, 25 minutes."

# CHAPTER 10

When the bus pulled up, Kitty made her way to an empty seat near the back, and sat down, keeping the bag containing her MacBook on her lap. A single episode, several years ago, of leaving a computer on a bus seat had permanently cured her of any tendency to set any electronics down on any form of public transportation.

If Annie was home and was okay, and especially if she had sent Dan/Don on his way, then the other questions ceased to be urgent, didn't they? But now a whole new set of questions took their place.

Should Annie be told, if she didn't know, that the ex-boyfriend was a federal fugitive? And what good would that do, if he was gone and she didn't know where? Or if she did know where but didn't want to turn him in. Would that make her a....what would it make her? Not an accomplice. Whatever you would call someone who aided and abetted after the fact? An aider and abettor? Kitty chuckled quietly, glad for a moment of lightness.

On the other hand, what if he was back at the Cocoa Factory? Now that Kitty knew his status, she herself might be in danger. It felt like a strange push-me-pull-you situation, with a whole set of different and confusing parameters. She leaned back against the seat and deliberately turned her attention to her breath. She put one hand on her solar plexus. Soon her breaths were coming longer, slower. She closed her eyes, then opened them suddenly as she realized the bus had turned under the BQE, on Park Ave. Not long until her stop, so better not drift off now!

Arriving at the bus shelter by Washington Hall Park, Kitty quickly disembarked. When the walk light came on, she made her way across the four lanes of Park Avenue, divided as it was by the expressway overhead and the empty space underneath that served as free parking for the whole neighborhood. She hurried across Washington and pushed her way through the iron gate that divided the courtyard of the Cocoa Factory from the sidewalk, admiring the well-groomed planters full of vines and flowering annuals. A welcome contrast to noisy traffic on grey streets, and someone was certainly taking good care of them this year.

James didn't look up from whatever he was reading at his desk. Kitty wondered what good the cameras did if no one ever looked at them. Were they recording? She doubted the management would pay for that kind of setup. So...a really great security system! Huh!

She stopped to check her mailbox. Nothing but fliers, it looked like. The elevator came quickly; Kitty punched 5, and was in front of her own door in no time. She dropped her things on the sofa, made a quick bathroom visit, and then stopped to assess.

If Annie was home, a call might be in order before she barged across the hall. No doubt the two women would have plenty to say to one another, and Gretchen might have changed her mind about a visit. Kitty hit Gretchen's number, and waited.

When Gretchen answered, it was to say that Annie had not yet arrived, and would Kitty come on over right away. When Kitty did so, she found Gretchen with a number of colorful cards spread over the tabletop. "Tarot reading?" she guessed.

"Yes, I had to do something to pass the time. Annie didn't say where she was, but it sounded like she wasn't sure just how quickly she could get here, so I'm assuming train changes."

"Probably, if she was in Manhattan somewhere. And this time of day, the trains will be starting to be packed.

"So what are you looking at here?" Kitty cocked her head and looked at the pasteboards, trying to remember anything she knew about what looked like a traditional card layout.

"Just a general check-in as to the situation of today, from my own perspective," Gretchen said. "I've got the 6 of Wands as the center card. That's the woman I always think of as sitting on the hot seat. Very fire-y, very sexy! That's the general topic or most important issue."

"So do you take that to be Annie?" Kitty asked tentatively, not wishing to push her own reading of the cards.

"Oh, definitely. And see the 'best possible outcome,' here at the top—the Priestess of Wands, walking with her familiar, or totem animal, the Lioness. That's clearly Annie, too. That's what I want for her, to come out of this with her head held high and no harm. The victor in whatever struggle she is in now."

"What do you take this card to mean?" Kitty pointed to a yellow card with six women floating in a circle, swords in hand.

"That helps" Gretchen said. "And this challenges," pointing to a card with strings of pearls spilling out of several broken pottery jars. "I take those to be, first, that it helps that we are both fighters, and magick will help us and our friends get through this together. And second, that there is danger and loss here, for us and perhaps for those around us. Probably more than we know right now. It will be a challenge to handle that without creating more trouble."

"So, it's all based on 'Strength,'" Kitty said, as the significance of the layout started to come back to her. "And over everything is the High Priestess. I guess that would be Annie, too. Right?"

"That's the card I chose to represent her. You do know that Annie is the leader of our coven?"

"Uh, no. No, I didn't." Kitty hoped she was showing neither her stunned surprise or her ignorance as she ventured to ask, "What sort of coven? Diannic?"

"No, not really," Gretchen shrugged. "We'd admit men if any wanted to join. We celebrate both the male and female principles. We just don't think you have to have the physical parts in order to represent either one or both." It sounded like a rote response, but Kitty had to admit she agreed with the philosophy.

Gretchen went on. "We celebrate the moon cycle, alternating among the phases—full, waning, dark, new, and waxing. And then of course the quarter and cross-quarter days of the sun cycle. You'd be welcome to come join us as a guest sometime if you'd like. Probably a moon ritual would be best to start—unless you've had some experience of Wicca."

"No, no direct experience. Just some reading, and hearing things from other people, some." She thought a moment, then added, "Sure, I think I'd like to come sometime. Let me know some possible dates, if you can."

Just then the loud "brap" of the outer door buzzer interrupted them. Gretchen stepped over to the intercom and pressed the "speak" button. "Yes?" she inquired.

"It's me, honey," an indistinguishable voice rattled. "Gretchen? Can you let me in, please, sweetheart?"

"Of course." Gretchen pushed the "open door" button. "What in the world? Why doesn't she have her keys?" she wondered aloud. "I'm going to go meet the elevator. I don't understand," she continued nervously. "Please stay here, Kitty?"

"Sure, okay," Kitty said, now feeling quite nervous herself. So much had happened since the last time she had seen Annie, it felt like she would be meeting the woman for the first time.

# CHAPTER 11

While she waited, Kitty looked around the apartment. It was similar to her own, but with what looked like a bigger bedroom. High ceilings, tall, deep-set windows overlooking Park Avenue and the BQE. Lovely old wood floors, carelessly sealed with polyurethane. Now she noticed for the first time the small scarf-draped altar between two windows. Candles, crystals, and a large scallop shell with ashes in the bottom were arranged on a little table, along with a large ceramic goblet, a delicate porcelain cup, a polished wooden stick, and a long silvery knife. And what looked like some kind of horn—not a cow horn, maybe from a goat?

As she heard footsteps nearing the door, Kitty moved away from the altar and turned her gaze on the Tarot layout still spread out on table. The door opened, and Annie came in, followed by Gretchen, who carried a small backpack. "Annie," Gretchen came forward. "You know Kitty, from across the hall?"

"Of course," Annie said pleasantly. "It's nice to see you, Kitty."

"Gretchen asked me to come over while she waited," Kitty said, feeling awkward. "I'll just slip out now."

"Oh, no, you don't need to go," Gretchen said quickly. "Kitty has been helping me when I was trying to find you," she addressed to Annie.

"Sure, I understand," Annie said. "Here, just let me sit down." She sat heavily in a nearby overstuffed chair. "Gretchen, honey, could you get me a glass of water?" She leaned back, closed her eyes and gave a loud sigh.

Kitty looked at the stocky gray-haired woman before her. In repose, Annie looked tired but actually quite pretty. She had a wide, generous mouth with crinkles that suggested she smiled easily and often. Wrinkles on a high forehead and between her straight dark eyebrows suggested she could also frown sternly when occasion called for it. Her eyes, now closed behind fashionable glasses, were (if Kitty remembered correctly) dark brown, and sparkled brightly when she was amused. Take off twenty pounds and 50 or so years, and yes, Kitty could just about imagine the innocent coed of the early 1960's. The years had been relatively kind to Annie, given what Kitty now knew about her hard initiation into the realities of sexual politics.

"Here you are, dear." Gretchen held out a glass of water.

Annie straightened up and took a long sip. "I'm too tired to think straight, but too geared up to rest," she said. "Maybe I can just fill you in on what has happened, honey."

"That would be good," Gretchen said, unsmiling.

Now that she knows Annie is safe, Kitty thought, she's like the parent who wants to blister the bottom of the child who wandered off and scared her to death.

"Well, I guess you know," Annie said, turning to Kitty, "that an old acquaintance of mine showed up a few days ago. I can't really call him a friend. We knew each other in college, and I hadn't heard from him for years.'

Kitty nodded. An old "acquaintance," she noted. She wondered what Gretchen was thinking of this bowdlerized version, and how much more of the story would be similarly cleaned up for present company.

"Anyway," Annie continued, "I think I introduced you to him, on the elevator. So, he stayed overnight with us, and then he started getting antsy and wanted me to take him somewhere where he said he could stay instead.Well, we went there Tuesday night, and that turned out not to work very well, and we spent all the next day and last night—would you believe?—in Central Park, just walking and talking.

"He told me he was hiding from someone, I didn't catch exactly who, but maybe an ex-wife or something like that. He was hoping we could help find him a place to stay. I said I didn't think we knew anyone with extra space.

"Well, then, Gretchen, I swear I didn't do anything to encourage him, but he started trying to put the moves on me. That was this morning. I kept fending him off. I told him I was married, but he didn't believe me. He kept coming on and coming on." Annie sat bolt upright. "The nerve of the man! I swear, honey, I didn't let him do anything, but he tried! Oh, man, did he try.

"Finally, I started to get scared. We were still there in the park. Nobody much is in the park early in the morning. I suggested we go get something to eat—anything to get to where people were. So we walked over to Broadway and found a diner. I felt safer there. And, honey," Annie turned to Gretchen, "believe it or not, the diner—they specialize in sandwiches—was actually called 'WonderWitch.'"

"You could have called me!" Gretchen said, her eyes wide. "I would have come!"

"Well, after we got some food, he seemed to settle down," Annie went on, staring off toward the window. "He got talking about what he had done after college. In the 70's, he went back to Hawaii and got involved in some protest movements. It sounded like he'd identified with Afro-Americans because of the way he was treated in Missouri. I had no idea they even had protests in Hawaii, but I guess they did. Then he got talking about his war experiences. When he left college, he got drafted and went to Vietnam. So, that got him all riled up. He was cussin' and shouting. I had to get him out of the diner, so there we were back on the street.

"He was still yelling and waving his arms, and then he started cussing me, saying I had ruined his life and now he was going to collect on that debt." Annie suddenly looked stricken, and Kitty would have sworn the woman was re-living the frightening days of her pregnancy and its aftermath.

"I told him I had no idea what he was talking about. If anyone had something coming, I would think it would be me—but I didn't dare say that. I was really scared, and I tried to head us toward where the streets would be really crowded, because....well, anyway, we roamed the streets of Manhattan for, it must have been hours! He kept saying I had to find him a place to live. Sometimes he said, 'a place to hide.' And then he would get all upset and start shouting again.

"Quite honestly, I didn't want to leave him in that condition, and yet I really wanted to get away. So we stopped, finally, at a little cafe, and he went to the restroom, and that's when I called you, honey." She looked at Gretchen. "I didn't know how or when exactly I could get away, but I knew I had to.

"So when he came back from the john, I told him I didn't know anyone who could take him in, and I didn't think we could have him live with us. I did say he could come stay the night tonight if he didn't find anything else. But I said that would have to be the end of it. I'm sorry, dear, I didn't know what else to do."

"It's okay, Annie," Gretchen soothed. "Maybe Joe would take him for tonight. Or maybe...."

"Why would you think of Joe?" Annie said, suddenly sharp.

"Annie, I've been out of my mind with worry! I would have called anyone I thought could help me find you! Joe was over here helping call the hospitals, because I thought you might have been in an accident. You didn't call, you didn't answer my texts...I was going crazy!

"Joe was a good friend in need. We even went to the police station last night to file a missing persons report." Gretchen stomped her foot. "Apparently you have no idea what I've been through!"

Embarrassed, Kitty half-rose from her chair. "Maybe..." she started.

"No, Kitty! Stay!" Gretchen was standing now. "I want you here. You deserve to hear the whole story. Go on, Annie. What else did you promise this freakin' freak?"

"He's no freak, Gretchen." Now it was Annie's turn to be soothing. "He's just a very troubled man. We have no idea what he's dealing with, and I am just trying to help him get on with his life."

"So he's coming here, tonight?" Gretchen was still standing, her small hands balled into fists.

"He may. I don't know. I went to the restroom, and when I came out he'd left. I don't know what to expect next." Annie sighed again. "But I think I really need to get some sleep. I'm totally done for."

"I probably should, too," Gretchen apologized to Kitty. "If you don't mind."

"Not at all," Kitty said, feeling exhausted herself. "I'll just let myself out."

# CHAPTER 12

So, Kitty mused, as she lay back in her own recliner, neither Gretchen nor Annie seemed to be aware of Daniel Oponuno's criminal record. Or if aware, they were not sharing the knowledge. And yet, if in fact this man was going to come back and be in their apartment again, they should know. Kitty actually didn't want him in the building at all, now that she knew. And if she saw him, would she be obliged to call the police herself?

She needed to talk to someone, and the only person she could think of was Joe, Annie's ex. She reached for her phone and quickly punched up Gretchen. "Hi, it's me, Kitty," she said when Gretchen answered. "Sorry to bother you, but I wondered whether you had told Joe that Annie is back safe."

"Oh! I told him she was coming, but haven't told him she made it back."

"Would you want me to call him? I'd be glad to do that. I'm sure he'd like to know."

"Oh, yes, would you? Please do," Gretchen sounded relieved.

"I'll need his number," Kitty said, reaching for paper and pen.

When she reached Joe, it sounded like he was in a restaurant or bar somewhere. "It's Kitty Toulkes, Gretchen and Annie's neighbor," Kitty said, hoping he could hear over the ambient noise.

"Kitty? Yes, of course. Just a minute. I'll step outside." She heard him excuse himself to someone, and then a few moments later he came back on the line. "Okay, now I can hear you. What's up?"

"Gretchen asked me to let you know Annie is home. She got home, uh, maybe an hour ago? She seems okay." Kitty paused, not sure how to proceed.

"Oh, that's great news, Kitty. And you? Are you doing okay?" He sounded genuinely concerned.

"I'm fine," Kitty replied. "But...well, there are some other complications I would really like to have your thoughts on. But I can hear you're busy...." She trailed off.

"Just down at a local watering hole."

"Oh."

"You could come and join us. We're just over in Williamsburg."

"No, thanks, I'm in for the evening, I think. I was going to invite you over here for a bite to eat. I've got some nice pork chops I have to cook. But...you're busy." Kitty felt reluctant to press, but realized as she spoke that she was very disappointed.

"Hey, that sounds like an offer. I haven't eaten. I can be there in half an hour or so. How about that?" Joe actually seemed eager.

Kitty smiled. "Sounds good to me. I'll see you soon, then. Bye-bye."

For the next half hour, she bustled happily, getting the pork chops browned, seasoned, and in the oven, running down to the store for veggies and a small pecan pie, and then quickly changing into a fresh pair of jeans and a slim-cut pale turquoise sweater she knew brought out her blue eyes.

Kitty was just setting the gateleg table with cotton placemats and two of her brother's hand-made plates when the outside doorbell bleated. "Yes," she spoke into the intercom.

"Joe."

"Come on up," Kitty said, and unlocked the door for him. "You know I'm right across the hall from Gretchen and Annie?" She finished setting the table and was just setting out two wine glasses when her doorbell dinged.

"Joe. I'm so glad you could come over." She opened the door wide, and stepped aside with a gesture of welcome.

"Me, too," he said. "It smells wonderful in here."

"It'll be a little while before the pork chops are done. I thought we might have a glass of wine while we wait. Would you like red or white? I have a nice Riesling, or a drinkable Cabernet. Or there is also a bottle of Cote du Rhone, I think."

"Oh, you choose, Kitty. Any one of those sounds good to me. I left a Margarita at the bar, but a nice sit-down with a glass of wine will be much better."

Kitty was curious about the circumstances that would lead to leaving a Margarita at the bar, but she suppressed the temptation to ask. "Let's have the Riesling, then. I think the chops are lean, and they're seasoned only with a little garlic, so it won't be heavy. We could actually start on the salad now, if you're hungry," she offered.

"No, I'm good. Let's talk. Shall I sit here at the table?" Joe pulled out a chair and sat without waiting for an answer.

"Here, you can open the wine, then." Kitty handed him the bottle. "You can be the first to use my new Foodlovers Classic Lever Corkscrew. I saw it on sale at Crate and Barrel last week and haven't even had a chance to try it!"

Joe seemed very much at ease. He opened the wine and poured it, while Kitty set out bowls of fresh salad greens and a bottle of sesame shiitake vinaigrette.

"So, you said you had some other issues come up?" Joe inquired.

"Let me tell you about what Annie told us when she got here," Kitty said. She summarized Annie's narrative briefly, ending with the information that Annie had told Dan he could stay the night. "She said repeatedly that she was frightened of him. But then she defended him to Gretchen as just a troubled man who needed help."

"It almost sounds like he has some kind of hold on her," Joe said thoughtfully. "Did you get the impression she was telling more or less the whole story? Did she seem to be keeping something back?"

"I couldn't really tell, Joe," Kitty said. "I don't know her that well, to be able to read her. I didn't notice any overt signs. But, I don't really know."

"Well, he could be quite the charmer when I knew him," Joe said. "He could wrap the girls—and actually guys, too, when he tried—around his finger. Some people thought he was using some kind of Hawaiian sorcery, he was that good. Most of the time, he didn't try, and he was…hmm…kind of distant, actually. Didn't have any real friends among the men, as I remember.

"So Annie is expecting him to show up tonight?" Joe looked troubled. "That could be a recipe for disaster, if he was mad at her earlier."

"Well, that's what she told us, that she had offered. And then, she said, he left without saying anything, so she didn't really know what to expect." Kitty frowned, trying to remember exactly what Annie had told them. "You know, she didn't have her keys! She had to buzz to be let into the building. I bet she gave him her keys!"

Joe stared at Kitty. "I can't believe she'd do that. Are you sure?"

"No, absolutely not sure. But why didn't she let herself in, if she had her keys?" Kitty frowned. "I suppose she might have left home without them, but that seems unlikely. Gretchen would have noticed if the apartment door had been left unlocked, and she didn't say anything."

Kitty stood up. "Well, we can ask, anyway. I'm going to get the food on. Pour yourself some more wine, if you like."

"It's good Riesling," Joe said. "Can I pour you some more?"

"Not right now," Kitty said. She set out a pair of hot pads and brought the pork chops and a dish of baked sweet potatoes to the table.

"Okay, dig in," she said lightly, seating herself and spreading a paper napkin on her lap.

# CHAPTER 13

The meal passed without further mention of Annie's situation. Kitty talked in general about her counseling at City Tech. Joe explained that, although retired from government work, he still kept in touch with some of his old friends.

"And with local law enforcement?" Kitty wondered aloud.

"Oh, some. I have some friends still there. I hope you aren't thinking we'll need the police tonight."

"I certainly hope not!" Kitty said. "But I am a little nervous." She hesitated and then plunged ahead. "The real reason I wanted to talk to you was, I googled "Daniel Oponuno" this afternoon. Have you tried that?"

"No," Joe said. "I didn't really think of it. What did you find?"

"Here, let me show you, rather than try to tell you," Kitty said. "If you're finished, I'll bring the computer over here and we can both look."

Joe scanned the on-line information with grim-faced intensity. "Does Annie know this?" he said finally.

"If she does, she didn't say anything. And neither did Gretchen," Kitty replied. "No telling whether either or both of them knew and were keeping it from the other. Or from me." Kitty smiled ruefully.

"Well, this puts a very different face on the whole matter," Joe said. "Knowingly helping a fugitive from a federal warrant to avoid arrest is a federal crime. If they know he's under indictment and then let him stay, that's a serious matter."

"And if they don't know, they are letting a guy accused of a violent crime stay in their apartment with no precautions whatsoever!" Kitty shivered. "I don't like the idea of his even being in the building, much less in their apartment!"

"Arguably, if we know where he is and don't call the authorities, we could be in violation of the law ourselves." Joe stood up and paced over to the kitchen. He turned back toward Kitty. "It's a tricky situation all right."

"Would you like a piece of pecan pie?" Kitty said hopefully.

"Oh, sure. Just a very small piece, thanks," Joe said. "Anything to put off doing something about this!"

"Coffee?" Kitty cut the little pie and put two pieces on small brown plates with bright yellow spots.

"No, thanks. But I'd take a cup of tea if you have it," Joe said.

"Sure. Black? or some kind of herbal?" Kitty filled the kettle and flipped the switch.

"Black tea, but with milk, if that's okay."

"Perfect. Would you like cream instead? I have it." Kitty set out a couple of mugs. "You don't mind your tea in a mug, do you? I have porcelain cups with saucers, if you are a purist."

"Not picky about my teacup. Maybe about some other things," Joe said with a crooked grin.

Kitty had just poured hot water over tea bags in the two mugs when loud voices sounded from outside the door. In the hall or in Apartment F, Kitty couldn't tell.

She looked at Joe. "That's not normal noise here. These walls are really thick, and we don't usually hear the neighbors much at all."

Joe rose to his feet. "I think I'll investigate. You stay here."

"It's my concern as much or more than yours. I'll come too," Kitty said. But she did let Joe lead the way.

He opened the door slowly at first, and then faster. No one was in the hall, and now it was quite evident the shouting was coming from the apartment opposite.

Joe knocked loudly on the door of 5F. "Annie, what's going on?" he called. "Is everything all right? Gretchen?"

The shouting stopped abruptly. A sharp noise, as of a piece of furniture being knocked into or knocked over, was followed by a disquieting silence.

"Oh, hi, Joe!" Gretchen appeared at the door. "Yeah, everything is fine. Sorry we were getting a little loud." As she spoke, clearly trying to keep her voice light, her brow was puckered in an exaggerated frown and her head moved slightly left to right and back again.

"May we come in? I'm just over visiting Kitty, and I'd like to see Annie for myself—seeing is believing, you know," Joe said smoothly. He didn't wait for Gretchen's response, but gently pushed his way past her and into the apartment. Kitty followed on his heel.

Annie was standing by the windows, seeming to look across at the traffic on the elevated expressway. Near her, his right hand clenched into a fist, was the man Kitty had met on the elevator what seemed like ages ago.

Backlit by the harsh gleam of the lights atop the BQE's huge stanchions, he looked both taller and darker than Kitty remembered. He appeared to tower over Annie. As he looked toward the door, he showed no sign of recognition of or even interest in the people standing there. The expression on his face was unreadable, blank.

"Hello, Annie!" Joe continued the light tone he'd used coming in as he strode across the floor. "I'm glad to see you! It's been a while!"

Annie turned from the window, stepping away from Dan. Her face was flushed. She raised one hand, in what could have been either greeting or warding off. "Hello, Joe. Nice of you to stop by." Kitty couldn't tell from the tone whether Annie meant the comment to be sincere or ironic.

However the response was intended, it didn't deter Joe. He continued forward, stepping close to Annie and putting his body between her and the other man. Without touching her, he somehow conveyed a possessiveness that under other circumstances, Kitty thought Annie and Gretchen would both probably have objected to.

"You doing okay?" he asked solicitously.

Annie just looked at him. She opened her mouth as if to speak, and then closed it again.

"And who is your friend?" Joe turned and stepped back a bit, still blocking Annie off from Dan. When Annie didn't say anything, Joe stretched out his hand. "I'm Joe Treacher," he said, his voice slightly deeper and stronger than it had been when speaking to Annie and Gretchen.

Dan took a step away, seeming literally taken aback by Joe's manner. "Don Forthright," he said, ignoring Joe's outstretched hand.

"Good to meet you. Any friend of Annie's, you know." Joe seemed determined to make conversation with the visitor. "You here from out of town?"

Dan looked at Annie, as though willing her to say something. But she didn't. She turned again toward the window. "Yes, from out of town," he answered finally. "But thinking of staying in New York. And you?"

"Oh, I live here," Joe said. "I've lived here for years. Hey, would you all like some pecan pie? Is there enough to share, Kitty?"

"I'm sure there would be, especially if Gretchen can scare up some ice cream to go with." Kitty looked to Gretchen, who was standing by the still-open door.

"That sounds nice," Gretchen said. "Will you bring the pie over here, or shall I?"

"Oh, I'll just go get it. Won't be a minute!" Kitty turned and moved quickly out the door and across the hall. She slipped the two pieces from their plates back into the pan and carried it back to the other apartment, where she and Gretchen busied themselves dishing up pie and ice cream.

"Won't you all sit down?" Gretchen indicated the sofa and chairs clustered near an antique wooden chest that served as a coffee table. Joe, touching Annie's arm lightly, urged her toward the sofa. When she sat, hugging the arm of the sofa, he sat down near her, in the center.

Daniel came slowly from the window and seated himself in a straight-backed chair across from Joe.

Gretchen and Kitty passed the dessert with forks and napkins.

"Anyone want something to drink?" Gretchen asked. Nobody did. Kitty took the remaining chair, and Gretchen sat on the empty end of the sofa.

With Joe leading the way, he, Kitty, and Gretchen kept up the semblance of a conversation. Gretchen chatted about her work, describing an amusing encounter with a confused customer who was looking for a theater, not a bookstore. Joe asked Kitty about City Tech, and a bit of conversation about colleges ensued.

"And where did you go to college, Don?" Joe turned to the visitor.

"I went to school with Annie, at a little school in western Missouri," Dan replied. Everyone looked him expectantly. But he volunteered nothing more.

"Well, this pie is really good," Annie said finally. "Did you get it downstairs, Kitty?"

"I did!" Kitty said. "I think they do a really good job on pastries."

"So do I," Annie agreed, seeming to shake off whatever state she had been in.

Suddenly, Dan set his plate on the chest and stood up. "Well, I can see we aren't going to get anything more accomplished now." He addressed Annie, looking directly at her. "Don't forget what we talked about. I will be back, and you need to be ready, one way or the other."

He put one hand in his pocket and jingled something as he walked toward the door. "I'll be back," he said, and walked out, leaving the door ajar.

# CHAPTER 14

Gretchen got up immediately and shut the door firmly, locking the bolt. She leaned back against the door. "Whew!"

"Well, that was interesting," Joe said. "Anybody want to tell us what's going on?"

Everyone looked at Annie.

"I wouldn't know where to begin," she said. She stood up and began to pace. "Gretchen, you tell them."

"Well, all I can tell is just what happened tonight," Gretchen said, coming back to the center of the room and taking the chair Dan had just vacated. "We were just sitting here talking when this guy opened the door, the locked door, I might add," she said with a sidelong glance at Annie. "And he just barged right in."

"I told you, Gretchen, he took my keys." Annie emphasized the word "took,' with both voice and a sharp, open-hand gesture. She sat down again, this time at the other end of the couch.

"Well, how exactly he got them, I don't know," Gretchen continued, "but anyway, he had them and he used them and he came into our apartment. He came in and came over to Annie and basically shoved me out of the way and began talking to her. I couldn't hear, or, more like it, couldn't make sense of, what he was saying. What was he saying, Annie?"

Annie shook her head and did not speak.

"It could have been sweet nothings for all I know," Gretchen said. "What did he want?"

"The sweet nothings? That was last night. Tonight, it was threats!" Annie blurted. Then she paused, two warring emotions, fear and anger, passing over her face in rapid succession. She turned to Joe. "He knows where Angela is," she said in a low voice. "Or at least, he says he does.

"Gretchen," her voice turned pleading as she faced her partner. "That's the only reason I left with him. I swear! If he could help us locate our daughter, that was the only thing on my mind."

"But he didn't help," Joe said, his voice husky with emotion. "Right? He only said he could, to get you out where he could work on you."

"And work on me he did," Annie said, anger now clearly in control, as her face contorted—jaw clenched, lips pressed tightly, and brows lowered. "It might have been effective when I was 19, but I've been around the block a few too many times since then. He started out telling me he'd been thinking of me, missing me, and thinking of how it might have been 'if only.' Well, I told him there wasn't any 'if only.' And that if he knew where Angie is, he had to tell me right away.

"Joe," she turned to face her ex-husband, "I haven't heard anything from her in months. Have you?"

"No," Joe said softly. "You know I would have called if I had." He paused. "Go on. What did he try to get you to do?"

"Well, first it was just to find him a place to sleep, a place to stay. He implied that there was someone, someone he said was looking for him...that he couldn't let whoever it was find him, and once they knew he was in New York they would look in all the Y's and missions and cheap hotels, so he couldn't go there. And the place he thought might work out, with some supposed friends, well, that was just a disaster, and neither one of us got any sleep that night.

"Then he began to tell me he needed me to help him get a job. He'd do anything, he said, just to have a job. I might have been willing to do that, if that's what it took to get whatever information he has about Angela, but when I told him definitely we couldn't have him stay with us and that I didn't know of anywhere else—well, then he started to get scary. He does have a way about him, always did. And when he gets a certain look, well, it's hard to not go along.

"I think I know quite a bit about magick, and spells, but...well, anyway, I wouldn't look at him, and that made him mad, and that's when he started grabbing me and trying to kiss me. This was in the early, early morning—and I had to fight to get him to go with me to a street where there were more people, to feel safer."

"And somewhere in that period, he took the occasion to grab your keys?" Gretchen asked.

"I may have had them out, I don't know." Annie shook her head. "But yes, he grabbed them and wouldn't give them back. Sort of teasing me with them. That's when I said he could stay one more night, tonight, with us. Well, you saw what that turned into."

"What did he want tonight? What did he mean by saying as he left that you had better be ready?" Kitty asked. "I guess he still has your keys, so he can come and go as he pleases."

"Tonight it was threats, as I said. He says he not only knows where Angela is but knows that she's in bad trouble, and if I can get him a job driving a truck with CSStudios, he'll tell us how to find her. The implication was that whatever she is doing, she'd be in trouble with the law if caught, and in real and immediate danger in any case.

"This from a man I thought was my friend, or used to be, anyway. I said as much, and he grabbed me by the arms and started shaking me. That's when you heard the shouting, I guess. Both Gretchen and I probably shouted at him and then he started shouting that I would do as he said. Otherwise, I would never see Angela well again. And that's when you guys came to the door." Annie slumped into the couch, exhaustion showing in every line of her face and body.

"Can I get you something to drink, Annie?" Kitty said, more to create a little breathing space for everybody than because she thought Annie would be thirsty.

But Annie said yes, she would like a glass of water. "While I'm up, anyone else want water?" Kitty asked.

"Yes, please," said Joe. And Gretchen nodded.

While Kitty fumbled around in the kitchen, hunting glasses, Gretchen got up, motioning Joe to scoot over, and went to sit beside her partner. Gretchen stroked Annie's hair and then let her arm drop to drape gently over the older woman's shoulder. Joe stood up and went to the kitchen to join Kitty. "Can you find a tray?" Kitty asked him. "I don't mean to pry," she continued softly. "But I'm assuming Angela is yours and Annie's daughter?"

"Yes," Joe also spoke softly. "We adopted her when it was clear Annie couldn't have children. Angela's bipolar, and she's also had trouble with substance abuse since her teens. This latest disappearance has lasted for months. I've told myself she was completely lost to us. But Annie keeps hoping. A crueler method of manipulating her could not have been devised," he finished with intensity.

"Do we have to tell Annie about the warrant?" Kitty asked, rattling ice cubes out a tray to cover her question.

"I'd like to hold off just a little," Joe said. "Now, with him threatening Angela, I want to go through some of my sources and see if we can't get some help from that angle. If we can, that will be the time to drop the AKA into the pot. No use exposing Annie and Gretchen to our suppositions until or unless we have to. We know we don't want this guy staying the night with them, even without that other business."

"And we also know he can get in anytime he wants to, since he has keys," Kitty reminded Joe.

"That's another reason I want to inquire of my friends. Maybe we can get him picked up before he tries to come back." Joe held out the bamboo tray he had plucked from behind the breadbox. "Talk more later," he whispered.

Joe carried the tray and Kitty served a glass each to the two women cuddled together. She and Joe took the other two glasses and sat down facing the couch. No one spoke for a while, as they all sipped.

Finally, Joe broke the silence. "I just told Kitty I'd like to talk to some of my law enforcement buddies, to see if we can get an APB on this guy before he does any more threatening. If I need backup, are you willing to talk to the police, Annie? Maybe Gretchen, too?"

"Certainly," Annie said. "Do you really think we can say he's done something to justify a pick-up, Joe?"

"I may have to bring Angela into it, Annie," Joe said. "If you object, say so now."

"If he's going to try to hurt Angela, I'll...." Annie raised a fist. "You know I can, Joe. Remember what happened to the guy who chopped down the tree across the street!"

"I do," Joe said, with a half-smile. "It was a beautiful sycamore tree," he explained, "that Annie particularly loved because it shaded our house in the summer. The neighbor had it cut down just because he didn't like the big leaves clogging up his flower beds in fall. When she heard it coming down, Annie ran out in the street and before I could stop her, she threw a spell at the guy." Joe gestured, two fingers pointing skyward.

"Two months later, this guy was hit by a train, crossing the tracks near our neighborhood. He didn't die, but he ended up paraplegic, in a wheelchair the rest of his life. You don't want to get our Annie too riled up." He leaned back in his chair, obviously relishing the memory of old times.

"But seriously, Annie," Gretchen interjected quickly, "please don't do anything to this guy. The police may not consider your spells to be deadly weapons, but if you have to do something, a binding spell would be much better from a karmic standpoint."

"I am concerned about the fact that Dan has Annie's keys," Joe said, leaning forward again. "If he comes back, I'm not sure what we can do. Maybe, just to be on the safe side, Gretchen, I should show you how to prop a chair under the doorknob. That's a reasonable door jammer, if done correctly. The door is steel, so he's not going to be able to break it down, at least not before you could call the police. And any attempt would make enough noise to rouse the whole hallway."

The women quickly accepted that offer. Joe stood up. "Well, I think we should go, and let you get some rest. Kitty, you go on home, and I'll stop by again after I give Gretchen a demo."

# CHAPTER 15

Back in the quiet of her own apartment, Kitty noticed there was still some wine in her glass on the table. She took it to the sofa and sipped thoughtfully. As she relaxed, she realized how tense she had been for the past hour or so. She was glad Joe was coming back over; she had too many unanswered questions to be able to settle in for the night without some further discussion.

She got up to stick a stopper in the Riesling bottle and place it in the freezer. She set the timer on the microwave for 5 minutes. Probably not what the wine gurus would recommend, but a little bit chilly was better than room temp.

Mentally reviewing the evening's events, she was impressed with the way Joe had taken charge of the scene in Gretchen and Annie's apartment. His presence, something about the way he inserted himself between Annie and Dan—very firmly, yet without creating any impression of being antagonistic or adversarial —made him seem physically larger than Dan, even though the two were probably about the same height. And Dan had clearly felt it too, judging both by his body language and by the fact that he left as he did, either unwilling or unable to continue what he had been pursuing when they arrived.

The timer dinged, followed almost immediately by the door-bell. "Come in," Kitty called, as she hurried to snatch the wine bottle from the freezer. Setting the now-cold bottle on the table, she started toward the door. Joe opened it just as she reached for the knob. "Hi, come on in," she repeated, stepping back.

Joe came in and looked at Kitty, eyebrows lifted in question. "I hope it was okay to come on back over," he said.

"Oh, absolutely. Hey, we didn't finish the wine yet," Kitty said, trying to keep the moment light, instead of collapsing into his arms in relief. She motioned toward the sofa. "Will you sit and help me finish it off?"

Joe moved toward the sofa. "Sure. I was hoping you'd offer," he smiled.

Kitty brought the bottle and handed Joe their two glasses so she could pour. It seemed natural, then, to sit not too far away from him on the sofa, the bottle on the floor between them. "It seems like we ought to drink to something, but I'm not sure what," she said.

"How about 'To us...all of us,' I mean?" Joe said.

Kitty couldn't be sure whether he colored up a bit. "To all of us!" she said cheerfully. "May we all be safe and well, including your daughter!"

They both sipped their wine.

"Did the door-jamming lesson go to your satisfaction?" Kitty inquired.

"Yes, it's really very simple," Joe said. "Want me to show you how?"

"I think I know," Kitty said. "My husband and I once stayed in a very dubious hotel, where the door lock on our room didn't work. We propped a chair under the door knob there. Pushed it up as tight as we could, and hoped the back legs wouldn't slip on the floor if someone should try to get in in the night. Nobody did, of course." She smiled at the recollection.

"You were married, then. But no longer?"

"He died ten years ago," Kitty said. She took another sip of the wine, which had chilled just enough to be pleasant but not really cold.

"I'm sorry," Joe said.

"Thanks. It was a long time ago," Kitty said. "We had a good marriage, but I'm fine. I had my work, and that helped."

"And your work was what? I think you told me you were at CUNY?"

"I taught in the Psychology Department at City College—that's part of CUNY, you know—for twenty years. Now that I'm retired from teaching, a few hours a week in the counseling center at City Tech is interesting, brings in a little extra, and saves a lot of time from commuting into Manhattan." After a moment, she added thoughtfully, "and I think we really do, as our website says, 'help students succeed in life.'"

"Are most of the students full-time?" Joe asked.

"A lot are, but we also have a large percentage of non-traditional and part-time students," Kitty said. "And a lot of our kids are the first ones in their family to go to college. So there are issues. Almost all of them tend to be highly motivated, but it isn't always easy to stay in school. It's really a challenge and a privilege to work with them, and I think most of our teachers look at it that way."

"Sounds like a great place to be," Joe said.

"Well, we have our problems, like anywhere. Administrative, financial, technological...but don't get me started on that!" Kitty shook her head, smiling. She continued more soberly, "I want to hear your take on what happened across the hall, and where we go from here."

"Yes," Joe said. "Well, I think we have a really delicate situation. First of all, there's the issue of Dan's having access to the building and to Annie and Gretchen's apartment. We can get the super to change the lock on their apartment, or get an additional lock put on. That's easy. But the outside door key, that's not so simple, and I don't know exactly how best to tackle that one. I'd sure like to see if we can't just get the keys back from him."

"Yeah, even if they have to get re-keyed over there, we surely have to do something about the outer door." Kitty frowned. "I don't suppose it's really possible to get that door changed. Or at least, it would be outlandishly expensive."

"Okay, well, that's one thing, and that may be taken care of, if the police become convinced they need to pick this guy up. So how to do that should probably be my highest priority. Gretchen can take care of getting their lock changed, and we talked briefly about her taking the day off tomorrow."

"What about your daughter?" Kitty asked. "Do you believe

Dan's story that he knows something about where she is and what trouble she might be having?"

"It's possible," Joe said. "It's also entirely possible he just made that up. Though how he learned enough about our situation with her to use that as a lever with Annie, I don't know."

"As far as that goes," Kitty said, "I've been wondering how he found Annie in the first place. She doesn't seem to have much of an online presence."

"I don't know," Joe replied, "and that worries me a little. But I don't think it's worth bringing up with her at the moment. He did find her."

"And he's not out to sell her life insurance or a piece of Arizona real estate! That's what I originally would have guessed when I heard the old college boyfriend was coming for a visit," Kitty said. "I had even thought maybe he was going to try to recruit her for some cult."

She chuckled at that idea, and Joe joined her. A less likely cult recruit could hardly be imagined. If anything, Annie could be considered a cult leader herself, as the High Priestess of a Wiccan coven.

"I'm going to, as I said, contact some of my law enforcement friends from the old days tomorrow, and see what they can do for me," Joe continued. "Starting with the threats, or implied threats, to Annie and Gretchen, the fact that he still has their keys, and going on to mention Angela if that seems necessary."

"Are you worried about the suggestion Annie mentioned that your daughter might be involved in something criminal?" Kitty wasn't sure she wasn't stepping out of bounds, but it seemed important.

"Not especially, compared with the need to try to make sure she's safe, or as safe as she can be." Joe turned and looked directly at Kitty. "You may think I'm unfeeling, but we've been dealing with this for many years, and after a while, you have to just get a little hardened."

"I've dealt with bipolar professionally," Kitty responded. "When I was in training, we called it being 'manic-depressive.'

It's a devastating condition, and very, very hard on families and loved ones. I understand, at least somewhat."

"Thanks, Kitty," Joe said. "Is there any more of that wine?"

"There is," Kitty said. She poured what was left into Joe's glass.

"Don't short yourself," he cautioned.

"No, I've got all I need," Kitty said. "So what about our knowing this guy's under a federal indictment? Aren't we still liable? I mean, aren't we legally obligated to tell someone what we know? And if we do, will that get Annie into trouble?"

"I'll give Dan's real name to my contacts, along with the name he's going by now. Remember, all we have is suppositions. We think we know who he is, and we think that's who we looked up online. He hasn't admitted in any way that he is Daniel Opon-uno. You don't know him at all, and I haven't seen him in over 50 years. But he didn't seem to recognize me, and I certainly couldn't swear it was the same person mentioned in the indict-ment. I think we'll be okay."

"I'll depend on you to keep me out of prison, then," Kitty said lightly. "What else do we need to do?"

"Well, I kind of hesitate to ask," Joe said, "but I wonder if you would be okay with my staying the night here?" He glanced at Kitty, and then went on. "I'm concerned that Dan may come back and cause a disturbance, and I'd feel better if I were here. Your couch looks pretty comfortable," he added quickly.

Kitty nodded, hoping she didn't appear too eager. "It makes into a full-sized bed, when you're ready. I'll feel better to have you here, too."

"The two across the hall will keep that door barricaded while they're home, until they can get the lock changed, but I'd rather be nearby, at least tonight." Joe tried unsuccessfully to stifle a yawn.

"I guess I'd better get the bed made up," Kitty laughed. "You're going to wink out on me soon anyway. And I'm tired, too."

"Here, let me help you clear up," Joe said. He picked up the glasses and wine bottle and carried them to the kitchen.

After the dishes were placed in the dishwasher, Kitty got out fresh sheets and towels, and she and Joe together made up a bed for him in the living room. "Okay," she said, "I guess that's it. You can have the first go at the bathroom if you like. But, actually, it might make more sense for me to go first." When Joe nodded, she continued. "I'll show you the light switches, and you can turn everything off and lock the door before you go to bed."

Joe came around from the opposite side of the bed, toward her. "Thanks, Kitty," he said. "You've been a real trooper, and even though it's not over yet, I feel like we're on the way to getting this taken care of." He stood awkwardly for a moment, and then held out both arms and took a step closer, smiling gently.

Kitty nodded and took a deep breath. Suddenly feeling very tender and vulnerable, she stepped forward and raised her arms for the hug he was offering to share.

Coming into Joe's arms, Kitty realized he was taller than she'd thought. She barely reached his shoulder, so that when she relaxed in the embrace, her head rested on his chest. She could hear his heartbeat. They held each other for a long moment, then both backed away slightly. Joe looked down at her and bent his head for a quick kiss on the mouth. "Goodnight, Kitty. May your dreams be sweet."

"Goodnight, Joe. The same for you."

# CHAPTER 16

The next morning, Joe had risen before Kitty woke up, and had already put up the bed before she came out of her bedroom. The sheets were neatly folded at one end of the couch. "I want to make some phone calls as soon as people will be at work," he said, "but that's not for at least another hour. Can I walk up to Myrtle and get us some bagels while you put on the coffee? That is, I hope you are a coffee person? If not, I can get a cup downstairs."

Glad to see he wasn't planning to leave right away, Kitty assured Joe she was a "coffee person," and sent him on his way with instructions for her bagel. She busied herself starting the coffee, and setting out plates and knives for the bagels, along with orange juice and coffee mugs.

When Joe got back, he held up the bag containing the Bergens Bagels like a hunting trophy. "Success," he announced. "One sesame bagel with tofu cream cheese, one everything bagel with sausage, egg, and cheese, and one egg bagel with strawberry cream cheese. Did I get it right?"

"You did!" Kitty laughed. "And I hope you like your coffee dark and rich." She poured the two mugs. "Cream?"

"Just some milk, if you have it," Joe said. "My doctor says I need to 'watch the saturated fat,' so I try, periodically."

After breakfast, Kitty took her waist pack from the rack near the door. "I have office hours today," she told Joe. "You're welcome to stay here to do your phoning, and there's a spare key to the apartment in the top drawer over there, under the tea towels." She gestured toward the kitchen cabinet. "I don't have a spare outside door key, but you won't need one as long as you aren't out past 7:00, when the doorman leaves. And even then, if any of us are here, you can just ring and we'll let you in."

She stopped, suddenly realizing she was proceeding on the assumption that Joe would be staying another night in 5G, even though he hadn't said anything about it. "That is, if..." She trailed off, embarrassed.

"That's perfect," Joe said quickly. "I'll keep in touch with you during the day, and I think I'll probably want to stay again tonight, if it's okay. I'll see what Gretchen decides to do about their door, and we'll just play it by ear."

"Okay, good. I'll be with clients most of the middle of the day, but you can always leave a message and I'll check in between. And now I have to run." She'd have liked another hug, but didn't see any way to make that happen.

Last night had been an unusual circumstance, she told herself, as she waited downstairs for the bus. No big deal, and certainly not anything to build a fantasy on. Still, she found herself thinking of Joe and his strong arms as the bus made its way toward downtown Brooklyn.

Once at her office, Kitty had little time for daydreaming. Her schedule was full, with two students she had not seen before and several with whom she had had previous consultations, including Serena, the girl she had spoken with on Thursday.

The day passed quickly.

The new clients all had issues Kitty recognized. Of course, each was different, too. That was what made this work so interesting. Kitty found that her years of teaching clinical psychology helped, but mostly because she was used to working with stressed college students, not so much the academic subject matter she had taught.

When Serena came in, as the last client of the day, she seemed a little less anxious than before, at least about school. The note Kitty had dashed off over her lunch break for Serena's teachers met with the girl's approval, and Kitty promised to send it to each one. From what Serena said, Kitty gathered that just the promise of uninterrupted study time in the library was bringing a measure of organization and stability to her schoolwork already, although it didn't, Serena emphasized, help the main problem, which she saw as her brother's drug use.

"Serena, I don't know that I can do anything directly about this situation," Kitty said. "What I would suggest, though, is that you—and if you think she would go, your mother—attend an Al-Anon meeting. This is a peer-to-peer organization for family members of alcohol and drug abusers, and they can really help. There's at least one group that's associated with the college, and I can give you a number to call. You can look online, too, for more information." She handed Serena a card with the phone number and a web address.

"And if you want to come in fairly regularly just to talk, that's perfectly fine. I'd like to know whether you find the Al-Anon useful, and also keep up with you on how your studies are going. Do you think that would be a good idea?"

"Oh, yes, if that's all right!" Serena sounded relieved and grateful. "I don't want to take up more than my share of your time, though."

"Not to worry," Kitty smiled. "It's all part of the service!"

After Serena left, Kitty realized she hadn't checked phone messages for several hours. And Joe had said he would keep in touch. She hoped she hadn't missed anything time-sensitive. As it turned out, she hadn't. Just a short voicemail from Joe at 2:30, saying he would be at the apartment later, and that he'd had some useful conversations during the day and hoped to have some more. And a text from Gretchen, asking Kitty to check in with them when she got home.

Kitty packed up her laptop, locked the file cabinet, and watered the plants she'd been neglecting. Happy her workday usually ended before the going-home rush, she locked the office door and said goodbye to the receptionist. "Have a good weekend, Alicia," she said.

"Goodbye, Kitty," Alicia replied. "You had a full day today, and it looks like another full calendar next Wednesday. You're developing a following, even though you are only part-time!

"Oh, I hope not," Kitty laughed. "Word gets around if you're a softie, I guess. I'll have to work at being more of a hard-ass."

"I think the students find seeing you really does make them feel better," Alicia said seriously. "I don't know what you say to them, but I can see the difference, when they come out, compared with when they went in. Lots of times!"

"Well, hmm! Thanks for the feedback, Alicia," Kitty smiled. "I hope you're right. And I won't complain about a full schedule. That's what I'm here for, after all. Okay, then, good night. See you Wednesday."

# CHAPTER 17

Entering the courtyard of the Cocoa Factory, Kitty realized she was very much looking forward to seeing Joe in her apartment. She'd just check the mail and go straight up. Through the lobby door, standing open as it usually was on nice afternoons, she could see Tressa, the afternoon attendant, chatting animatedly with a man who had his back to Kitty. As she walked past the desk on her way to the mailboxes, the man turned and spoke.

"Hello. Kitty, isn't it?" he said, smiling broadly. "I'm glad to see you." Turning back to Tressa, he continued smoothly, "Thanks so very much, Tressa. You've been a great help. And I'll look forward to seeing you again soon.

"Let's go up, shall we, Kitty?" He smiled again and gently but firmly took her arm.

Kitty allowed herself to be steered toward the elevator. She didn't want to go up with Dan, she didn't feel safe getting on the elevator with him. But somehow she went along. Once the door closed, he let his hand slide from her forearm to her wrist, and then to her hand. His hand was very soft.

Turning to face Kitty as she stood near the back wall of the elevator, he leaned slightly forward and looked directly into her face, still holding her hand. "You have beautiful eyes, Kitty. I could get lost in them," he half-whispered. "You really shouldn't be worrying about Annie. She doesn't need your help. I'm the one who needs help, and she's going to give it to me. You can help me, too, if you want to. I'm sure she's told you, I need a job and a place to stay. I'm sure you want to help, Blue Eyes.

"You can help me, starting right now," he continued, as the elevator reached the 5th floor. The door slid open, and Dan, still holding Kitty's hand with a firm grip, stepped out, half-pulling her with him. He slid his hand back up to her wrist and pulled her so close that she could smell an acrid odor and feel the angular hardness of his body. "You can help me by returning these keys to Annie." He laid in Kitty's hand a keychain with an enameled gold rose at one end and two keys at the other. "I don't need them any more. Tell Annie I'll be by a little later to see how she's decided."

He dropped Kitty's wrist and stepped back into the elevator just before the door closed. Kitty noticed the directional arrow pointed up.

What had just happened? She felt disoriented and decidedly wobbly. She made her way down the hall, stopping twice to lean against the wall. Her heart was pounding, and her breath was coming in short, hard gasps. When she came to her apartment at the end of the hall, she reached for the doorknob and in so doing, dropped the rose keychain, which fell to the floor with a clank. Only then did it really become clear to her that Dan had given her back the keys he had taken from Annie.

Her hands were shaking so badly that instead of pulling out her own keys, she rang the doorbell, praying that Joe would be inside.

He was, and came quickly to the door. Seeing Kitty so obviously distraught, he drew her inside and wrapped her in his arms. The door drifted shut.

Joe held her silently, while Kitty leaned against him. Finally, remembering, she spoke in a whisper: "The keys. Annie's keys. Dropped them...outside the door." She twisted in Joe's arms, feeling an urgency to pick up the dropped keychain.

"We'll get them in a minute," Joe said gently. "Come and sit down. Here, let's take off your things." He helped her out of her waist pack, and guided her to the couch.

"I'll see about the keys." He retrieved the keys and, after looking closely at the keychain, laid them on the table. Back at the couch, he sat down next to Kitty. "Can I make you some tea, or a glass of water?" he asked.

"Maybe some tea," she said. She closed her eyes and leaned against the backrest.

Joe got up and turned on the kettle. But he came right back and again sat next to Kitty, his shoulder touching hers. "Whenever you are ready to talk, I'm ready to listen," he said, his voice level and quiet.

"Could you just hold me a little?" Kitty asked. She looked at him. "I'll be okay, I've just had a scare. I'll be all right in a minute."

For answer, Joe turned to her and, as she leaned slightly forward, put both arms around her. One hand went to her head and lightly caressed her hair. He leaned down and rested his lips on the top of her head. Kitty relaxed and closed her eyes again.

"Shall I get the tea?" Joe asked after a few minutes.

"That sounds nice," Kitty said. Her breath had stabilized and her heart was no longer pounding.

Joe got up and fixed the tea. "Milk?" he queried.

"Yes, please," Kitty said. "Here, I'll come to the table."

Seated across the table from Joe, Kitty stared silently at her tea. Finally, she took a sip and then began to tell him what had just happened.

He looked directly at Kitty while she talked, saying nothing until she finished with, "I guess I'm a real wimp, huh?"

"No, I wouldn't say so. It was a frightening situation. And one of the more disturbing things you've told me is that he went up rather than down after you got off. We need to try to scope out where in the building someone could hide. Because if he's given us back Annie's key to the outside door, that limits his coming and going somewhat. Even assuming, as we must, that he's copied the apartment key, getting the one for the front door done wouldn't be easy."

"We could try talking to Tressa," Kitty said, "but I don't know that she could tell us anything. And maybe she wouldn't, anyway, if he was charming her. He was chatting her up when I came in. Better maybe to talk with the super tomorrow. He'd know if there are any hidey-holes.

"At least, we can give Annie back her keys," she added after a moment.

"I think we'll wait a little while to give this back to Annie," Joe said. He was unfastening the clasp that held the keys on the rose keychain. "Do you have a paper clip or a large safety pin we can put through these?" he asked Kitty.

"Yes, of course. I'll get something. But why are you taking them off the keychain?"

"Because the keychain isn't Annie's, it's Angela's. I gave it to her for her birthday over two years ago."

# CHAPTER 18

Kitty felt a sinking in the pit of her stomach. "Then he does know where Angela is! Perhaps is even holding her?" She shivered.

"Not necessarily,' Joe said neutrally. "He's giving us evidence he knows something about her. But there are any number of ways he could have gotten hold of her keychain without actually having been directly involved in whatever situation she may be in. There's no point in speculating about that, since we can't know."

Clearly, Kitty thought, Joe was detaching from his personal concerns to concentrate on problem-solving. A skill he no doubt learned in his professional life. And one she should be practicing as well.

"You said you were going to make some calls today. How did that go?" she asked.

"I talked to some people," he said.

"The police?"

"Well, I contacted the 88th Precinct and told them that the lost lamb had returned to the fold. That needed to be done. Of course, for them, that's just a bookkeeping note.

"I also talked to a friend of mine who's a little higher up in the NYPD. He was more interested in the implied threat to Angela, and I got the impression he might get someone working on tracing her." He paused, and for a moment Kitty could see the pain of a worried father in his rugged features.

"Well, that's good," Kitty said, wishing she could say something more helpful.

"Yes, it's good," Joe said. He breathed deeply and straightened in the chair. "So, anyway, I left calls for a couple of other fellows, and went around to see a friend who is ex-CIA. I gave him the complete run-down, not because I thought he could do anything himself, but because he might have some ideas." He looked at his hands. "I'm expecting to hear back from him yet tonight. And probably I'll hear from the other guys, too. Nothing that helps us in the immediate situation, but if they run him, and I have no doubt they will, they'll find the warrants and then they may have more interest."

"I would think the federal authorities, if they've been looking for this guy and you tell them he's here...." Kitty began.

"You'd think they'd be right over?" Joe said. "Well, yes, you might think so! But the Department of Justice is a huge bureaucracy, and sometimes it takes a long time for the word to get to the right place."

"You mean the left hand of Justice doesn't always know what the right hand is doing?" Kitty quipped.

Joe nodded, without smiling. "Supposedly the Homeland Security changes make it easier to share information from different agencies, but there still has to be someone who really wants to make that happen in a given case. We may have more luck with the NYPD, if we can figure out the right button to push."

"The fact that this scary guy may still be in the building is probably not enough cause for them to send someone over, I suppose," Kitty said, discouraged.

"I'm sorry. I'd hesitate to call the precinct with that," Joe said. "Especially since we just deleted a missing person report. Somebody will get interested eventually. I just hope it's in time to prevent any more harassment here."

"Well, it sounds like you've done what you could for now. Have you seen Annie and Gretchen?" Kitty was starting to feel more normal, and was curious how her neighbors might be doing.

"I've talked to Gretchen a couple of times. She's getting new locks put on, but not till tomorrow. And I haven't actually talked to Annie," Joe said. "It might be a good idea for the two of us to go over there after a while. Or at least offer. But meanwhile, I'm getting hungry. Are you feeling like getting something to eat?'

"Yes, now that you mention it, I am," Kitty acknowledged. "We could order in, or get take-out. There's a good Italian place just across the street. If you are hungry for pizza, they do really good pizza, or their regular meals are excellent. Or, there's also a good Chinese up at the corner. Those would both be take-out. Then, of course, there are dozens of places that deliver."

Kitty opened a drawer under the tabletop and pulled out an unruly handful of colorful menu fliers. "Here. See if anything appeals," she said. "We can look online, but I kinda prefer paper."

"Right off the bat, let me say I'd much rather order in." Joe spoke quietly but firmly. "I'm not interested in going anywhere while we think Daniel Oponuno is in this building." He looked very serious. Kitty cocked her head, listening intently

"Kitty, I don't want you to think for one minute that I'm minimizing either his threats to Annie or his treatment of you," he continued. "These are not the actions of a man we want to mess around with. The other thing I did today—and I hope this is all right with you—was to pick up a few things from home." He stood and walked over to the couch. He opened a small case and held up what looked to Kitty like a very serious handgun. "Including this," he said.

Kitty stifled a gasp.

He put the pistol back in the case, and coming back to the table, he continued. "I'd like to stay here until we get this wrapped up, unless you don't want me in your way. If you say so, I'll figure out something else. Most likely Annie and Gretchen would let me bunk on their couch for a while if necessary."

Kitty hadn't thought of his staying as an extended possibility. But as she quickly considered it, it sounded more reassuring than anything. And, actually, kind of nice. Joe was looking at her. "Oh, by all means, stay! I'd be really glad to have you here," she said.

"So, no take-out," she said, changing the subject to cover what she suspected was an over-eager response on her part.

"And the Chinese place doesn't deliver?" Joe asked.

"No, but there is a pretty good Thai place that does," Kitty said. "Do you like Thai?"

After pouring over the brightly-colored menu, they settled on Pad Thai, PIneapple Fried Rice, and fresh Spring Rolls. While they waited for the delivery, Kitty described (without naming any names) some of the situations her day's clients had brought. "I don't know what I can do about the family with the drug issue. It's clearly affecting the student's progress, but unless her family member wants to get help, there's not much she can do."

"I think you did the right thing suggesting Al-Anon," Joe said. "I've had some experience with that organization."

"Oh, I suppose maybe so," Kitty said, chagrined that she hadn't made that connection with Joe's daughter's problems. "I'm sorry if I brought up a painful subject."

"S'okay," Joe said. "It never goes away very far." Just then the intercom bleated. "Make them identify themselves, Kitty, before you buzz them in," Joe said.

When the delivery man came to the apartment door, Joe insisted on hearing from what restaurant the order was coming before he opened the door. He paid the bill without giving Kitty a chance, and when she tried to pay her half, he said it was only fair he should pay, since he was staying at her place.

"The logic of that escapes me somehow, since you are here partly to help keep me safe," Kitty said, "but I'll get the next one."

Joe smiled. "We could call this a date, if it would make you feel better. Or would you still insist on paying your own way?"

"No, I'm old-school on that," Kitty said. "If it's a date, then you can pay. Next time I'll invite you, and I'll pay. That's only fair, don't you think? We used to call that 'Sadie Hawkins'!" She chuckled.

"Oh, I remember Sadie Hawkins Day!" He began serving out the food. "The girl was supposed to ask the guy, pick him up, and pay for everything! It was a hoot! One year I got asked to the Sadie Hawkins dance by one of the prettiest girls in my high school."

He smiled, remembering. "I would never have had the nerve to ask her out myself. It was one of the dullest dates I ever had! She had looks but she was a terrible dancer, with no sense of rhythm. We didn't find much of anything to talk about all evening, and she took me home early."

"So not even any hanky-panky?" Kitty teased.

"No hanky-panky, and no return engagement," Joe laughed, picking up a spring roll.

While they ate, they chatted animatedly, as though there was nothing more important on their minds than the local sports teams and whether the much-heralded new movie Joe had seen and Kitty had not was really worth all the hullabaloo.

Cleaning up after the meal, Kitty asked again about Annie and Gretchen. "Should we go knock on their door?"

"I'm thinking call first," Joe said. "I'll call Gretchen. I think she'll want us to come, but we'll give them a chance to say no."

# CHAPTER 19

She didn't say no. In fact, she said, "Yes, please! Come on over. We're going stir-crazy!"

"I should maybe tell them about seeing Dan?" Kitty wondered aloud. "I don't really want to think about it, but yet...it seems like they should know he is in the building."

"They should. If you want a suggestion, "Joe said, as they locked Kitty's door and crossed the hall, "you could summarize very briefly. That way, you don't have to re-live it."

Kitty nodded as they heard locks being unlocked in 5F. Annie opened the door. "Come in," she said, smiling for what Kitty thought might be the first time in several days. "It's good to see somebody other than ourselves for a change!"

Gretchen, standing at the window, gestured toward the couch. "Please, have a seat. We don't have much in the way of food to offer you, but I could get you a beer, or a can of seltzer."

"Seltzer sounds good to me," Kitty said. "Don't worry about the food. We just ate Thai, and as usual there was way too much! We should have invited you over."

"Seltzer for me, too," Joe said. "Have you heard anything from our friend today?"

"No, thank Goddess," Annie said. "I hope to never hear from him again!"

"Probably unlikely," Kitty said, taking her cue. She accepted a cold can of Canada Dry Lemon-Lime seltzer from Gretchen, popped the top, and took a slow sip. "I saw him today."

"You did?" Annie was astonished. "Where?"

"Down at the front desk, when I came home from school," Kitty said. "He was chatting Tressa up."

"Typical," Annie muttered. "Did he recognize you?"

"He called me by name and then got on the elevator with me. It was kind of scary. I see what you mean by his being very persuasive."

"Tell me what he said to you," Annie said flatly.

"More or less that you were going to have to do what he wanted, I guess. And implied that he expected I would, too. I don't really know—"

"He's turned into a monster!" Annie said. "I should never have let him come here."

"He might have come anyway," Joe reminded her. "Do you know how he got your phone number? He called you on which phone? Mobile or landline?"

"The landline," Gretchen said. "She turns her mobile off at night."

"The landline is listed in my name, my maiden name, so that would have made it entirely too easy, I suppose, for him to find me," Annie said. "Did he say anything else, Kitty?" she prodded.

Kitty glanced at Joe, who gave her a slight nod of encouragement. "He said to tell you he'd be by soon, and for you to be ready."

Annie, who had been sitting throughout this conversation, jumped up from the chair and began shaking her fist while pacing back and forth in the small living room space. "I can't let him get away with this. I will do something about it!" She stamped her foot: "I will!"

"Easy, sweetheart!" Gretchen cautioned. "It's not going to help to get excited."

Joe's phone jingled, startling them all. He looked at the caller, and asked to be excused to the bedroom. "If you ladies don't mind," he nodded to Gretchen and Annie.

"Go," Annie said. "I want to hear some more from Kitty."

When Joe closed the bedroom door, Annie sat down again and turned to Kitty. "So, I can tell there is more to this than you've said. I know it's painful, but please—tell me what else happened." She glanced at the door. "Did Joe tell you not to tell me?"

"Joe is trying to protect me from thinking about it too much," Kitty said. "It was kind of awful, really. He touched me. Not anywhere the children's manuals would call 'private,' but in a way that felt both intimate and threatening at the same time."

"And then?"

"When I got off the elevator, he went on up, instead of down! So we think he might be intending to hide somewhere in the building."

"By Goddess! I will hex him," Annie burst out. "Someone has to stop this guy. Gretchen, you can help, and Kitty, too, if you want to." She rose from the chair and walked quickly over to the altar, where she began rearranging statues and candles.

"Annie, hold it!" Gretchen pleaded. "You know this isn't the way to go. I don't need to remind you—the Three-fold Law!"

Kitty frowned, puzzled. "What's that?" she asked Gretchen.

"The Three-fold Law? Witches believe—and we've seen it prove true—that whatever you send out comes back, three-fold. So, if you send out good, it comes back and if you send out bad...well, that comes back to you, too."

"It's like the Judeo-Christian concept of casting your bread upon the water." Annie turned from her altar. "You're right, of course, honey. But I'd almost risk it, just to get this guy, before he does anything more.

"If we have to do something—and we do have to do something —a binding's definitely more appropriate, as you said, and not so risky," she continued. "I just get mad when I think of how he is using people—all just to get a job?"

"I'm not sure that's all there is to it," Kitty said quietly. "Although I have no reason to think that. It just doesn't seem to quite fit."

Joe came out of the bedroom at that moment. He looked grave.

"Was that one of your friends?" Kitty asked.

"It was," Joe answered. "And I've learned some things. Let's all sit down, and I'll tell you what they are saying."

# CHAPTER 20

Joe explained briefly to Annie and Gretchen about the contacts he had made with his former colleagues and connections. "This call was from an FBI guy," he continued. "He had the information about Angela—I had to tell them about that threat, Annie—and they were treating it as a possible kidnapping."

Annie's face grew pale.

"I know," Joe said, speaking directly to her now. "To cut to the chase, what they are wanting us, or rather mostly you, to do is not to resist. To go along with what Dan wants. This agent said to tell you they think that if Dan is allowed to go ahead with whatever he has in mind, he will inevitably trip up somewhere and they'll be able to find Angela through him, whether he actually has her or just knows where she is."

No one spoke for a long moment.

"I guess from what I've heard," Kitty said, to break the uncomfortable silence, "that what he wants is a job with the film company down at the Navy Yard?"

Annie nodded slowly, her face expressionless.

"Can you do that?" Kitty asked doubtfully.

"Probably she can, actually," Gretchen chimed in. "She teaches a horticulture class down there, and she has become quite chummy with the personnel office. They're always advertising for drivers and guys to move stuff around."

"A horticulture class at the film studio?" Joe sounded disbelieving.

"The class isn't for the film company," Gretchen explained. "It's for the neighborhood. CSStudios is just letting the neighborhood group use the yard in front of their building, and one of the rooms they have vacant."

"The room has big windows on two sides, which means they can't use it as a sound stage, but it's just right for growing things," Annie said. She seemed to have regained her composure. "So what are we supposed to do?" she asked Joe.

"Wait for him to contact you. Stay safe, but agree to help him, short of letting him stay here, of course. Do you have a phone number for him?"

Annie shook her head.

"It's only reasonable to ask him for it," Joe suggested. "You'll be trying to get him an interview, I suppose. Right?"

"I suppose so," Annie said, hesitantly. And then, with more energy, "I don't want to let him in this apartment! Especially after what he did to Kitty."

Joe glanced sidelong at Kitty with raised eyebrows, and then responded to Annie. "No, and I don't think you should. You can talk through the door, or maybe if we are lucky, he'll phone you rather than come.

"And it will be better if he assumes I've gone on home," Joe continued. "I'll be out of the way at Kitty's, unless we have any reason to think he'll come by here soon. If it turns out you have to let him in before we leave, I can be in the bedroom with the door closed.

"Gretchen," he went on, "you should go ahead and get the lock changed as soon as you can! Tomorrow, right?" Gretchen nodded. "Until then, use the chair. Actually, we should have it in place now." He got up and suited action to his words.

"So you are saying we just wait, and when he contacts me, let him think he's won. I assume the FBI is going to be watching him or us or something?" Annie sounded skeptical.

"That's what they are asking us to do. I'm sure they've run him for warrants, and for all we know there may be some outstanding for who knows what." Joe threw Kitty a warning look. "Of course, the film company may not be willing to hire him, if that's the case. They probably have someone who vets their applicants for criminal records."

"Do *you* think Dan has Angela, or is involved somehow with her?" Annie asked pointedly.

"I don't think he has kidnapped her, based on the fact he's very vague in his threats. But he may know where she is. And if he is arrested—for kidnapping or anything else—something might shake loose. It's probably our best option at this point." Joe shook his head and grimaced. "It's also possible that if you do what he asks, he'll actually tell you what he knows. That could be a win-win."

"I hope so, but I'm not counting on it," Annie said.

"Neither am I," Joe agreed. "But by 'cooperating with law enforcement,' he said, giving a pseudo-smile and miming the quotation marks, "we will at least have a chance of locating her, and getting her back into whatever kind of care she will tolerate this time."

He stood and walked over to Annie, laying a hand on her shoulder. "Chum, it's not so different than it's been for years. We just do the best we can for her, when we get a chance, and let the results take care of themselves."

Annie reached back and laid her fingers on Joe's hand. "I know, Chum," she said, "I know. Thanks for being here, once again."

"Kitty, are you ready to go?" Joe asked.

"Yes, I'm tired," Kitty said, "and I bet these gals are, too."

"Okay, ladies, we'll go, and you be sure to re-set the chair up behind us," Joe said, moving to leave.

Then they heard a fumbling at the door. The bolt turned, and there was more noise, as someone turned the knob and tried to push his way in. The four held their collective breath. But the makeshift door-wedge held tight.

"Annie!" came an all-too familiar voice. "Annie, sweetie, what's going on here?"

Annie looked at Joe, who nodded, and then mouthed, "Just don't let him in."

"Annie, I just want to talk to you. Let me in, so we can talk."

Joe was shaking his head firmly.

"Dan, we can talk through the door. I can't let you in, but we can talk through the door," Annie said. She moved toward the door, but kept far enough from the chair to avoid any possibility of touching it.

"Okay, Annie, if that's what you want. For now. You are going to help me, right? You're choosing to help me." It was a statement, not a question.

Annie hesitated, looked around at the others. Even Gretchen was nodding. "I will, Dan," she said finally. "I will, but you'll have to help me help you. And then, you'll tell me where to find my daughter, right?"

"That's after I get what I need, Annie. Let's talk about how you are going to help me. I need that job at the movie company, and I need it now." His tone was rougher now.

"Dan, I'll need to have you fill out an application. If you'll give me your phone number, I'll call you as soon as I can get one." Annie's voice cracked, betraying the strain she was feeling.

"How about I call you?" Dan said.

"That will be awkward," Annie persisted. "It will be quicker if I can call you. But it's up to you," she added. She glanced over her shoulder at Joe, who nodded encouragement.

"Okay." Dan sounded off-hand about it after all. He gave Annie the number, adding, "I'll be expecting to hear from you soon. Oh, and Annie, why don't you just go ahead and fill out the form. It doesn't matter what you put down. You're going to be the one getting me the job!"

"I'll do what I can," Annie said. "Tomorrow being Saturday, I don't know whether the Human Relations office is open or not. But I'll do what I can, as fast as I can."

There was no answer. Everyone in the apartment waited. Annie backed quietly away from the door, and Gretchen came up to embrace her tenderly.

Joe reached an arm out and drew Kitty toward him.

Finally, Joe motioned toward the far corner of the room. When everyone was gathered around him, he spoke quietly. "Let's wait a little while longer. There's no telling whether he left or is hanging around. Gretchen, when the super comes to put in your new locks, see whether he'll put in a peephole, too."

Gretchen nodded.

"You did good, Annie," Kitty whispered. "I think he was convinced."

"Well, at least he did give me a phone number. It remains to be seen whether it's real or not," Annie said.

"Can I get everyone a drink now?" Gretchen said softly.

"I'd appreciate something," Joe said.

"Beer?" Gretchen asked.

"Actually, if it's not too much trouble," Joe said, still keeping his voice very low, "I'd really like a cup of tea."

"Oh, sure! Good idea," Gretchen said. "I'll make a pot, shall I?"

Annie and Kitty both nodded, and Kitty went with Gretchen to the kitchen.

Eventually, after a pot of tea had been brewed and quietly consumed, Joe stood up. As he moved toward the door, the gun Kitty had seen earlier was suddenly held discretely at his side. Quietly and quickly, he removed the chair and jerked the door open. Gun first, he moved to look out the door and then down the hall. Just like in the movies, Kitty thought. He does know what he's doing.

"Okay, ladies," he addressed Annie and Gretchen. "I think we'll go. I have some calls to make. Gretchen, I saw you writing down the number he gave us. Can you read it off to me, so I can pass it along?"

Back in her own apartment, Kitty realized she was near the point of exhaustion. "Joe," she said, "I think I have to go to bed. I'm sorry; I know you are going to be up a while, but I don't think I can."

"Don't worry. You go take a hot shower and go to bed. I'll be fine," Joe said. "I won't be far behind you, anyway. Just a phone call or two, won't take long."

"At least I can make up the bed for you," Kitty said.

"Here, we can do it together," Joe volunteered. They worked smoothly as a team and the sofa-bed was ready in no time. "Okay, my fair lady, time for beddy-bye," Joe said with a twinkle. He held out his arms and this time Kitty went without hesitation for a hug that lasted a bit longer than necessary, and a goodnight kiss that went a little beyond just friendly. If she hadn't already declared she was ready to drop, Kitty thought she might have stayed for more. But there would perhaps be time for that later, if things went on the way they seemed to be going.

She moved away reluctantly and went to get the prescribed shower. Not a cold shower, although as she lay alone in her own bed later, she wondered whether that might have been a good idea.

# CHAPTER 21

The sun was streaming in when Kitty finally woke. She thought she heard kitchen noises, and when she opened the bedroom door, she certainly smelled fresh-brewed coffee.

Joe waved to her from the kitchen. "Good morning, Merry Sunshine!" he smiled. "As soon as you're ready, there's coffee, and I'm going to run downstairs and get cream and some fresh croissants. Would you like me to get anything else?"

"Sounds great," Kitty said. "Why don't you pick up a copy of the *Times*? I don't subscribe, because I don't have time to read it regularly, but I do like to catch up on the weekends."

"Done," said Joe. "And I'll be back in a jiff."

Kitty took a quick shower and washed her short wavy hair. She pulled on a pale blue sweatshirt and finger-combed her hair before tugging on a pair of jeans she knew helped flatten her stomach, and showed off her buns. By the time Joe got back, she had laid out plates and knives, and poured herself a cup of strong black coffee.

"Here's the cream." He opened the carton and handed it to Kitty. "And here are the *croissants*." He pronounced it in the French way. Kitty creamed her coffee and wondered if Joe had needed multiple languages in his mysterious working past.

"Shall we eat at the table?" she asked, "or lounge over there and read the paper?" She nodded toward the sofa and recliner, while putting butter and a jar of strawberry jam on the table.

"Oh, I'm for lounging, I think," Joe said. "Unless you'd prefer the table?" he queried politely.

"No, I think a Saturday morning eating croissants and reading the *New York Times* is about as delightfully decadent as I care to get!" Kitty responded. "There's also orange juice, if you want some."

"Not right now," Joe said, helping himself to more coffee.

They settled themselves in the living room, Joe in the recliner and Kitty on the couch, sharing the small end table between them for their coffee mugs.

"Mmm! I do love a fresh, well-made croissant," Kitty murmured. "I don't know who does their baking, but whoever they are, they do a great job!'

"I agree," Joe said. "And to have it right in the corner of the building! That's a real perk! I might just decide to stay here instead of going back to Williamsburg." He made a sound like a little chuckle, meant to indicate, Kitty surmised, that the comment wasn't to be taken seriously.

"Did you know the Navy Yard still has an active shipyard?" Joe asked after a while, looking up from the paper.

"No," Kitty said. "I thought that was all closed down, and that was why they have all those other businesses in there."

"No, apparently there's still a shipyard. It's private now, of course, not military."

Joe read from the *Times*: "'Brooklyn Navy Yard is home to COC Shipyard Corporation, a private full-service shipyard, servicing vessels which meet air draft requirements for the Brooklyn Bridge. A channel (depth 35 feet) from Throggs Neck to the yard is maintained by the Federal Government.'"

"What's 'air draft'?" Kitty asked. "It has to have something to do with how big the ship is, but I've never heard that term before."

"It's the height above the water," Joe answered. "'Draft' usually means the depth, or, if you will, the height, of the part that's in the water."

"So," Kitty finished, "the 'air draft' is the height of the part that's in the air. How cool! Learn something new every day!"

"So, they repair Coast Guard ships and all kinds of private shipping from tugs to Holland America cruise ships," Joe continued. "They have the largest dry dock in New York Harbor, and it sounds like they do all kinds of repairs. They work mostly on cargo ships of various kinds, but they're bringing in a small fancy cruise ship this week."

"Which ship?"

"The *Queen Europa*," Joe said. "She was damaged below the waterline in a trans-Atlantic crossing, so they're going to fix her here."

"That would be interesting to see," Kitty said. "I think my husband and I might have sailed on that ship. I wonder if a person can get in close to where they're working? I know there are parts of the Navy Yard that are wide open, but I don't know if there are other parts that are not."

"We could go down there and look around later," Joe said. "It'd be good to get out and stretch our legs. Do you know whether we can just walk in?"

"At least one gate on Flushing you can." Kitty frowned. "I think so, anyway. I'm not sure about the gate that is closest to us, straight down Washington. It's a really big piece of land."

"The article said 300 acres," Joe said. "Only if you'd like to," he continued.

"You can't walk all the way around the outside, of course," Kitty said, "because it opens on the water. But we could walk along the Flushing side, or alternately, if we weren't set on going in, we could just cross Flushing and keep going on Washington. I don't really know how far you can go that way, before you either run into the East River or get stopped by some other barrier."

"Where is the film company?" Joe asked.

"Well, I think it's actually down near where the dry docks must be," Kitty said. "So if we can go see the studios—I mean the outside, I'm sure they don't let you go inside, unless there's a real tour—but if we can walk around near the studios, we ought to be able to go to the shipyard. I'd be up for that after a while. But not right now." She stretched and yawned expressively. "I'm going to enjoy being lazy for a while longer."

"Sounds good to me," Joe agreed. "I'm getting some more

coffee, though. Want a refill?"

"Yes, please," Kitty said. She handed him her mug. "With cream, please."

#

An hour later, Joe got up and folded the piece of the paper he'd just been reading. "I'm going across the hall," he said. "I'll be back shortly."

Kitty heard him knock on the door, and then heard him say sharply, "NO! First, you ask for ID, and satisfy yourselves that you know who is standing there. Only then do you touch the chair."

Uh-oh, Kitty thought. You don't want to get this guy upset with you!

When he came back in about ten minutes, Kitty inquired about his visit with Gretchen and Annie. "Gretchen has arranged with the super to get the locks changed today. He'll put in a peephole as well, but the peephole doesn't go until Monday, worse luck. He's supposed to be coming soon about the locks, so I think this would be a good time for us to go walk-about."

"Walk-about Wallabout!" Kitty chanted enthusiastically. "You know about Wallabout, right? Much better than 'Not Quite Clinton Hill.' The bay, and by extension this area of Brooklyn."

"I've seen Wallabout Bay on maps. I guess there used to be more of a bay there, before the Navy Yard."

"I've read that the early settlers on the Bay were Belgian. The term 'Wallabout' is supposedly from the Dutch phrase for 'Walloons' Bay,'" Kitty got up and carried the coffee mugs and plates to the kitchen. "I should run the dishwasher today. But it doesn't have to be right now, I guess." She rinsed the mugs and put them, along with the plates, in the dishwasher.

They walked the short block down Washington toward Flushing—past the tiny upscale wine store with its wrought-iron door screen, past the garage with yellow school buses labeled in Hebrew parked in front, and past a couple of other spaces optimistically being renovated for leasing to new retail establishments. The Brooklyn Roasting Company on the corner was humming with business. "We could stop here for lunch on the way back," Kitty suggested.

"Sounds good," Joe said. "Which way shall we walk?"

"Let's try going on down Washington," Kitty said. "I want to know what's down there. It looks like you can't go through, but let's go see."

When the walk light came on, they crossed the four lanes of Flushing Avenue. "I guess we have to go down the other side of Washington," Kitty said, noting the absence of sidewalk on their side. On the far side, they found themselves passing a fenced parking lot and a six-story brick building of relatively recent construction before coming to a guard post. Kitty walked over to the guard hut, and inquired whether they could walk through.

"Only on a tour," was the reply.

"And what is in this area?" Kitty asked.

"The road here leads to the piers at the eastern edge of the bay, and also accesses the shipyard," the guard told her. "That's why it's not open to the public."

Returning to Joe on the sidewalk, Kitty relayed what she'd learned. "Let's walk down Flushing in the Williamsburg direction, and around the corner a little ways. We'll come to water eventually if we go far enough, but it'll make a nice walk."

While truck traffic on Flushing kept it from being quite the idyllic stroll it might otherwise have been, Kitty noticed with pleasure that Joe quickly accommodated his long strides to her shorter legs.

A tall fence, woven of heavy wire, showed signs of having been overgrown with trees and vines, which had been cut out in many places, giving glimpses of 19th century buildings in various states of disrepair. Joe and Kitty took turns trying to guess the original purposes of the buildings they saw. "We'll never know who was right, unless you want to do the research—because I certainly don't," Kitty teased.

"I'd probably enjoy it," Joe replied. "But whether I ever get around to it, that's another question. Are you getting about ready to turn back?"

"Let's go on just a little further, if you're game," Kitty said. "I see some trees up there, and maybe there is a place to sit down, before we go back."

"That's fine. I just didn't want to wear you out," Joe said.

"Hey, I'm a New Yorker!" Kitty retorted, smiling. "I walk."

When they reached the trees, there was indeed a small wooden bench set back from the sidewalk. Kitty sat gratefully at one end, noticing for the first time that her feet were hurting a little. Joe sat down near the middle, and stretched his arms over the back of the bench. Within a few moments, the arm that had come across behind Kitty was gradually brought around her shoulder. She sighed happily and scooted just a little bit closer, basking in the comfortable companionship.

"Ready to go back?" Joe said after a few minutes.

"Uh-huh," Kitty agreed.

Joe stood up and reached a hand out. Kitty took it and then it seemed perfectly natural to keep hold after she stood up. They walked along hand in hand for ten yards or so, but the difference in length of stride prevented a comfortably rhythmic arm swing. They both noticed this at the same time, and began to swing their joined arms artificially high and in rhythm with neither's steps. "Okay," Kitty laughed. "This isn't working."

"No hand-holding?" Joe mimed deep disappointment. "Well, then, how about smooching?" He grabbed Kitty's shoulders playfully and pulled her close enough to plant a quick but unequivocal kiss on her upturned lips. She snuggled in a little closer and Joe wrapped his arms around her in a firm hug. "I like the feel of you in my arms," he whispered in Kitty's ear.

She smiled up at him, earning another kiss, a little longer than the first.

"We should move on, I imagine," Kitty said, stepping back. "Don't want to shock the natives. Are you ready for lunch, if we stop at Brooklyn Roasting?"

"Ready," Joe said. "Have you seen what you wanted to see of

the Navy Yard?"

"Not really," Kitty said. "What I've seen is that you can't get to the shipyards from this end. Maybe from the Sands Street side. I'll have to look more carefully when the bus goes by there. Or maybe from going further down Flushing the other way; I know there's at least one more public gate there. It doesn't really matter. I just would like to see the *Queen Europa* out of the water. It would be a kick."

Lunch at the coffee shop was simple sandwiches and good coffee, followed by lemon bars and more coffee. Conversation was pleasant, if a bit desultory. And then they walked together back up the hill to the Cocoa Factory.

# CHAPTER 22

Arriving back at 5G, Kitty unlocked her door, while Joe inspected the door across the hall. "Looks like the super has been and done," he said. "I want to check with the ladies."

"I'll come, too," Kitty offered. "Unless you'd rather I didn't."

"No, by all means," Joe said, knocking on the door of 5F.

"Who is it?" they heard Annie call from inside.

"Good girl, Annie," Joe said. "It's the plumber. I've come to fix the sink, and I've got my helper with me!"

Annie opened the door, laughing. "It's good to see you, Mr. Plumber, and Ms. Plumber's Helper," she said. "Come in. We have, as you see, been visited by the super, who grumbled a bit but agreed to try to get the peephole in first thing on Monday."

"I don't know that we need to come in," Joe said. "I just wanted to see that your new locks were working well, and that you were still remembering to ask for ID."

"It's our new protocol, at least until we get the peephole," Gretchen said, coming up behind Annie.

"And even after, until we know this business is completely over," Joe cautioned. "It's always possible to mistake a voice, or even—I am sorry to have to suggest this—but it's possible a person shows up in front of the lens who is not alone and not able to speak freely."

Kitty shuddered. "You really think—"

"I don't know!" Joe said, interrupting her brusquely. "And that's just the point! I'd rather take some common precautions than be sorry because we didn't!"

"Sure," Kitty said, shrinking back a little at his tone. "I didn't mean...well, sure, better safe than sorry." She wasn't sure she liked this professional Joe all that much.

"Annie, Gretchen," Joe said, "now that you can lock your door and trust it will stay locked, I was about to suggest that you both get out of the house for a while. At the very least, go get your new key copied at the hardware store." He sounded both encouraging and directive at the same time.

Kitty could imagine him using this tone with his troops when in the military. If he had any "troops," which she didn't know, of course. "Go on up to Ft. Greene Park," he continued, "anything to get some fresh air and stretch your legs."

"Yeah!" Gretchen said eagerly. "There's really no reason we need to stay cooped up now, is there? I could use a good walk, and we need groceries, too."

"Sounds good to me," Annie said. "As long as we stay together. I don't want any chance of running into Dan on my own."

"Good idea," Joe nodded. "Stay together, and keep an eye out, but I think you'll be fine. You've agreed to do what he wants, and he knows you can't do anything til Monday, so I doubt he'll be around before then."

"Well, have a good walk," Kitty said, "and stay safe. It's beautiful outside; you'll enjoy it, especially after being cooped up for so long!" She yawned and stretched extravagantly. "Me, I've had my exercise, and I'm going to take a nap!"

"Sounds like a good exit line to me," Joe smiled. "Have a good afternoon, ladies."

Back in 5G, Kitty moved to make good on her declaration. "Do you need anything, Joe, before I go lie down?" she asked.

"No, I guess not," Joe said, "if you're definitely committed to sleeping."

"Was there something else you had in mind?" Kitty said, hoping she didn't sound too coy.

"Well, I was thinking there are other things two people can do on a beautiful Saturday afternoon besides nap," Joe said speculatively, "some of which might involve lying down…." He trailed off, looking at Kitty, his head cocked to one side.

She smiled. "You think?"

"I do," Joe said, moving toward her. He reached for her shoulders and drew her close in a tender embrace. She tilted her head up to receive his kiss. After a moment, he moved one hand down to pull her lower body close to his. As the kiss grew, she could feel that something else was growing, too.

Finally, Joe moved his hand back up to Kitty's shoulder and lifted his head. "If you want to try out my idea for afternoon entertainment," he said, looking down at her, "you'll have to let me make a quick run to the drug store. I know I'm healthy and safe, and I'm sure you are, too, but you don't really know me that well yet." He waited for her answer.

"Sounds right to me," Kitty said, her inner tingle giving more passion to her voice than the words alone might have seemed to warrant. "I'll be here when you get back."

"I won't be long, you can be assured," Joe said. "Just don't open the door to anyone else!"

Kitty showered leisurely, enjoying the silken slide of the body wash over her skin, as heart and yoni throbbed in anticipation. She dug a tiny bottle of Chanel #5 from the bottom of a drawer and selected a pink t-shirt, deemed after an appraisal from all sides in the full-length mirror to have optimal coverage versus un-coverage, both top and bottom. A vining rose embroidered diagonally through the middle of the front was one of the reasons she didn't usually wear that shirt in public.

By the time Joe got back, Kitty was putting a Mel Torme CD in the player. "I hope you like The Velvet Fog," she said.

"I do," Joe answered enthusiastically. "I heard him once in concert before he died. It was a real highlight of my cultural life—not that that's saying much!

"Speaking of highlights," he continued, "you look splendid! Let me catch a quick shower. I'll be right with you."

When Joe came out of the bathroom, a towel wrapped decorously around his hips, Kitty thought she had never seen, in person or on-screen, a better-put-together "older man." She smiled warmly at him as he stood, rather timidly, she thought, near the bedroom door. "Come into my parlor," she said, beckoning him toward the bed.

Their lovemaking was both slow and passionate. Joe was a gentle and attentive lover, lingering over one spot before swooping to another. When Kitty felt she could wait no longer, he surprised her by gliding in a finger, coated with something slippery, which touched her in places she thought had never been touched before.

"We now pause for motion indemnification," Joe said. He slipped a condom package from under the pillow and tore it open. "Want to help me with this?" he said playfully.

She did.

Joe came fully into her now, and they merged in the kind of timeless rapture that can never be adequately described or even exactly remembered, but which is also never forgotten.

*** 

The rest of the day passed in a pleasantly hazy muddle. They went across the street to the dimly-lit little Italian place for dinner. Gretchen called to say they had had a good outing and were going to bed early. Joe suggested watching something on TV but the movie they found was not lively enough to keep either of them really awake. When Kitty turned the set off, Joe lifted his head from his chest.

"You want to come sleep in the bedroom?" Kitty asked him.

"Save making this one up," Joe answered. He smiled wearily at her.

"Then come along, sleepy-head, no sense dozing on the couch while pretending to watch TV."

"If I snore too much, you can send me back out," Joe said, as he put his arm around her. "I don't hear myself, but I have been told that I might snore just a little."

"If you do, I'll just kick you, and you'll wake up enough to quit," Kitty teased. "That's a trick I learned long ago."

# CHAPTER 23

Sunday morning, Kitty woke with a start. Eyes still closed, she searched mentally for what could have wakened her, only to feel an unfamiliar movement in the bed. Oh! she remembered, and then an arm came over her and pulled her in close as Joe nuzzled her shoulder. "Good morning," he whispered hoarsely. "I'm still here, darling."

"Good morning," Kitty whispered in return. "So am I." She rolled over and kissed the tip of his nose.

"No need to get up right away, is there?" Joe asked.

"Not by me," Kitty said, snuggling closer.

"I might as well admit up front," he said, "the brave little man is probably not good for another round right away—at least, not without a blue pill. But I'm good at cuddling, and could probably come up with some other means of making a pretty woman happy, if you are in that sort of mood."

"If you don't mind my asking, were you using 'the little blue pill' last night?" Kitty asked.

"No, my dear, that was your charms entirely," Joe said, stroking her hair. "I don't have such a prescription. But I'm certainly willing to get one, should there prove to be a need." He smiled fondly at Kitty. "Tell the truth, I do not know at this point."

"I like that we are able to talk about it," Kitty said. "That's important to me."

"Probably lots of things we might want to talk about," Joe said. "Or not, at least not right now."

"It's Sunday, isn't it?" Kitty asked. "Are you a church-goer?"

"Not so much," Joe said. "Are you?"

"Sometimes I go over to the Quaker Meeting on Schermerhorn," Kitty said. "Not this morning, I think. I'm too lazy. And I need to do laundry."

"I could help you with that," Joe offered. "And then—actually, one of the things we do need to talk about—I need to get some more things from my place if I'm going to continue to stay here for a while longer. It's probably not strictly necessary from a security viewpoint." He paused, watching Kitty closely. "I'd still like to stay, for at least a couple of reasons, one of which has nothing to do with the purpose for which I came in the first place." He had propped himself up on an elbow, and now glanced across the room, as though Kitty's response had little to do with him.

"I'll tell the truth and shame the devil," Kitty said. "I would really like you to stay, because I'm not convinced that this guy won't be back, or isn't still in the building. But I also like having you around. So there!"

"Well, then, maybe you'd like to take the bus with me back to Williamsburg to pick up a few more things. And I might bring my car. It could make it easier should I need to liaise with someone over the next few days."

"'Liaise'!" Kitty almost laughed aloud. "I actually know someone who can say 'liaise' with a straight face. Amazing!"

"What's wrong with 'liaise'?" Joe asked. He stuck out his lower lip in an exaggerated pout. "Are you saying it's not a kosher word?"

"No, I think it probably is. It's just that I've only ever read it in British crime novels. I guess I didn't know real people actually used it."

"Well, now that you mention it, I may have picked it up from a couple of English professional contacts I have lunch with sometimes. They are always liaising with this person or that organization. Funny how you pick up words like that without even noticing."

"Right," Kitty said. "Well, to answer your question, yes, I will go with you to Williamsburg. Could we do laundry first, or would some of the clothes you need to bring like to visit the laundry, too? We do have a nice laundry room here. It's one of the other perks." She smiled conspiratorially.

"Ok, to put things in order, breakfast first, laundry second, Williamsburg third. Right?"

"Sounds good. We are out of OJ, and I don't know what else we have of a breakfast sort of food," Kitty said, stretching and rolling toward the edge of the bed. "Shall I go hunting and gathering while you make coffee and get beautiful?"

"Good idea, ma'am," Joe said, giving her a left-handed salute from the bed. He rolled out of bed, too, and together they quickly spread the bedclothes and pulled up the quilt.

"You haven't kissed me good morning," Joe complained, as Kitty turned to leave.

"Have to do something about that," Kitty said, and they proceeded to remedy the situation nicely before Kitty dressed quickly, grabbed a canvas shopping bag, and headed out the door.

A few minutes later, she was adding yogurt, whole oat flakes, and orange juice (lots of pulp) to the shopping cart that already contained the carton of organic fresh fruit chunks she had selected. She turned a corner in the tightly-stocked little store and came face to face with Dan Oponuno, standing next to the Tom's of Maine toothpaste, just past the recycled paper towels and biodegradable soap powder.

"Why, hello, Kitty," he said. "How nice to see you here!" His voice was low and compelling as he stepped forward, his handsome face split by a broad smile that failed to reach his eyes.

Kitty turned her head away so as not to meet his gaze. Backing her cart out of the tight aisle, she fled toward the checkout counter, whatever else she might have intended to purchase now completely forgotten. As she reached the counter area, she looked behind her to see whether the man had followed— knowing that if she glimpsed him she would abandon her cart and run for the front door of the Cocoa Factory. When he didn't appear, she unloaded her few items as quickly as possible onto the little counter, paid in cash, and made her escape, half-running to the street and into the courtyard of the apartment building.

She rushed through the outer doors, inserted her key to open the inner doors and watched them snap shut before dashing to the elevator and punching "5" and "Close door" in quick succession. Once safely inside the door of her apartment, she stopped short, out of breath and shaking. "Joe!" she called urgently. "I need some help." She dropped the grocery bag and bent over, hands on her knees.

"Are you okay?" Joe came rushing from the bedroom. "Kitty! What happened? Are you all right?" He gently lifted her head to look in her face.

"Yes, I'm okay," she said crossly, now annoyed with herself. She caught her breath and straightened up. "Just had a fright is all. I'm sorry!"

"Sorry about what? What happened?" Joe was concerned but understandably puzzled. "A traffic accident?" he guessed.

"No," Kitty said. "I saw our guy, in the Food Friend! He was just standing there, like he belonged." She tossed her head. "I'm okay. I was just so startled to see him!"

"Did he see you?" Joe wanted to know. He stepped around the grocery bag and took Kitty in his arms.

"Oh, yes! He spoke to me! And then I ran!" She tried a laugh that didn't come off. "Heh-heh! What a pantywaist!"

"No, not at all! You did exactly the right thing. Did he follow you?"

"I don't think so. I didn't see him again, and I was able to check out without his coming up to the front," Kitty said.

"Well, at least he can't get into the building on the weekend, because he gave back Annie's keys and the building key can't be duplicated without lots of paperwork." Joe began picking up the spilled groceries.

Kitty looked at him thoughtfully. "Not true, actually—that he can't get in—if he's figured out that you can get into the building through the Food Friend."

"You can?" Joe was surprised. "That sounds decidedly insecure."

"Well, it's through the back, and most people, unless somebody showed them, wouldn't think of going through what looks like a service door. It leads to a kind of catacomb through stocks and cleaning equipment and such and then you come out in the lobby of the Cocoa Factory, just by the security desk," Kitty explained.

"And there's nobody on the desk on the weekend," she added. "Not that they'd be likely to question anyone coming through that passage anyway. I don't know whether they would or not. Most of the time it doesn't seem like they are paying any attention to who comes and goes."

"Can you show me how that entrance from the store works?" Joe asked.

"Sure," Kitty said. "Right now? "

"No, let's have breakfast now. We can do it later. But we have to assume he does have access to the building any time he wants."

"Okay," Kitty said. She had regained her composure, and began setting out bowls and flatware."I hope you like yogurt?" she asked.

"A little goes a long way with me, but if you've got fruit and cereal, I'll take a little yogurt on top." Joe poured coffee and offered Kitty the cream.

They were just finishing breakfast when Joe's phone rang. He excused himself to the bedroom, leaving Kitty to clean up.

When he came back, he was frowning.

"What's up?" Kitty inquired.

"That was the FBI. They want to put a bug on Annie's phone. I'm elected to tell her they're coming over."

"Well, I suppose that makes sense," Kitty says. "I don't think Annie will object. What if Dan were to call her from a phone different from the number he gave us?"

"If they just wanted the phone calls," Joe explained, "they only have to get a court order to tap the line. A bug on the phone itself will transmit everything said in the apartment. I don't like the implications."

"That means they don't trust Annie and Gretchen? And by association, us too?" Kitty was wide-eyed.

"Seems likely," Joe said.

"Another way to look at it is," Kitty mused, "if Dan were to get into the apartment somehow—if anyone were monitoring a bug, it might be a safety factor for Annie and Gretchen."

"Humph!" Joe sounded his skepticism. "One of the things I like about you, Kitty, is that you're always looking for the good in any person or situation. Don't lose that!"

"I've been wondering," Kitty ventured, "why they needed Dan's phone number, anyway. Couldn't they just have tapped Annie's phone, and that would have been easy because she probably would have given her permission right away?"

"I don't know," Joe said. "It's become clear there are things going on that we don't know about. I'll make some phone calls later and see what I can find out. Maybe nothing, but it won't hurt to try. So, let's get at that laundry, shall we?"

"Okay, it won't take long for me to get ready. Do you have anything you want to toss in?"

# CHAPTER 24

Later, finishing up the laundry, Kitty realized having Joe with her was reassuring to a degree that she hadn't really counted on. The laundry room was a clean, well-lighted place, but it was also very isolated, and she had often thought it could be spooky if she let herself dwell on that aspect. Yet she hadn't worried a bit today.

The trip to Williamsburg was postponed so that Joe could alert Annie and Gretchen about the bug.

Gretchen was relatively calm in hearing the news. Annie grasped immediately the implication that Joe had mentioned to Kitty. "Why do they need to hear what we are saying in our own apartment?" she demanded, squinting at Joe, her chin thrusting forward.

"Don't ask me," Joe said. "I'm just the messenger boy. Of course, you can refuse permission," he continued. "But I imagine if they wanted to they could use some of that fancy listening equipment that goes right through the wall."

Annie gaped. "What do you know about that? Joe, you never told me about that!"

"Hey, babe!" Joe said, smiling. "There's a lot more than that I never told you." He paused. "But seriously, this is a technology that's been around for a while, though it's probably only since 9/11 that it's available for use in domestic snooping. I don't like the idea of it, but you can be sure they're using it in cases where national security is at risk."

"How would this situation qualify?" Kitty puzzled. "It's being treated as a kidnapping, right?"

"So far as we know," Joe said. He didn't say anything more, and

Kitty wondered what else he knew or suspected.

"Well, I don't see why we would object," Gretchen said. "The phone is in the living room, not the bedroom, right? And we don't intend to do anything illegal or even suspicious."

"I don't want our upcoming moon celebration being monitored," Annie protested.

"I'm sure someone else will host," Gretchen soothed.

"Would you want to do it at my place?" Kitty offered. "I could move things around however you needed."

"See," Gretchen said. "It will be no problem. It's next Wednesday night, Kitty," she said. "I'll come over before then and we can talk about how to make the right kind of space, and you'd be welcome to join us if you like."

"Okay, sounds fine," Kitty said. "And of course, by then this may all be over and they will have taken the bug out."

"We hope," Gretchen said, fervently.

"You want me to be here when they come?" Joe asked.

"Thanks, but I don't see why you'd need to be," Gretchen said. "Do you, Annie?"

"No, if we have to do it, it's just a technical thing, right?"

"Right," Joe said. "They just wanted you to know before someone showed up at your door. Speaking of which, when did you say the super is coming to put in your peephole?"

"Not until Monday," Gretchen said. "We'll be really careful about identifying the FBI people when they come. Do you have a name for us?"

"I don't, but you can count on their saying who they are from downstairs, and again when they come to the door. And use the chain guard when you ask them to show their badges," Joe cautioned.

"We will," Gretchen assured him. "Thanks, Joe. You've been a good friend."

"Yeah, thanks," Annie echoed, less enthusiastic. "I don't like this whole thing, and I especially don't like the bug.

"But it's none of it your fault," she conceded grudgingly.

"Okay," Joe said to Kitty once they were back in the hall. "Let's go to Williamsburg. We can have a nice lunch and then go rummage through my stuff for some presentable duds."

"If you don't mind my asking," Kitty said as they stood waiting for the elevator, "how do you come to be living in Williamsburg? I think of it as more of a hipster neighborhood these days."

"Well, I had a job there a while back, and, I guess, like you, I just like being around young people." Joe hesitated. "I'm a sound sleeper," he added.

Another "can't talk about it" answer, Kitty thought. But she only said, "Do you want to see the secret passages in and out of the Food Friend?"

"Might as well do that now," Joe said. "The Sunday crowds in Williamsburg won't be any better or worse for a slight detour."

"Okay," Kitty said, as they reached the first floor and walked past the empty reception desk. She pushed the red button to unlock the thick glass inner doors leading to the entry-way, and Joe held a door open for her. "So," Kitty continued, pushing through the second set of transparent doors, "to start with, that door over there leads directly into the Food Friend. It's unlocked whenever the store is open." She pointed to an unprepossessing steel door in the courtyard wall.

Joe pulled the door open and followed Kitty into a dampish hallway that quickly turned into the fish and seafood section of the little grocery. "So, you see where we are now," Kitty said. "The bakery and deli counter is right over there, and this is the entrance they use to bring in the fresh baked goods every day. I don't know exactly where they bake, but it sure smells good if you're coming out of the apartment house at the same time."

"Speaking of bakeries, I could actually use a cup of coffee about now," Joe said. "Would you like a little something?"

"Sure," Kitty said. "I'd share a croissant with you, or a Danish."

"I'd just as soon have my own," Joe smiled, as they reached the bakery counter. "Which would you rather have?" he asked, opening the self-service cabinet door.

"Oh, a Danish, I guess, if they have something other than cream cheese," Kitty answered.

"Looks like raspberry," Joe suggested.

"That's good. I"ll go get the coffee, shall I?" Kitty asked, already heading to the little coffee bar.

Joe turned to say, "Make mine French Roast!" as he slipped two pastries into little brown waxed paper bags.

"Okay," Kitty said, once they had paid and were each carrying a paper cup in one hand and a goodie in the other. "Now for the really cool part. You go past the cereal—and come to think of it, this was about where I saw el-Creepo earlier—so, past the cereal and the crackers, and straight ahead through this door.

"It doesn't look like it would go anywhere but to storage for the Food Friend, or maybe a staff restroom," she continued, leading the way. "But you wind around and down (watch the steps!), past the cold storage locker, and eventually you start up this little ramp—and here we are, back inside The Cocoa Factory." They stepped from the dimly-lit hallway into the brightness of the apartment building lobby.

"And you think most people don't know about this?" Joe asked. He sipped his coffee.

"I almost never see anyone use it," Kitty said. "From either end. I don't think even most of the people living in the building know about it. I use it once in a while, and it's really handy in bad weather. But I don't think I'll be using it with el-Creepo still on the loose!"

They exited the building again through the front door, and walked through the courtyard to the sidewalk.

"Do you want to walk, or take the bus?" Joe asked. "It's about twenty minutes, either way."

"Since we're going to be doing a bit of walking after we get there, why don't we take the bus?" Kitty suggested. "We can always walk back if we feel like more exercise."

"Sounds good to me," Joe said, heading for the corner to cross the street toward the bus shelter.

***

Williamsburg was a treat. The sidewalks were crowded, but after a few blocks of window-shopping, they found a little cafe with a back garden. The waitress was friendly, cute, and very efficient, and the menu offered free-range chicken, baked with an apricot glaze and served with bok choy and baby carrots. For dessert, Joe had a piece of flourless chocolate cake which he declared the best he had ever eaten, while Kitty enjoyed a very nice creme brulee, along with a perfect cup of coffee.

After lunch, they walked a few blocks, past The Front Room Gallery to Kent Avenue, where Joe lived in a condo apartment in another old factory building someone had renovated.

"Please don't look too closely," Joe pleaded, as he ushered Kitty into a small, bright loft apartment with light wood floors and one red-brick wall. "I'm not the world's best housekeeper."

"I'm certainly not a connoisseur of housekeeping," Kitty laughed. "Don't worry about me!"

Joe quickly gathered up clothes and sundry, as well as a laptop. "If you don't mind, I'll figure on using your laundry soap and such," he said. "I don't want you to think I'm mooching, but I also don't want to feel like I'm 'moving house,' either."

"No problem," Kitty replied, looking up from examining a sad-looking philodendron. "How about we take this plant with us, too? Philodendrons can take a lot of neglect, but this poor baby looks like it could use a little TLC, if you don't mind my saying so."

"I'm not insulted, if that's what you mean," Joe laughed. "That's one of the few lingering left-behinds of a relationship that went south about 4 years ago. I liked the plant, so I kept it, but I tend to forget I have another living thing in the house with me. Poor little guy! By all means, if you want to rescue him, please do!"

"Do you have something, maybe a bread sack or something similar that I could carry it in?" Kitty asked, picking up the plant.

Joe found a plastic bag and Kitty carefully slipped the pot containing the philodendron into it and zipped the bag.

Joe picked up the suitcase into which he had put his clothes. "I need to grab my mail, too," he reminded himself aloud. "When we said we might walk home, I'd forgotten about getting my car. I still think that might be a good idea . So if you want to walk some, how about driving over to East River State Park? It only takes a few minutes to drive there."

"I've never been there," Kitty said. "Sounds like fun."

"Let's go down, then, get my mail, and get the car. The garage is in the basement." Joe opened the apartment door, and gestured to Kitty. "All set?"

"All set," she said.

The car was a silver MX-5 Miata. Joe put the suitcase in the tiny trunk before opening the door for Kitty. "You okay with that plant at your feet?" he asked.

"Sure," Kitty replied, settling into the deep bucket seat. "Nice car!" she added.

"An old man's indulgence, I know," Joe replied, folding himself under the steering wheel of the sports car. "But I've driven so many pieces of crap for so many years in so many different places, after I retired, I decided I'd have something nice for a change."

"Why so many bad cars?" Kitty wondered.

"Government issue, and if you didn't need a good car, you didn't get one," Joe said briefly, turning his attention to starting the car and pulling out of the garage. He really wasn't going to talk about what he had done, Kitty surmised. Oh, well, might as well try another fraught topic while she was at it.

"You mentioned a relationship gone bad," Kitty said. "Do you mind my asking how long you've been divorced from Annie?"

"Not at all. It's not sore anymore, though it was for a while, for sure. We divorced twenty-some years ago. She couldn't tolerate my unpredictable absences and the fact that I really could not talk about where I was going. I don't blame her. Most women wouldn't. Most women can't." He paused. "There were other things, too, of course. Not least of which was the stress of Angela's illnesses, which were just starting to get out of hand about then. We did some counseling, but it mostly helped us separate relatively peacefully."

Kitty wanted to ask more about the recent relationship, but couldn't think of a reasonably polite way to do so.

"You were married for a long time, I gather," Joe said. "Do you have children?"

"No children," Kitty said. "I was focused on my career and so was my husband. He was a doctor. So I know a little bit about sudden and unpredictable absences—though probably not much like yours."

After a moment, she continued. "So you really actually can't tell me who you worked for after the army, or anything about what you did?"

"Really actually," Joe mimicked her, "really actually, I cannot. But I don't work for them anymore, so I am here in Brooklyn, bored and bad-tempered most of the time."

"I haven't seen any of the bad temper," Kitty said. "I don't know about the bored. Are you really bored?

"It's been a challenge," Joe said. "Even near the end, when I was at a desk job, the tension was fairly high most of the time, so I guess since retiring I've just had to adjust to a lower level of adrenalin."

"What do you do with your time?"

"I have a couple of weekly study groups I go to, I work out regularly, I explore the city some, especially Brooklyn." He paused. "And believe it or not, I'm trying to write a novel."

"What are you—" Kitty began.

Joe interrupted her. "Can't talk about that, either. Write it, don't talk about it, is the advice I've been given. But we're here, anyway."

They walked along the estuary, enjoying the late afternoon sun and the views across to Manhattan. Then, as the sun sank lower in the sky, the breeze off the river began to feel cool, and they agreed it was time to head for Park Avenue.

# CHAPTER 25

Joe parked his car under the BQE, and plucked his suitcase from the trunk of the Miatta. "I assume this parking area has the same alternate side of the street rules as most places in the city?" he guessed.

"Yes," Kitty said. "I think there's a sign somewhere that tells which side for which days. But Sundays it doesn't matter. We can come out tomorrow and look for the sign in daylight."

They crossed at the light and walked past the Food Friend. Joe pushed open the gate and then reached for Kitty's hand as they walked into the courtyard of the apartment house. She smiled and gave his hand a little squeeze.

Then, looking toward the lobby from the darkened courtyard, she squeezed harder and pulled Joe to a stop. She nodded toward the door, through which they both saw Dan Oponuno, just stepping warily into the brightly-lit lobby from the ramp. He looked around and ran his hand across the vacant security desk. They saw him smile, and walk over to the wall near the door, where he evidently hit the door release. He pushed the inner door open and then, with a satisfied air, let it close and turned to walk out the back door of the lobby.

"Well, I guess that proves your theory, my dear Kitty. He's discovered your secret passage all right. And quite pleased with himself, by the look of it."

"I wish I'd been wrong," Kitty said with a shiver. "Do you think he saw us?"

"Fairly sure he couldn't," Joe said. "We were mostly in the shadows, and it's lots lighter in there."

"Shouldn't we go in now, in case he would come around here

or anything?" Kitty asked, starting toward the door.

"Sure," Joe said, "and after we unload stuff, I think we should see if the gals next door are home, and tell them."

Back in 5G, they agreed to phone Gretchen before knocking on the couple's door. She didn't hesitate inviting them over.

"So, you see," Kitty explained after Joe described what they'd just seen, "he's found the passageway, and that means he can get into the building whenever the Food Friend is open. Which is most of the time," she added.

"Yeah, every day until midnight now," Gretchen said.

"Hey, Annie, I've been meaning to give you back your keys," Joe said. "Dan gave them back to Kitty that day on the elevator, and I purely forgot I had them." He reached in his pocket and handed her the two keys on their paper clip key ring. "I apologize."

"Well, I haven't needed them," Annie said. "And of course the apartment key is of no use to anyone now, anyway. But," and she shook the paper clip, "where's my keychain?"

"I don't know," Kitty said.

And Joe echoed, "We don't know. They weren't on your keychain. I don't know what happened to it."

"That's way strange," Annie said. "Well, I liked that keychain, but after he's handled it, now I'd like it a lot less."

"Good excuse to buy yourself a new one, honey," Gretchen encouraged.

"To change the subject just slightly," Joe said, "are you going back to work tomorrow, Gretchen?"

"I have to," Gretchen said. "I can't stay away any longer. But I don't like the idea of Annie going out by herself, or being here by herself, for that matter. "

"I don't either," Joe agreed. "And I'm going to be busy most of tomorrow, with various things."

"Well, I'd like to be macho and say I can handle whatever, but I really don't relish the idea of any one of us dealing with that guy alone," Kitty said. "I wonder," she continued thoughtfully, "whether Annie and I could hang together if you two are both going to be gone?"

"That was going to be my suggestion," Joe said. "What do you think, Annie?"

"I think it sounds like really our best bet," Annie said. "I'll probably need to go over to the Navy Yard, at least to pick up an application from the studios. I might call first. I don't have a class to teach tomorrow, but I'll need to talk to my friend in HR. So, Kitty, if you don't mind going over with me, I'd be glad of the company," she finished.

"Sounds like a plan to me," Kitty said. "What about the super coming to do your peephole?"

"Oh, I can call him in the morning and make an appointment for sometime when I know I'll be planning to be here," Annie said.

"So, give me a call in the morning when you know what time you want to leave," Kitty said, moving toward the door. "I'll be glad to go along, and we can sort of plan the rest of the day after you pick up the application."

"So, are we all squared away?" Joe asked." Everyone comfortable for the time being?"

"I think so," Annie said. "You okay, Gretchen?"

Gretchen nodded.

Everyone said their goodbyes, and Joe and Kitty returned to 5G, where a pick-up supper of bread and cheese was all either of them wanted to eat before spending the rest of the evening peacefully reading and catching up on email.

# CHAPTER 26

The next morning, Joe left early for the gym. Kitty took her time over breakfast, but was ready and eager to go when Annie called. Together, the two walked down to the Navy Yard and in through the second Flushing Avenue gate. The sidewalk, once they got past the entry, followed a meandering curve of street behind several 20th century buildings in this relatively new part of the Yard. Low bushes lined both sides of the street, and old-fashioned electric light posts, imitating gas lanterns, appeared at regular intervals. The street and sidewalks were deserted except for the occasional truck with the CCStudios logo, passing to or from loading docks that came into view on the right as the sidewalk took another curve.

As they walked, Annie talked. "It seems like a nightmare to me, Kitty," she said. "This is a man I knew so long ago that all I had left were my fantasies about him. I thought at one time back then that he loved me, and that we would make a life together."

Kitty wondered at the mood that seemed to have come over Annie, usually so reserved on personal topics. But come to think of it, she realized, Annie might not have anyone else she could talk to about this topic. Probably not Gretchen, to whom it would almost certainly be painful. And, of course, clearly not Joe. So she resolved to listen sympathetically for as long as Annie wanted to talk.

"And then, when I needed him most, he threw me aside." Kitty started to try to say something encouraging, but Annie seemed not to need that, or even any assurance that Kitty was listening. She continued in a rush of words: "And I still loved him. I went on loving him. Even after Joe and I were married. Or, maybe not loving, but fantasizing about him. Wondering where he was, what he was doing. Was he well? Was he married? Was he happy?

"He tried to contact me a couple of times over the years. I didn't answer back. I was afraid to, really. Afraid the old flame would flare up again."

She paused. Kitty couldn't contain her curiosity any longer. "How did he know how to contact you? Before?"

"Well, he knew Joe, from college. And while Joe was in Vietnam I lived in a town near the college, so in those days, I suppose he simply looked me up in the phone book. And now, with the internet, anyone can find anybody. You know he called on the landline, which is a listed number. Under my birth name," she finished.

The Human Resources office for CSStudios was in a plain three-story red-brick building with white window frames. Kitty guessed it to be of mid-19th century construction. A small uncovered porch in front seemed out of place, but was graced with two wooden benches.

Inside, the personnel office was directly ahead. Entering through a door marked "Please come in," they were in a small room with several straight chairs. In a connecting room, Annie introduced Kitty to an attractive African-American woman Kitty guessed to be in her mid-forties. "Cathryn, I'd like you to meet my friend Kitty Toulkes. She lives across the hall from me."

"I'm glad to meet you, Kitty," Cathryn replied in a deep contralto. "What can I do for you ladies?"

"Are you still looking for drivers?" Annie asked.

"Always," Cathryn replied. "They leave as fast as they come. Either they're completely incompetent to get around the city or they find better jobs. Sometimes they just disappear with no notice."

"I know a guy," Annie began. "He wants a job driving. I might take an application for him if that's okay."

"Sure," Cathryn said. "You can print one off the website, if

117

you'd rather, but I have some here for people who just walk in off the street." She opened a file drawer in her desk and pulled out a sheet of paper with printing on both sides. "He does have a commercial license, doesn't he?"

"I think he must. He seemed very confident about being able to handle the job." Annie took the application. "Now," she said, her face coloring a bit, "I want to be sure you understand I'm not personally recommending him as a driver. But I have no reason to think he couldn't do it, or that he wouldn't stay for a while. He's in very good shape."

"Of course," Cathryn said. "I understand. We'll vet him in the usual way. You're just picking up an application for him." She smiled.

"Okay, thanks," Annie said. "Kitty, let's go get this application delivered. Cathryn, I'll be back this afternoon to do some gardening, unless something intervenes. I don't have a class until tomorrow."

Once outside the building, Annie took out her phone. "She doesn't know I'm lesbian," she said. "Did you see that she thought maybe this was a guy I was interested in?"

"I thought that's what she was thinking, and I wondered," Kitty said. "You and she aren't that good friends, right?"

"Right," Annie said. She grimaced. "Okay, I guess I should call Dan now, and let him know I have the application."

"Don't you want to go back to the Cocoa Factory?" Kitty asked. "It's seems kind of weird to call him just standing here." She pursed her lips and frowned. "I guess I'm really afraid of meeting up with him."

"We could go to Brooklyn Roasting. I can call him from there. I think he's going to tell me to fill out the application and turn it in for him." Annie started walking.

"That's kind of bizarre, don't you think?" Kitty said, hurrying to stay alongside Annie. "If he wants this job, you'd think he'd want to do the application himself."

"Who knows?" Annie said flippantly. "And I don't really care. I just want to get him satisfied, so I can forget about him. Oh, and maybe get some information about Angela." She was striding determinedly toward the coffee shop.

When they arrived, Annie went straight to one of the funky wooden booths in the back. "Would you get us something to drink?" she asked Kitty. "I want to get this over with."

"Coffee?" Kitty asked.

"Fine. Americano, black." Annie punched a button on her phone.

Kitty went over to the high old-fashioned counter and ordered an Americano and a decaf soy latte. While she waited she looked around the little cafe. The floor had gaps in the tiny white tiles, either where something had once stood or where the tiles were simply gone. The story was that in the days when ship-building at the Navy Yard was going strong, the building had been a "hotel" of the sort that accommodated sailors and other unattached men for short visits. Presumably, the first floor where the cafe was now had been a bar in those days. The roasterie had come in and cleaned up, but had left much of the hard-looking structure in place, supplementing it with equally old, unmatched furniture and decoration.

When Kitty walked back to the booth, Annie was already off the phone. Kitty raised her eyebrows, questioning.

"As I expected," Annie said, "he instructed me to fill it out and sign it for him. I have his license number, and anything I don't know, I'm supposed to make up!"

"Can you do that?" Kitty was flabbergasted.

"I can. And I will," Annie said firmly. "Here, sit down. You can help me make up stuff. He's counting on that they won't check any references. And they probably won't!"

"Which name are you using?" Kitty asked, suddenly aware that she, at least, had never told Annie about the bank robbery charges.

"'Don Forthright' seems to be what he is going by now," Annie said. "He said that was the name on the license and would be what he would use. I don't care. I just want to get it done."

The two women spent the next half hour working on the

application, making up most of the details. Previous jobs were especially interesting. To concoct the kind of work history that would lead a reliable and competent man in his early 60's (they agreed that he could easily pass for 60) to be looking for a job driving short-haul trucks was a bit of a challenge, but creativity prevailed and they were proud of the result.

"Now what?" Kitty asked.

"Now we take it back to Cathryn and wait," Annie said. "And hope!" She began to bus the table.

"If he gets an interview, he'll have to do that in person," Kitty said, picking up paper napkins and tossing them in the trash. "I guess that goes without saying."

"I was instructed to give my phone, not his," Annie said. "So we'll know if he gets an interview."

# CHAPTER 27

Out on the sidewalk again, they made short work of the trip back to the studio personnel office. A stocky, rather roughly-dressed man was sitting in a straight-backed chair in a corner of the reception area, making hard work of filling out an application form. After turning in the form they had forged, the two hurried outside.

"Did you see—?" they both started at once! Giggling, they moved quickly away from the building. "If that's the competition," Kitty said, "I'd think Dan would be a welcome change. He should be a cinch to get a job." She chuckled, thinking of the surprise Cathryn might have when Dan/Don walked into her office.

"I suppose they don't hire on looks," Annie said, "but I know enough to know it does influence our thinking, whether we mean to or not. That's why you usually dress up for a job interview!"

"Maybe that was dressed up, for that poor guy," Kitty said. "It isn't nice to laugh at him, but I couldn't help it."

The two of them walked back toward the Cocoa Factory, still amused both by their audacious application-forging and by the idea that Cathryn would have another sort of applicant on her hands if she chose to interview the man going by the name of Don Forthright.

At the corner of Park and Washington, having passed the wine store and the ramp to the little Caribbean bistro, Annie said she'd decided to go into the Food Friend. "I'll come with you, then, shall I?" Kitty said. "The whole idea here was for us to stay together."

"Oh, right! I'd forgotten," Annie said, shaking her head. "Well, then, do you mind?"

"No, it's fine," Kitty replied. "I can't think of anything I need, but I'll go in with you."

Annie's shopping took only a few minutes. After she had paid and was starting for the front door of the store, Kitty asked, "Shall we go through the back way?"

"Oh, sure, I guess," Annie said. "I'm not sure I've ever gone that way."

"Well, follow me." Kitty led the way through, and they were soon in the lobby of the Cocoa Factory.

James, at the desk, looked up as they walked by. "Good morning," Kitty said.

"Morning," he muttered, before turning back to his video game.

"You want to come to my place?" Kitty asked, as they arrived at their end of the hallway.

"Sure. I don't have anything here that needs to be put away immediately, except for the cold cuts and lettuce." Annie said. "I thought we could make some sandwiches, if you have bread. Or salad, if you don't."

"I do," Kitty said, unlocking her door and motioning Annie inside, "but salad sounds good, too."

They were just setting out the food when Kitty's phone rang. It was Joe.

"Just checking in," he said. "Is all well with you?"

"All is well," Kitty said. "Are you coming home soon?"

"Not right away," Joe said. "Are you and Annie together?"

"We've been together all morning. We have filled out an application for the driving job. Made it up out of whole cloth—quite a creative writing project. We just turned it in. Annie put her phone number on it, as instructed. So now we wait, I guess."

"Okay, I think you should continue to stay together. I hope that's not becoming difficult."

"Not for me," Kitty said. "I think we had fun doing the application, and now we're going to fix a little lunch." She turned to Annie, "Are you getting too much togetherness, Annie? Joe wants to know whether we are getting tired of each other." She smiled.

"No problem," Annie said. "Tell him I quite approve of his new lady friend, and we're getting along just fine."

Kitty blushed. "Did you hear that?" she asked Joe.

"I did," he said. Kitty could hear him hm-hming fondly, whether for her benefit or Annie's she couldn't tell. "So, okay," he continued. "I'll be back later this afternoon. Call me if anything happens, or if you need me sooner."

"See you soon, then. Bye-bye," Kitty said.

"Bye," Joe said.

They fixed sandwiches, and Kitty poured orange juice for herself and water for Annie.

Helping clean up after lunch, Annie yawned broadly, and announced she was ready for a nap.

"Me too," Kitty said. "All that fiction writing was tiring, I guess. If you don't mind sleeping on the couch, or you can stretch out in the chair if you like." She gestured.

"Chair looks good to me," Annie said.

About an hour later, Annie's phone rang. She answered, listened for a moment, and then said brightly, "Hi, Cathryn, it's Annie Wellington. Donald isn't here right now. May I take a message for him?"

She paused again to listen and then said, "Okay, I'll give him that message. And if you don't hear from him, you'll assume he's coming at ten tomorrow?"

After Cathryn rang off, Annie heaved a sigh. "Now I have to call Dan again. And remember to call him 'Don.'"

"I'm sorry you are having to go through all this," Kitty said. "I can only imagine how it is for you."

"Mostly, I'm really, really angry. At him. But also at myself for ever getting involved with him.

"I'm putting this on speaker," Annie continued. "It'll make me feel you are there with me." She made a face. "Okay, here goes!"

"Well, hel-lo, Annie!" Kitty thought Dan sounded full of good will and sunshine. "What do you have for me, my dear?" he continued.

"You've been scheduled for an interview with CSStudios," Annie said. "At 10:00 tomorrow. Bring your commercial driving license, and your union card. You know where to go, right?"

"I could probably figure it out, but I'd rather you tell me," Dan began.

Annie cut him off. "Well, you can figure it out, then," she said briskly. "That's all I needed to tell you."

"Oh, Annie. I'd much rather we had this conversation in person. Look, I'm in your building, actually, so I'll just come on up and we can talk like old friends should."

Kitty shook her head frantically, mouthing "no, no, no."

"That won't work, Dan," Annie said, her voice husky with the tension. "You can't come to my place, and I'm not meeting you in the lobby."

"Well, Annie, I don't know that you have a whole lot of choice," Dan said smoothly. "Not if you want to see your angel again."

Annie looked at Kitty and shrugged. Kitty pressed her lips together and continued to shake her head. Then she mouthed "Food Friend," followed by "coffee," as she mimed sipping from a cup.

Annie nodded. "Dan, I would be willing to meet you in the store downstairs. We can sit in the little deli-coffee bar area for a few minutes." Her face was white, but she managed to keep her voice steady.

"As you wish, my dear," Dan said, managing to sound both ironic and smarmy at the same time. "I'll be there before you." He clicked off.

The two women looked at each other. Finally, Annie spoke: "I hate to ask it, but will you come with me?"

"Of course I will," Kitty said quickly. "I wouldn't think of letting you go by yourself." After a pause, she continued. "Let's set a time-period now. We tell him we have to leave in, say,15 minutes, to meet someone. In fact, let me call Joe. Maybe he can be who we have to meet—without saying so to Dan, of course."

She called Joe as they made their way toward the elevator. "I'm actually on my way back to the Cocoa Factory now," Joe said. "I should be there in about ten minutes. I'll hang out in the lobby until you come back through. And don't hesitate to call me if you need me to come into the store."

"You know we will," Kitty promised. "Thank you!"

When they reached the deli, Dan was, as he'd predicted, already there, seated at one of the tables, a steaming cup of something in front of him. "Ladies, welcome!" he purred. "How nice to see you, Kitty. To what do I owe this pleasure?"

Neither woman spoke. Annie looked at him with an expression of utter disgust.

"Please! Have a seat," Dan said. "Or can I get you something to drink?" He looked at Kitty, who shook her head.

"Dan, what do you want?" Annie said coldly, taking a seat across the table.

"Now, is that any way to begin?" he replied with a smile. "I just wanted to see you, Annie. I haven't seen you for so long, and it's so good just to be with you for a little while."

"What do you want now?" she asked again.

"Okay, if it's going to be all business." He sat back and stretched, a smirk on his handsome face. "Tell me about the studio and the job. Who is the interviewer? Your friend? What will they be looking for? And what am I supposed to have been doing for the past ten years or so?" He laughed quietly. "Tell me who I am, Annie!"

"Oh, I could tell you what you are," Annie snarled. "But to answer your questions—I think the interviewer is the personnel officer, Cathryn, my acquaintance. And as to your history, you drove a school bus for six years in Indian Country, long hours morning and evening, on the Hopi Reservation. Long since forgotten the phone number, but your supervisor was Ed Bengay. That's such a common name, she'd have a hard time tracking down any particular man, even if he existed.

"Then you moved to Phoenix, where you drove delivery trucks for a couple of small, local haulers: Madison & Sons, and Harmon Haulers. We looked up area codes and gave phone numbers for those."

"But if she checks and it's a wrong number or not in service, they were small outfits and maybe gone out of business," Dan said. "Good thinking, my girl!" He reached across the table to pat Annie's hand.

She jerked it away. "Not your girl anymore!"

"Anything else I should know about my past?" he asked, ignoring her reaction.

"I made you only 62, so I doctored what I knew of your real college dates to match. But I left it that you didn't finish college. And you might want to think about why you left Phoenix for New York City about 3 months ago. I didn't give any jobs in between. Your address is the one you gave me."

"You did good, Annie. Now we just have to sell me in person."

"What do you mean, 'we'?" Annie said, her eyes narrowing.

"Oh, you're coming with me tomorrow." Dan smiled broadly. "I'll do the interview, of course, but I want you along as backup. Makes it apparent that you are really eager to see me get the job."

"If you think that will make any difference, you are greatly overestimating my importance," Annie said.

"Let's just call it insurance, then," Dan said lightly. Then his tone hardened. "I want you to come, Annie," he said.

"If I come, you'll tell me how to find Angela," Annie said firmly.

"Let's just see how it goes," Dan said. "No point in planning too far ahead." Turning toward Kitty, he smiled. "Now that the business part is over, are you sure I can't get you something to drink? A *cafe au lait*, perhaps, or maybe an Italian soda? You look like an Italian soda kind of girl to me."

"Actually, Annie, we've got to go," Kitty said abruptly. "That appointment, I almost forgot. We're going to be late as it is." She stood up and brushed her hands together. "Excuse us for rushing off," she said over her shoulder as she started to leave.

"I'll see you at the office a few minutes before ten, Annie," Dan said smoothly. "Right, Annie?"

"I'll see you there," Annie said, her voice soft and sad. She stood and followed Kitty out of the front door of the store.

Joe was waiting by the mailboxes in the lobby of the Cocoa Factory. He gathered Kitty under his arm and placed the other hand gently on Annie's shoulder for a moment. Together the three walked to the elevator.

Once in the safety of Kitty's apartment, the two women described their recent experience. "The man makes my skin crawl," Kitty said.

"How are you holding up, Chum?" Joe asked Annie, who had collapsed into Kitty's recliner.

"I think I can get through tomorrow morning," Annie said. "And then I hope we'll be rid of him!"

"Maybe, or maybe not," Joe said reluctantly. "I spent my day talking to people. There's something else going on. I haven't figured out what, yet. Annie, did you know about Dan's federal indictment? For bank robbery?"

"What!" Annie reared up in the chair so hard the footrest came down with a crash.

"It was some years ago," Joe said. "I can't give you an exact date. But there's something else, too, and I don't know what that is. Something more current or even yet to come. People—agencies—are involved that shouldn't be if it were just the armed robbery charges and possible kidnapping."

"This is too much for me," Annie said. "I'm going home." She stood up.

"Annie, are you okay?" Kitty asked.

"No," Annie said. "I'm not okay. I'm furious! But I'm also sad, and exhausted. Gretchen will be home soon, and I'm going home to wait for her."

"Okay, but no hexing," Kitty said, trying to lighten the mood. "You remember the Three-fold Law."

Annie didn't smile. "That's the only thing keeping me back.

Tomorrow after the interview, I'm doing a binding. If anyone wants to join me, so much the better. But I'm doing it! Period!"

"I'll let you out, and see you safely inside your door." Joe rose from the sofa. "Don't open for anybody!"

"Except us, of course," Kitty called out. "Bye, Annie. Let us know when Gretchen gets home."

When Joe came back, he sat down next to Kitty again and drew her close. "Quite a day, huh?" he said.

"We had some fun making up Dan's movements of the past ten years. Annie decided to make him a Native American. Or at least imply that he is. She thought that might help him get the interview, because they wouldn't want to discriminate."

"As soon as Gretchen gets home, I'd like to take you out someplace nice for dinner. Unless you're too tired." Joe looked suddenly concerned.

"No, I think that sounds nice," Kitty said. "But tell me more, if you can, about what you said, about there being something more going on. And by the way, good move slipping in about the bank robbery as if you'd just learned that today! You are a sly one."

"All those years doing all those secret things, I should have learned a thing or two," Joe laughed. "I can't really tell you much more, because I don't know much more. Someone actually asked me to keep an eye on Dan." He stopped talking and leaned over to give Kitty a kiss on the forehead.

"Sounds to me like there is more to tell," Kitty said. She turned her head to snuggle under his chin, and Joe kissed the tip of her nose.

"If I were going to guess," he said thoughtfully, "I'd say maybe he's gotten mixed up with some kind of sabotage plot. Some important people are interested. I don't think Angela being missing or kidnapped is in the forefront of anyone's mind but ours any more, if it ever was." His kisses moved down a little further.

When Kitty's phone rang, it startled both of them, interrupting what had been a pleasant interlude without any further discussion. It was Gretchen, saying she was home safely and did they need anything more before she fed Annie and packed her off to bed. Kitty assured her they did not, and wished the two of them a good night. "Tell Annie I'm going along tomorrow. If Dan doesn't like it, he can jolly well lump it!"

# CHAPTER 28

The next morning came early. Kitty offered to make bacon and eggs, but Joe allowed that he'd really been thinking pancakes. So the two of them agreed to walk up to John's Diner on Myrtle for breakfast. They hiked up the hill, past the Washington Hall Park basketball court and a series of more-or-less well-kept brownstones, most divided into multiple apartments. Behind old-fashioned wrought-iron gates, the small areas in front of the buildings varied from carefully-tended postage stamp gardens to scrubby grass patches to mere collections of garbage cans on dirty concrete or brick pads.

As they walked, Kitty tried with little success to get Joe to talk more about his knowledge and/or suspicions about what "more" there might be of interest to federal authorities related to Daniel Oponuno.

"I really don't have anything solid to go on," he avowed, scanning the sidewalk for rough spots and other hazards. "It's just, as I said before, that the people who seem to be keeping an eye on things, and—watch out, dog poop!—and, frankly, asking me for information about what he's up to, information I simply do not have, some of those people are neither local police nor FBI. They're more from the realms I used to work in; I'd say maybe NSA, in the current lingo. And if that's who's watching him, then at least some of his friends, if not Dan himself, are being seen as greater threats, threats to more than just a single bank or a single missing woman."

At the corner of Myrtle and Washington, they took a left, and proceeded past a sequence of small shops, including the Chinese carry-out, a coffee bar, and the package shipping/copy place, which was already doing a brisk business. When they reached the busy little diner, they squeezed through the narrow entryway and looked around. "I think it's the counter or a wait," Kitty said. "Do you mind?"

"The counter?" Joe led on. Halfway down the row of stools, he found two empty together. "Okay?"

"Okay by me," Kitty said. She climbed up onto a stool and put her elbows on the counter. "I'm ready," she said.

On the way back, after a meal of John's deservedly-famous pancakes, Joe turned serious. "I want you and Annie to be extra careful this morning," he said, "if you are going with him on his job interview."

"It didn't sound like we had much choice," Kitty said, "if we're still expected to help him with getting this job. And if we're still trying to get him to give us information about your daughter?"

"I know," Joe said. "So just don't let him persuade you to go anywhere with him or do anything besides that office visit."

He rubbed his chin. "I am going to be hanging around," he said, "and if you feel anything is going amiss, or about to, just give me a quick text. You don't need to even say anything, just send a blank text, and I will come immediately, with backup!"

"You could do that? The backup, I mean?"

"I can, and I will, if necessary." He sounded definite.

By the time they got back to the apartment, Kitty was feeling anxious. She puttered around, putting away dishes and straightening placemats. She even got out a dust cloth and worked for a while swiping at the layer of grime that collected so regularly on all horizontal surfaces. Finally, she called Annie. "What time are you thinking we should leave?" she asked, when Annie answered.

"About twenty to would be plenty early," Annie said. "I don't think we want to be waiting around down there."

"And how are you going to dress?"

"Just slacks," Annie replied. "There's no need for us to dress up, that I can think of."

"Okay then. Come ring my doorbell when you are ready to leave." Kitty clicked off the phone. As she headed into the bedroom she noticed Joe had gone into the bathroom, but without closing the door. When she came out, having changed into a pair of dressier slacks and a cotton sweater, she saw he was still there.

"May I ask what you are doing?" she ventured.

"Muf-tuh minuf," came a muffled reply. "Iwl be wid oud."

Kitty frowned. What could he be up to?

Very shortly, a man came out of the bathroom, but he didn't look much like the man with whom she had recently been sharing her bed. He had ill-cut gray-blond hair sticking out beneath an I <3NY cap. Bushy eyebrows with a gray mustache and goatee added to the look, as did a noticeable but not disfiguring scar on one cheek. When he saw Kitty, he adopted a slight limp as well.

"Uh, Joe?" she said, startled.

"What do you think?" The familiar voice was reassuring and at the same time very strange, coming as it did from a mouth she could hardly recognize, since it twitched up at one corner in a very un-Joe-like manner.

"I hardly know what to say!" she stuttered. Gathering herself, she added, "I think the limp might be a bit much!"

"Hard to keep up," Joe nodded. "Anyway, I wanted you to see me now, so you wouldn't worry when you see me on the street."

"You weren't kidding about hanging around," Kitty said, shaking her head in wonderment. "Is this an art you learned on the job?"

"You might say so." Joe tossed it off. "It's sometimes useful not to be known."

Just then, the doorbell rang. "That will be Annie," Kitty said. "Better let me go to the door; she might freak out if you do."

"Be sure it's her, before you open up," Joe cautioned. "And that she is alone."

Kitty peered through the peep-hole, and saw Annie's face. "Are you alone?" she asked through the door, slipping the chain on as she spoke.

"All by my lonesome," Annie announced promptly, her face up close to the lens.

Kitty opened the door cautiously, and when she felt assured it was just Annie, she slipped off the chain. "Come on in," she said. I'll be with you in a minute." She stepped aside so that Annie could have the full benefit of Joe's transformation.

"Oh, hi, Joe," Annie said, with hardly a pause or change of pitch. "Are you going with us?"

"Not with, exactly," Joe said, smiling at Kitty's expression. "I'll be around."

Annie turned to Kitty. "You ready to go?"

"I guess so," Kitty said. "Sure! Let's go."

# CHAPTER 29

Out on the sidewalk, neither of them said much as they made their way down Washington and along Flushing toward the HR office of CSStudios. The wind had kicked up since earlier, and Kitty imagined she could feel a chill off the East River as they neared the estuary.

When they reached the office, Annie spoke. "I don't think any explanation will be required for why you're with me." Checking her watch, she continued. "We should be here a few minutes before Dan, aka Don."

They opened the door to the Human Resources office, and just as Annie had predicted, they had arrived a little early. "Cathryn, you remember my friend Kitty?" Annie said, sticking her head around the open door of the inner office.

"Sure," Cathryn said warmly. "How are you, Kitty? I understand it's getting a bit windy out."

"It is," Kitty agreed. "I thought I could feel the first hint of fall in the air."

"Well, it can't come too soon," Cathryn laughed. "This has been the longest summer on record, by me. I love a four-season climate, but summer is my least-favorite of the four."

"Have you lived where there were not four seasons?" Kitty wondered.

"I grew up in Southern California, so, yes, I have," Cathryn replied. "But, excuse me, did you two want something in particular? Because I have some appointments back to back here soon." She glanced down at the papers on her desk. "In fact, the first one is that friend of yours, Annie. Donald Forthright?"

"Yes, well..." Annie hesitated. "More of an acquaintance I'm trying to help out. Anyway, that's why we are here. To lend moral support, I guess you could say." No sooner were the words out of her mouth than they heard the outer door open.

"Mr. Forthright?" Cathryn stood up.

"Indeed!" Dan strode through the inner door, brushing past Annie, and reached out to shake Cathryn's hand across her desk. "How do you do?" He smiled confidently and reached behind him to pull a chair past the corner of the desk, where he could sit just a couple of feet from Cathryn.

"We'll wait outside," Annie said, backing toward the door. The two of them hurried outside and found a place to sit in the sun on the porch.

"Whew!" Kitty whistled. "The man is a force of nature. If only he were using his powers for good instead of for not-good."

"A force of nature is what he has always been," Annie said with a sigh. "I wouldn't wonder if rather than being immoral he is maybe simply amoral, without any sense of right and wrong. You're a psychologist. Do you believe there are people like that?"

"Well, there certainly are sociopaths. There's been research lately to suggest there's something different about their brains. They might really not have the built-in automatic tendency to empathize that even animals like rats and apes have. They literally don't put themselves in someone else's place and imagine what it must be like to be that person in that situation. Something little kids normally learn at three or four.

"So, while the true sociopath might sometimes try to empathize, most of the time he—it's most often a man—truly doesn't 'feel for' someone else whom he might be hurting. But, sorry, I'm lecturing," Kitty said. "And I really don't have any evidence to suggest that Dan is a sociopath. They're actually quite rare. Just plain garden-variety 'mean' accounts for most of the nastiness in the world."

"Well," Annie sighed again, "I don't really need a label. I just want him out of my life!"

"I know," Kitty said sympathetically. "I want him gone, too. Maybe this will be the last of it." She thought of what Joe had said and wondered whether his official friends might be completely wrong and Annie's wish could come true without any further complications. But instead of mentioning that, she simply said, "Where do you suppose Joe is?"

Annie didn't appear to have heard.

They looked out at the trucks coming and going at the loading dock. "Why do they need all these trucks? Where are they all going?" Kitty mused.

"I think they make lots of commercials, in addition to feature films," Annie said. "So they send crews out all over the city for shoots, and they have to truck not only props and possibly costumes but also all the cameras and sound and sometimes lighting equipment. You see them coming and going all day every day."

"And every driver has to be union, I suppose," Kitty said. "So the cameraman can't drive the truck."

"Right," Annie said.

The two sat in silence. Some lengthy minutes later, the door opened. "Hi, ladies," Dan said cheerily.

They jumped up, and then looked with surprise to see Cathryn coming out immediately behind him. "Well, that's all the paperwork done. You see where the dock is, Don. You can start this afternoon. Just show up at 1:00, and give that card to the foreman. He'll want to see your union card and your license, of course. Thank you very much for coming in." She shook his hand vigorously.

"Thank you, Cathryn," he purred, holding her hand after she stopped shaking, and releasing it slowly with a kind of sliding motion. "The pleasure has been entirely mine," he added, looking directly into her eyes.

Cathryn dropped her eyes and pulled away from him. Then, recovering her composure, she turned briskly to Annie. "See you this afternoon, I expect, Annie?"

"Oh, yes, I expect so," Annie said. "I'll probably be in about 2:00."

"Okay, well, goodbye, all." Cathryn turned and fled into the building without waiting for anyone to reply.

"Ah, lovely ladies and a lovely day," Dan said, turning his full attention on Annie and Kitty. "Shall we walk?" It clearly was not meant as a question. He stretched an arm behind Kitty, who was standing nearest. His hand on her back, he herded her down the steps, then reached out to take Annie's arm and half-guide, half-propel her along the same path. Together, then, Kitty in front and Annie still held in Dan's grip, they moved quickly away from the CSStudio building.

Once out of sight of the studio, Kitty stopped and turned around. Annie stopped, too, and shook off Dan's hand. "Let's not keep this up," she said hoarsely. "You promised to tell me what I needed to know to help my daughter. So you got the job; now keep your promise!"

"Oh, yes, your angel," he said, grinning. "Well, there's no hurry. Let's wait and see how this job works out."

"What do you mean, there's no hurry?" Annie was shouting. "You've been promising for days now."

"Well, it can wait a few more days, then, can't it." Dan reached as though to put an arm around Annie's shoulder and she jerked away. "Oh, touchy are we? Now, now!"

"I don't believe you know anything about Angela!" Annie's hands were doubled into fists at her sides.

"Oh, but I do, my dear, and you know it. That's why I sent the keys home on a different key ring." He stepped closer to Kitty. "I don't know why you are so suspicious, Annie." He reached out in a sudden move and slipped his arm around Kitty, roughly pulling her toward him. "See," he said as Kitty staggered against him, "your friend isn't nearly so stand-offish." He chuckled deep in his throat.

Kitty broke his hold and started to turn away, but Dan stepped behind her and grabbed both shoulders in a painful grip that might have appeared from a distance to be a friendly gesture. "Here, here, Kitty," he said. He was purring again. "I want us to get much better acquainted. Annie has to work this afternoon, but you can ride with me when I take my first afternoon on the job. I'm sure the foreman won't mind, and if he does, well, at least we will have a few hours before then to spend together."

Kitty found that, with her back to him, she could resist whatever strange psychic force Dan seemed to exert. However, the grip he had on her shoulders was not only painful but very, very firm. She struggled to get loose, but his arms now moved downward so that he was holding her tightly just above the waist, his arms pressing upward against her breasts.

"Annie, please...." she started.

But just then someone else appeared on the sidewalk, apparently out of nowhere. "Say there, fella," the stranger boomed heartily. "Can you tell me where to find the Human Resources office around here?"

Startled, Dan let go of Kitty. Both women began to run down the sidewalk.

"Looks like your lady friends wasn't as friendly as ya thought," the newcomer chuckled. "That's the way with women, huh? Always fickle. About that office, though; am I headin' in the right direction?"

Kitty stopped running and leaned over, panting so hard she didn't hear Dan's reply. From his gesture, however, she gathered he had affirmed that the man she now recognized as Joe-in-disguise was, in fact, headed toward the HR office. Joe-in-disguise bowed his thanks, and walked casually on, with just the hint of a limp.

Seeing Dan turn as if to follow her, Kitty began to run again, ignoring her heaving lungs. Annie had kept moving, and was waiting up ahead, so Kitty quickly joined her. Together, they continued at a brisk pace, and soon left Dan behind as they made their way back toward the Cocoa Factory.

# CHAPTER 30

Annie came into 5G with Kitty, both having agreed there was no guarantee Dan wouldn't follow them, but that it seemed less likely he'd try to get into 5G than into F.

"I've got to have a shower," Kitty said, after double-locking the door and adding the chain. "I can't help it; I just feel dirty all over."

"You go right ahead," Annie said. "I'm going to try to call Gretchen."

When Kitty came out of the bathroom, a towel around her wet head, she found Annie still on the phone. "Yes, dear," Kitty heard her say, "I'll be home by the time you get here. Don't worry! Nothing happened, and nothing is going to happen. We'll be fine, and tonight you and I will go over the moon ritual with Kitty, if she's still okay with holding it." She glanced at Kitty, who nodded in return. "So, bye now, sweetheart. I'd better let you get back to work. Yes, me too. Bye."

"Gretchen," Annie said by way of explanation. "She's worried, of course."

"Of course," Kitty agreed. "I wish Joe would get back."

"I think I'd like a wash, too," Annie said. "I don't need a full bath, just a washcloth and towel, if you don't mind. I'd like to get the scent of him off my head and arms."

"Yes, certainly. The linen closet is right there. Just help yourself," Kitty said. "I'm going to sit down out here."

Both women jumped as they heard a key in the lock. Before they could move, they heard the second lock click and the door was pushed against the chain-guard. Then Joe called out: "It's me, Kitty. Good girl! Now, please let me in!"

Annie dropped back onto the sofa, while Kitty hurried to the door. She peered around the edge of the frame just to be certain the voice was whose she thought. It was, and she opened up gratefully.

The towel fell off her head as she grabbed him. A kiss proved problematic, given that Joe was still wearing the makeup and goatee, but they managed a semblance thereof. "I can't even say how glad I was to see you!" she said into his ear. "You managed to put him off without causing any fuss." She backed away, picking up the towel. "Thank you, thank you, thank you!"

"Jus' doin' my job, Ma'am," Joe said, in character. "Give me a minute, ladies," he continued. "I'll be right back." He stepped into the bathroom.

When he came out a few minutes later, he smelled slightly of rubbing alcohol, but the beard, mustache, and scar were gone. "Do you have some good moisturizer, Kitty?" he asked. "I think I'll be doing this again, and it's a little hard on the skin."

"Sure." She got a bottle from the bathroom cabinet and watched in silence as he spread the lotion generously over his face. "Now you'll smell like lavender and mint," she said fondly.

Annie got up and silently kissed Joe's newly-moisturized cheek. "Yes, he does, indeed. Not exactly macho, but 'clean and fresh,' for sure." She moved to sit again, heading for the chair. "I'll leave the couch to you two," she said.

"No," Joe said, "keep your seat. I have something to talk to both of you about. But first, bring me up to date. What happened at the office?" He pulled up a straight-backed chair and motioned for both of them to sit down.

Kitty summarized the experience at the personnel office and then the aftermath. "So Dan was telling me I would be spending the next several hours with him!" She shuddered. "And then you came along and rescued me. Now I'm half-expecting him to show up here any minute. I can't understand what he wants with us." She looked at Annie. "Can you?"

"Not really," Annie said. "He always liked to have a woman on his arm when I knew him. He'd have said that about himself. But now—who knows?"

"Maybe cover," Joe said. "I was telling Kitty last night that there seems to be something more going on than we know. Or at least the powers-that-be suspect something more. And now I've had a call from my FBI contact inviting us to come to downtown Brooklyn and meet with someone who is flying in from D.C. It was suggested that we can keep clear of any implication that we might be involved in whatever it is by 'cooperating.'" He shrugged and shook his head.

"And since we have no idea whatsoever what might be going on, I think we don't have much of any choice other than to show up for this meeting." Joe looked from one woman to the other. "Are you going to be okay with this?"

"Doesn't really make any difference whether we are okay with it or not," Annie said, sounding glum. "Your reading is that we don't have any choice, and I don't know enough to judge for myself. Do you, Kitty?"

"I'm still shaking from....well, you know," Kitty said. "I'll do whatever Joe says we ought to do, I think. When is this meeting, then?" She looked at Joe and held out her hand to show that it was, indeed, shaking.

Just then, Annie's phone rang. Kitty held her breath as Annie pulled the phone out of her bag. "It's Dan," she said. "Do I answer it?" Then she answered her own question: "I don't dare not." She punched "speaker' and said "Hello," her voice flat and uninviting.

"Hello, Annie. How are you?" Dan's voice penetrated the silence in the room.

"I think you can guess, Dan," Annie said. "Glad you got the job, waiting for you to keep your promise."

"And I'm waiting for one of you lovely ladies to accompany me on my first set of rounds this afternoon," Dan said. "Where shall I meet you?"

"You know I can't, Dan. I have a job to do this afternoon."

"Then it will have to be Kitty, I guess," Dan said. "I'll need you to put her on the phone, darlin'."

"I don't think she wants to talk to you," Annie said.

Kitty was shaking her head vehemently. She pointed to her chest and mouthed "work, work."

"She says she has to work today, too. It isn't going to happen, Dan, that's all."

"But it's what I want, Annie. Though, actually, if I have your promise that one of you will be here tomorrow morning, that would be just as good, maybe even better. Can I have that promise of a rain check?"

"And if we don't?" Annie was bargaining now.

"If you don't, if I'm not getting what I want—well, I think you know what that would mean. Giving up all hope of finding your daughter. And you don't want to give up hope, do you, Annie?"

"If we can talk here, we'll figure something out, I'm sure," Annie said, desperation creeping into her voice.

"You do that, Annie," Dan said. "I'll be calling back about tomorrow morning. Bye now."                And Annie's phone began to beep as Dan rang off abruptly.

"Now what?" Annie sighed, her expression bleak.

Kitty closed her eyes and sat silently, hugging herself.

"Now, I'm afraid, we need to leave to go meet with Papa Bear," Joe said. "I'd do anything I could to keep you from having to go to this meeting or to have anything more to do with Dan Oponuno. But I don't see that being in the cards, either. We'll have to hurry if we're going to make this meeting. Annie, can we take your car? Mine's a little small for three."

# CHAPTER 31

Joe drove Annie's aging dark blue Corolla to a small house in a residential neighborhood near downtown Brooklyn. "Now I don't know the name—or the agency—of the man we are meeting," he said as they pulled up to the curb. We'll ask for some ID and then we may or may not know. But I feel quite confident he will be representing the government of the United States. That may or may not mean he'll be telling us the truth as he knows it —but we might as well assume he has the blessing of higher ups, up to and possibly even including the President."

"Wow! Really? You're not pulling my leg?" Kitty was amazed.

The whitewashed stone house was partly covered with English Ivy. They stepped over ivy going up the flagstone walk and Joe brushed aside a strand of the vine to press the doorbell. The man who opened the heavy wooden door was disappointingly unlike the stereotypical English butler, however. He looked more like a bouncer in a nice suit. Joe said his name and showed the man a photo ID card which he had pulled from a special case, not from his wallet.

"Right this way, Mr. Treacher," the man said. "And ladies," he added, including them all in a sweeping gesture. The room he led them was small, and darker than it might have been owing to the velvet drapes covering what appeared to be large windows or French doors along one side. "Mr. Harris will be with you shortly," he said. "Please sit down." He indicated several comfortable-looking arm chairs of the sort that might at another time have graced a conference table.

The bouncer having left quietly by means of the door

through which they had entered, the three of them sat down in silence and looked around. A wooden desk with an American flag and several pens on a blotter stood opposite. A plainly-framed photograph of the President hung on the wall behind the desk. On the same wall, to the other side of the desk, was a door. The walls were papered with something that looked old but showed no obvious signs of wear.

"Well, I—" Annie began to speak, but Joe cut her off, shaking his head and putting his finger to his lips. She raised her eyebrows, but stopped talking. Kitty too looked a query at Joe, who merely shrugged and again tapped his lips with one finger. Then he tapped his ear with the same one finger. Kitty's mouth formed an "Oh" as she realized what he was suggesting.

Presently, the door behind the desk opened and a fiftyish-looking man with curly steel-gray hair came in. He carried a pipe (which soon proved itself to be unlit). Joe stood up immediately and stepped forward. "Mr. Treacher?" the man said. "I'm Bill Harris." He extended his hand and the two men shook briefly. "And ladies?"

Both women stood automatically, and Joe quickly introduced them. "Ann Wellington Treacher, and Dr. Katherine Adamson Toulkes. I assume you don't need to see our ID." Bill Harris shook his head. "But if you don't mind, I'd like to see yours," Joe continued.

"Not at all," Harris said, and reached into his inside jacket pocket for a small leather case. He handed the case to Joe, who passed it in turn to Kitty and Annie. It identified William S. Harris as an agent of the Federal Bureau of Investigation. Kitty felt a little letdown of relief. Surely if it was just the FBI, the situation couldn't be too terribly grave.

"Now what can we do for you, Mr. Harris?" Joe asked, as he and the two women settled back into the leather-covered arm chairs.

"First, let me tell you what we think we know," said Bill Harris, seating himself behind the desk. "Daniel Oponuno has been of interest to federal authorities for about twenty years. We had lost track of Mr. Oponuno, aka Donald Forthright, aka several other names, until you came to us a few days ago.

"We have been watching him for the past several days and have connected the man you call Dan Oponuno or Don Forthright with a man using the name Sam Sly who has been of interest to the National Security Agency for some months because of communications with certain other parties known to be or suspected of being involved in conspiracies to commit violence against the United States."

Annie gasped softly. Kitty reached for Joe's hand and, finding it, squeezed hard.

Mr. Harris continued. "That being the case, we are quite interested in what he is doing and with whom he is speaking. We'd like to know, for example, from you, Ms. Treacher, how long you had been in touch with Mr. Oponuno prior to his coming to New York. And what subject or subjects your conversations were in reference to."

Annie looked perplexed. "Prior to...? But surely Joe has told you, Dan just called me a few days ago, out of the blue."

"I'd like to hear it directly from you, if you don't mind, please." Harris flashed a brief smile that seemed intended to be reassuring. "None of you is under suspicion, for now. It's just that any information we can get about Oponuno's activities, habits, even what he eats for breakfast—any of this kind of information might prove to be useful. We don't know at this point, but we believe we have little time to discover what he and his co-conspirators are planning."

"So you really think Dan is into some kind of plot?" Kitty couldn't help interrupting.

"It's very probable, based on the electronic traffic, that someone is. And this group is one of our best targets," Harris said. "We are grateful to Mr. Treacher—and to you ladies—for alerting us to this possible entry point."

Joe frowned and leaned forward, suddenly suspicious. "What entry point? I thought this was purely an information-consolidation meeting."

Harris pivoted his chair to look directly at Joe, and then turned back to the two women. "My team needs to know where Oponuno goes, what he is doing, and why he wants a job at CS-Studios. A delivery truck of the size and type he is going to be driving is perfect cover for any number of illegal activities."

He turned back to Annie and Kitty. "It's not the sort of thing we would normally ask a civilian to do, but if either of you could get close enough to plant a bug in his truck or on his person somewhere, it might make the difference in allowing us to save lives, potentially hundreds or even thousands of lives."

"Get close enough?!" Kitty was incredulous. She and Annie looked at each other and Annie laughed shortly. "We were plenty close this morning!" Kitty continued. "And this is not a man I care to ever be close to again, if I can help it! Not at all."

"I understand that," Harris said calmly. "Let me explain a little more what we have in mind." He proceeded to lay out surveillance options and the role either Kitty or Annie could play.

"So if you agree, we would fix you up with a wire—"

Joe, who had been listening silently, suddenly spoke. "A wire would be detected. There isn't anywhere you could put it that this man is unlikely to touch." He turned to Kitty. "You don't have to do this. Nor you," he continued, fixing Annie with a grim look.

"Harris," he now addressed the man behind the desk, "I know you're doing your job—and in this case trying to prevent what might be a terrible attack—but what these women have already gone through at the hands of your suspect has been harrowing. A wire is out of the question!"

"Sir," Harris said, "with respect, please listen to me. First, the definition of a wire has changed in the past few years, and it doesn't actually include any physical wires." He smiled, again, briefly. "Our devices now are so small they can be hidden in a couple of buttons, or a pair of earrings. I think the odds are very good—in fact, I would say I can assure you—they won't be detected."

Both Kitty and Annie were staring at Harris intently,

mouths slightly open. Joe, too, seemed to be listening closely.

Seeing that he had his audience's attention, Harris continued. "The primary reason for the wire is the protection of the wearer. We will have people stationed within close proximity at all times, and if the need for an extraction occurs, we will take whatever measures are necessary."

"There must be some other way," Joe said. "I know this man, too. Maybe I can get closer to him, get him to take me into his confidence." Kitty stared at him.

"There isn't time, sir," Harris said firmly. "I would have preferred that also, but based on what we're hearing, we have only a few days at most before whatever it is, is due to go down. So it's really what these ladies can do for us, or we take our chances with picking Oponuno up prematurely and the attack very likely goes forward without him. We don't know where, what, or how. Only that he is involved somehow, and that what is planned may be very, very big. Daniel Oponuno is our only confirmed on-the-ground conspirator."

"Okay," Kitty said. "Suppose we were to agree to help. Not saying we do agree, you understand.   But how would it work? This morning he was insisting I go with him on his first set of rounds, whatever they might be. When Annie told him I had to work, he said he'd settle for tomorrow. But we don't know whether he'll ask for me or for Annie. He's going to call us in the morning, if not before."

"All right." Harris nodded. "That's actually better than we were anticipating. I think, because of the variables in the situation, that we would expect to have either of you ready to go—meaning, if you both agreed, that you would both be wired, and fully briefed," Harris said. "If only one of you is willing, then the other one would have to be firmly unavailable to Oponuno, across town or at work downtown, something like that."

"Does anyone have any idea why Dan wants one of you to come with him?" Joe asked. "If he's innocently starting a new job, it makes no sense at all. And if he is really plotting something, I can't see that it makes any sense that way either. Any ideas,

Annie? Kitty? Anyone?"

"I just figure he wants to torture us. He clearly likes hav-ing people—at least women—in his power. It seems sexual, even though so far he hasn't tried to do anything really sexual to me, not that you could pin down." Kitty was amazed at how calm and rational she sounded, when inside she was roiling with anx-iety.

"It's another ploy to put off telling us where Angela is," Annie said. "He either doesn't know where she is, or maybe if he tells us, it will turn out to be to his disadvantage somehow. That's all I know. And Mr. Harris, what can you tell me about my daughter? Do your people have any idea where she is? Is anyone even looking for her?"

"We are looking for her. We suspect she may be with some of the other co-conspirators. But since we only know them as electronic signals—we don't know who they are, or where— we're having slow progress. That's another reason for concen-trating on Oponuno. If we can get him to lead us to some of the others, even one, that may give us the information we need to locate your daughter." Harris paused, and picked up the pipe that had been lying on the desk for most of the interview. He stuck it in his mouth and pulled at it thoughtfully.

"The only idea I would have about why he would want one of you in the truck with him, and is willing to risk violating any "no riders" clause in his contract, is that he wants to go some-place where having a woman in the vehicle with him would be disarming." Harris shook his head and laid the still-unlit pipe back on the desk. "Where that would be, we haven't come up with as yet. Hence, again, the need for one or both of you to help unravel that piece of the puzzle."

"I don't want to pressure you at all," Kitty said, looking at Annie. "But I'm going to say yes to this crazy idea. If I don't, and something bad happens, I'd always be haunted by the feeling that I had a chance to help and didn't do anything."

"Count me in, too," Annie said. "I can see the best way to help try to find Angela is to bring this so-called plot to an end, one way or another. But I want to be really sure the people who are 'around' in case of emergency really will come running if something goes very wrong. Because if the bugger tries with me again some of the things he's tried with me before, I may kill him with my bare hands before they get there!"

Harris assured Annie that the surveillance would be both close and "hair-trigger." He went on to spell out more of the necessary details, including requesting they accept the presence of a female officer in Annie's apartment overnight, to ensure both their interim safety and the ability to respond quickly in the morning to whatever Dan's new demands might be.

Annie insisted on calling Gretchen to check this out. "You're going to what?!" They all heard Gretchen's screech through the phone as Annie jerked it away from her ear. "Calm down, sweetheart," Annie tried, her voice low and gentle. "I know, I know," they heard her say. And then, "But, listen. Just for now, just say it's okay to have the officer come sleep on our couch. We can talk about the other part when we both get home."

Gretchen must have agreed to that, because Annie soon clicked off the phone. "It's okay," she said. "I won't say I can be the one to go with Dan, because if Gretchen is dead set against it, I may choose not to. You understand, I hope," she said, looking at Kitty and then at Harris.

"I do," Kitty said, and Harris nodded.

"I hated Joe's field work the whole time." Annie had a faraway look for a moment. "I can understand Gretchen's feeling."

"It may be," Kitty said, "that if we tell him I'm the one coming, he'll just accept it with no questions." She felt something like panic rising in her chest. "I want to be able to do it, but I don't know whether I will be able to or not." She looked at Joe. "You may have to help me get ready," she said softly.

"Kitty." Joe leaned closer and put his arm around her protectively. Gently cupping her chin in his hand to look her directly in the eyes, he continued. "You don't have to do this. I respect and will support to the fullest your decision, whether you want to go through with it, or if you decide"—he looked pointedly at Harris—"even at the very last minute, not to do it."

"Absolutely," Harris agreed. "Ms. Toulkes, as a civilian member of the public, you are being asked to do this as a public service, and you have every right to decline. If you choose to co-operate, we will give you every protection we possibly can." He stood up and walked around in front of the desk. "We wouldn't ask it of you if we didn't think it was reasonably safe. And balanced against the value of the information, I hope you'll decide to help. But you are free to decide.

"And now, unless any of you have questions, I should contact my people and make sure everything is in readiness. And, sir," he nodded at Joe, "I'll be in touch if we have any more information to add, or if the situation changes in any significant way. And I would ask you to do the same"

"Very well," Joe stood up. "Kitty? Annie? Any final questions or comments?"

Both of them shook their heads. Joe gestured toward the door. "I've thought of one more little thing," he said lightly. "You gals go ahead. I'll be right out."

"Thank you for coming," Harris said as the two women exited.

A few moments later, Joe came out. "Let's get out of here," he said.

The Bouncer who had let them in appeared again and escorted them to the front door. "May I say, Mr. Treacher...," he said hesitantly. Joe looked at him quizzically. "May I say, it's a privilege to have met you. I have, of course, heard a great deal about you from colleagues who served with you." Joe nodded gravely and shook the man's hand before leaving. The Bouncer watched them to Annie's car and then closed the door.

On the way back to the Cocoa Factory, there was little conversation. Annie placed a call to let her assistant gardener know she would be a little late for the afternoon's class. Kitty in turn called the Counseling Services Center to say that she needed to take the next two days off. "If someone else can take my open office hours on Wednesday," she told Alicia, "that would be great. And if I have any scheduled appointments, either call and cancel them or make sure whoever takes them knows if he or she wants to call me about them, it should be today, not tomorrow."

Joe drove efficiently, but the trip seemed much longer going home than it had coming. When they reached the Cocoa Factory, Annie took her keys from Joe and excused herself to go by the Food Friend. "I'm hoping Gretchen can come over to talk to you about the moon ritual," she said as Kitty and Joe prepared to go into the courtyard. "Our coven will be gathering on Wednesday night, and if it's okay we'd still like to have it at your place."

"Sure thing," Kitty said. "Tell Gretchen to come on over. It'll help pass the evening."

# CHAPTER 32

Back inside the apartment, Kitty dropped onto the couch. "This all seems completely unreal," she said, her voice barely rising above a whisper.

Joe came to sit beside her. "Do you want to talk about it?" he asked.

"Not really," she said. "Maybe we should, though—but really, I don't even want to think about it." She looked at Joe, her face full of questions.

"Then let's not think about it for now," he said. "Let's find something else to occupy us." He gathered her into his arms and began stroking the back of her neck and shoulder. As she relaxed, his stroking became more intimate, until abruptly, with no warning, he pinched her derriere.

"Hey!" Kitty sat up, surprised. "What was that for?'

"Want to go to bed?" Joe asked, playful now.

For answer, Kitty took his face in her hands and kissed him thoroughly. Then she stood up and took him by the hand and headed toward the bedroom.

This time, Kitty took the lead, undressing first herself and then Joe, slowly, with lots of stops along the way. As she stripped off his shorts, she asked casually whether he had ever studied Tantra.

"You mean the ancient Indian science of Tantric Yoga?" Joe asked. "Where all the dirty pictures come from?"

"Yes, what you said," Kitty replied. "But not dirty, just very, very sexy."

"And very, very athletic," Joe added, skeptically.

"So, did you do the workshops and all that?"

"Nope," Joe said. "Never had the time."

"Well, I did," Kitty said boldly. "Let me show you some of what I learned. It isn't all athletic. Some is very useful for 'older people.' It's all about using your energy in the most effective ways."

A few minutes later, she asked, "You know about the G-spot. You showed me that a couple of nights ago. Tantrikas call it the Sacred Spot. Did you know you have one too?"

"No," Joe said. "Didn't know that." Kitty proceeded to show him.

Some time later, Joe stretched languorously. Kitty, propped up on one elbow, used a finger to trace spirals on his chest, stopping at a small silvery scar under his left collarbone. "What's this?" she asked, circling the scar with her finger.

"A scar," Joe said.

"I can see that," Kitty laughed. "From what?"

She could feel Joe tense a bit. "A piece of metal that I got in the way of," he said finally. "You know, my darling, I really was hoping you'd say no to Harris. The idea of your being in harm's way turns my insides to jelly."

"But you'll help me be brave if I have to do it, right?"

"I will. And I'll do whatever I have to do to help keep you safe." Joe rolled over and sat up. "Let's go to the park," he said.

In the end, they decided to have something to eat on the way to Ft. Greene Park. Walking down Myrtle toward the park they passed several small restaurants and bars before Kitty suggested stopping at Maggie Brown's. "They have excellent burgers, nice salads. And the biscuits are as good as I can make myself," she concluded modestly.

At a little table near the front of the small café, they studied the menu and finally both settled on burgers, sweet potato fries, and house salads. After a filling meal, they strolled on down the street, past the little alternative health store with its wheatgrass dishes, past the middle-aged security guard standing lethargically on the sidewalk outside a bank's plate glass facade, and on past the discount drugstore across from the brick wall with a boldly-painted mural commemorating the spot where a young man was shot, back when Myrtle was known locally as "Murder Avenue."

In due time, they arrived at the park, where they strolled under ancient trees on grassy hillsides that made terror plots and missing loved ones seem like a bad dream from which one might soon awaken. They walked up the hill to the Prison Ship Martyrs monument. "But let's not go into the visitors' center," Kitty suggested. "I don't want to read about more awfulness today."

Heading back some time later, Kitty got a phone call from Gretchen, saying she was home, and asking when she might come over to talk about the moon ritual. They arranged for seven.

"Kitty," Joe said as they neared the Cocoa Factory, "I should really go back to Williamsburg to get some things. Would you be okay if I go now? Or do you want to go with? Or, I could wait until Gretchen comes over later."

"Oh, I'm fine for now, I think," Kitty said. "I might take a little nap. But..."

"But what?" Joe was all attention.

"Just...maybe you'd walk me back to the apartment, if you don't mind. I hate being a wimp, but I'd feel better. I'm kinda spooked about going into the building by myself."

"Of course," Joe said immediately. "No problem, and don't think anything of it." He walked her to the door of 5G, and unlocked it. "Let me come in a minute until you get settled," he offered.

"I won't say no," Kitty sighed. "You can call me when you're on your way back," she continued when they were both inside. "I'm fine now, and I will take that nap."

***

By the time Joe got back, it was nearly 7:00. Kitty had remade the bed and was straightening up the living room, in preparation for Gretchen's coming. "What did you bring?" she asked Joe. "Anything for me?"

"Not directly," he answered. "Just some things I might need for tomorrow."

"I think you are not going to tell me what you plan on doing tomorrow," Kitty said.

"And you'd be right, partly because I don't know myself until it happens," Joe said.

"And partly because you don't want me to know. Why?"

"Old habits," Joe replied. "Information shared on a need-to-know basis. What you don't know can't hurt you, and you can't accidentally share it with someone who shouldn't know."

"Like Mr. Harris?" Kitty probed.

"Or Dan," Joe said gravely.

"Oh." Kitty thought about that. "Oh."

Just then the doorbell rang. Kitty startled, even though she was expecting Gretchen. Joe opened the door after confirming that it was, in fact, the next-door neighbor arriving for the briefing on the moon ritual. He excused himself and went into the bedroom, shutting the door.

"Okay," Kitty said with as much enthusiasm as she could muster, "tell me what you'll need for this ritual."

"Well, first let me tell you a little bit about moon magick in general and the importance of the moon in our style of Wicca," Gretchen said. "You know what Wicca is, I assume."

"I think I do, but tell me anyway," Kitty replied.

"Modern-day Wiccans, or Witches, as we sometimes call ourselves, are the spiritual descendants of our biological ancestors in pagan Europe. Although most of the pagan religion was wiped out during the Christianization of Europe, enough survived in isolated pockets, secret family teachings, and hidden-in-plain-sight public ceremonies and icons such as the May Pole, Halloween, the Easter Bunny, and the Green Man carvings to verify the truths that were our heritage.

"The sun and moon were both important to the people of ancient Europe. The solar year, with its four major quarter points—Spring and Autumn equinoxes, Winter and Summer solstices—and the four cross-quarter days in between, tell the story of the Sun/Son as he passes through the cycle of birth, growth, decline, death, and rebirth. The lunar month charts the cycle of the Lady Goddess, as she appears, waxes, comes to fullness, wanes, and finally disappears again before starting the cycle all over again.

"Each part of each cycle has appropriate types of celebration. For example, the Autumn Equinox, which we've just celebrated, is a time of giving thanks for the harvest, gathering in the fullness of what we have learned in the months past, and preparing for the winter to come. Anyone living in a temperate climate feels these changes in her bones, and even those who aren't overtly pagan often celebrate in their own ways. Spring the same way—who doesn't feel renewal, relief, a kind of 'hooray, let's begin!' in the spring, or a sacred kind of hush at the first snowfall around the time of the winter solstice?

"The moon changes can be more subtle, especially for those of us living in cities, where the night sky is hardly a major feature of our lives. But paying attention to the moon's cycle can make us appreciate that it does affect us, and it can help us stay in tune with our bodies and our psyches.

"Wicca 101 lecture over now," Gretchen laughed. "I'm sorry. I get wound up!"

"No apology needed," Kitty said. "I'm fascinated. That's lots more than I knew. So what are we celebrating this week?"

"The Dark Moon," Gretchen explained, "when the moon is so close to the Sun that it's not visible from Earth. Usually we celebrate the New Moon, when the first slip of a crescent is visible in the sky. But given what's going on right now, Dark Moon magick seems more appropriate. The Dark of the Moon is a time for searching the dark places in ourselves for old angers, sorrows, and passions we should let go of, getting rid of physical things we don't need anymore, casting binding spells, and bringing balance or justice into all kinds of situations."

"Well, that certainly sounds fitting," Kitty said. "So how do we proceed? I'm willing to move furniture around, whatever is needed to make this go smoothly. Are there many people in your group?"

"For the moon celebrations, usually not more than ten," Gretchen estimated. "Since it's mid-week, maybe not even that many." She looked at the large open space that served as Kitty's living room, dining room, study, and library. "So the way you have your living space arranged, we won't have any problem. Annie and I will bring a few chairs over, and the altar. If you have any extra candles you'd like to put out, that would be great. Since it's Dark Moon, we'll try to get by without any artificial lights—you know, electric, I mean. But candles we need to see what we are doing!"

"I certainly have candles," Kitty said, "especially if they don't have to be new ones."

"No, partially-burned ones are fine," Gretchen said "Just set them out wherever you feel like, and we'll bring some, too."

"Can you give me an overall plan for the evening?" Kitty asked.

"I'm sure Annie and I will be here early," Gretchen said, "so we can set up, and we'll be able to greet people and introduce you as they arrive. Once everyone's here, we'll cast a circle, probably do a check-in, and then some rituals according to what comes up. A binding for sure. But other people may have some specific things they want to work on. Once we're all finished, we'll open the circle, and have some refreshments. Everybody will have brought some food, and we'll bring some wine when we come."

"Should I..." Kitty began.

"You don't need to bring anything," Gretchen interrupted, "but if you could set out some plates and glasses that would be great. And don't worry about anything. It's all informal, and Annie will be explaining things as she goes along."

"What do you wear?" Kitty wondered.

"Well, some covens work sky-clad—that's mostly those who can really work outdoors, though. Urban witches, like us —we wear whatever. Something comfortable. Some of the girls wear long skirts and such; I'll be in slacks and a t-shirt, most likely."

"Sky-clad?" Kitty repeated, frowning. And then her eyes opened wide. "Oh!"

"Right," Gretchen smiled, as her phone began to ring. "Hi," she said into the phone. "Okay, we'll be right over." As she snapped the phone off, she spoke to Kitty. "The woman agent has arrived. Annie thought you'd want to meet her tonight, rather than just in the morning."

"You go ahead, if you want to," Kitty said. "I'll get Joe and we'll be coming."

The agent sent by Harris was a thirty-something woman in slacks and a dark leather jacket, who introduced herself as Letitia Brown. Like the Bouncer, she seemed to know of Joe, although she didn't give any more context than the Bouncer had. Kitty made a mental note to ask Joe what he had done to earn such a reputation with the younger generation.

"I understand that either of you may be the one called on to make this contact tomorrow," Letitia said, addressing Annie and Kitty. "So both of you need to be ready. Right?"

"Right," Annie said. "I'm the one whose daughter he claims to know something about. Joe, do you think he really does know where Angela is? Or is he just saying that to get us to go along with him?"

"He does know at least something, Chum," Joe said. He reached into his pocket and pulled out the rose key-chain. "When he returned your keys, remember he didn't give back your keychain?"

"I certainly do. It was my favorite keychain!"

"Well, they were on this chain instead. I don't know whether you recognize it, but I gave this to Angie for her birthday a while back."

For a moment, it looked to Kitty as though Annie was about to collapse. She caught herself, however, and simply stared at Joe. "You didn't think to tell me?" she said finally.

"I thought of it, and thought better of it," Joe said. "I'm sorry if I made the wrong choice. We still don't know how he got the chain, whether he actually has seen Angie or whether he picked this up from someone else. Nor do we know how long he has had it. He may have seen her months ago, under who knows what circumstances. We already know he snatches women's keys—right?"

"That settles it, then," Annie said, ignoring Joe's last comment. "Gretchen, I'm going through with this, no matter what! I hope you understand. But even if you don't, I have to do what I can."

"I do understand, honey," Gretchen said. "Don't worry. It'll be all right, I'm sure of it."

"Anything more tonight, then?" Joe asked, his gaze taking in all four of the women.

"Nothing from my side," Letitia said. "Except to settle on a meeting time for tomorrow morning. What time are you expecting to hear from the man?"

"We don't really know," Annie said, "but I'm guessing before his workday starts, so maybe 7:00, or even earlier."

"Then we might start here at 6:15?" Letitia suggested.

"Sounds about right," Kitty said. "We'll be here."

"And in that case, we should leave now," Joe said. "Good to meet you, Letitia, and we'll see you all in the morning."

Back in the hall, Kitty stopped before opening her door. "I'm not quite ready to call it a day, are you?" she asked.

"Not necessarily," Joe said. "Are you hungry?"

"No, just restless. Would you be interested in going up on the roof for a little while?"

"Oh, you have a roof garden?"

"Not a garden, exactly, but a nice little space, with great views," Kitty explained.

"Let's do it, then," Joe said, taking off down the hall.

They took the elevator as high as it went and then climbed a flight of stairs, to come out on a dimly-lighted platform, ringed with waist-high railings.

"Very nice," Joe said.

"It's spectacular from up here when there's a good sunset," Kitty said, gesturing toward the East River below and lower Manhattan beyond. "And sometimes at night you can see the full moon, hanging over the city. It's really beautiful."

"Moon over Manhattan," Joe crooned.

"Shining on one I love," Kitty continued, making up words to the familiar tune, and they both laughed with delight.

"No moon tonight," Joe said.

"I guess we are heading for the dark of the moon," Kitty said. "I think that's what Gretchen was saying."

"Well, it's a pretty sight, even without the moon. You're lucky to have this rooftop." Joe slipped his arm around Kitty as they stood together, taking in the iconic view.

Finally, reluctantly, Kitty broke away. "We'd better go, I guess. Morning will be early tomorrow." She reached out her hand and together they walked across the roof, and made their way back to the apartment.

# CHAPTER 33

At 6:15 next morning when Gretchen opened the door of 5F to Kitty and Joe, Annie was already being instructed on the placement of her "wire."

"It looks to me like the two optimal placements for you," Letitia was saying, "would be either on your shoes—these buckles—or in a watch. Do you think our man might notice a change of watch?"

"I doubt it," Annie said, "but I really don't know."

"Well, I don't usually prefer shoes, just because there is so much ambient noise. But, you may be mostly in a vehicle, as I understand it?"

Annie nodded. "That seems to be his plan."

"Then without a lot of walking, the shoes should be fine. We'll use two devices, one on each shoe, with two different channels, so what one doesn't transmit clearly, the other one perhaps will. Hello, Kitty, Joe," she tossed over her shoulder. "I'll be with you in just a minute." She placed the buckle clips on Annie's black wedge loafers. "Look okay?" she asked.

"I think they look fine," Annie said. "Can I keep them after this is over, minus the spy hardware, of course?

Everyone laughed.

"Okay," Letitia said. "Let's see you, Kitty." She looked Kitty over from head to toe. "Hmm! No headband—your hair is too short. No shoe buckles on your sneakers, although we could put something in a fringe if need be. Earrings! That's a winner. I assume you carry a phone? That's easy to bug...but the phone could get dropped, or taken from you, in a pinch."

Kitty looked dismayed. She turned to Joe for reassurance.

"Hey!" Letitia saw the look. "We're talking worst case scenario here! That's really what this is all about. Not what we *think* will happen, but what *could,* but probably won't, happen."

Joe nodded. "Absolutely right," he affirmed. "'Be prepared' is more than just a scouting motto."

"So, here's what we'll do," Letitia continued, reaching into a black cloth bag. "I'll trade you out these earrings for the ones you've got. Hope you like them. You'll find them just a little bit heavier than you may be used to. That's the battery. But they're kind of pretty, I think."

They were, actually, rather pretty. Filigreed antiqued metal, with little balls dangling. Posts, not the wires Kitty normally chose. But not uncomfortably heavy.

"And then we'll just make sure we can track you by your phone. Do you know whether it has location enabled?" Letitia was looking at her digital tablet.

"I think so," Kitty said. "I mean, it shows me where I am when I go to the subway map or whatever."

"Okay, good," Letitia said. "Here, give me your phone for a minute, will you?" Kitty did, and Letitia took down a couple of different numbers.

Kitty could tell Joe was watching everything closely. "You look like you wish you could get into this equipment," she said, giving him a little nudge in the ribs.

"Just amazed at how the technology's changed in a few years," he said. "And how that expands what they can do."

Letitia handed Kitty back her phone. "Okay, ladies, I think we're ready to roll. Now we just wait for our boy to call. Is that right?"

"That's what he said," Annie confirmed. "There's more coffee, and Gretchen has been down to get rolls already. Anybody hungry?"

"Not really," Kitty answered. "My stomach is talking to me, but 'hungry' is not what it's saying."

"I know," Annie said. "More like 'what were you thinking of when you got us into this?' Right?"

Just then, Annie's landline rang. "That will be Dan," she said. "Are your people listening?"

"They are. Go ahead and answer," Letitia encouraged.

Kitty held her breath. Joe put his arm around her. Gretchen came close to Annie and put her ear near the phone.

"Hello," Annie said. "Yes, Dan, we're here, both of us...."

"I'm giving the phone to Kitty, then, if that's what you want. But don't forget your promise to me—you promised to.....yes, giving the phone to her now!"

Kitty reached for the phone. "Good morning," she said, doing her best to keep her voice even.

"Good morning, my dear," she heard. "And how are you this fine day?"

"No comment," she said shortly.

"My, my! Hostile already? That's no way to treat a friend who just wants to take you for a ride in his car-car."

"Okay, what is it I need to do?" she asked.

"Have it your way, then," Dan said. "Please meet me at the loading dock in twenty minutes. Just you, we don't need Annie, and three of us wouldn't fit in the truck very easily anyway."

"Twenty minutes?" Joe shook his head, as did Letitia. "I can't make it that soon. It takes twenty minutes to walk over there, and I haven't had any breakfast yet. And..."

Dan cut her off. "I'll give you half an hour. No more. If you can't make it by 7:30..., well, just be here by 7:30!" He broke off the connection.

Kitty felt sick. Her heart was pounding, and her stomach clenched as though someone had punched her, hard. She closed her eyes and concentrated on her breath. Breath in, breath out. Breath in, breath out.

Gradually, her breath slowed and became more even. When she opened her eyes, she found everyone looking at her, various expressions of concern on their faces. Gretchen and Annie were clutching hands. Joe had come close, the effort he was putting into self-control showing in his posture. Letitia was simply looking, no doubt trying to determine whether Kitty was

163

going to decline to carry through.

"Okay," Kitty said finally. "I think I can go. And it really will take me almost 20 minutes to get there, so we only have a few more minutes. He wants me there by 7:30 and he's threatening—who knows what—if I don't make it by then."

"Kitty," Letitia asserted her authority. "Our people are in place, near where you will be meeting him. We have your position from your phone, the bugs in the earrings are working, and all you need to do is just drop either or preferably both of these little location transmitters in or on his truck somewhere." She handed Kitty what looked a little like two tiny dust bunnies. "I suggest you put them in your purse or pocket, whichever you can get into the most casually. Plant them as soon as you can, so as to get them off your person. If you have a tissue, you can put them in that and just pull it out and let them go. They're magnetic and will stick wherever you drop them."

"Am I supposed to get him to talk about what he is doing?" Kitty suddenly felt completely inadequate to the job assigned her.

"No!" Letitia was very firm. "You just take care of yourself, act like you would if none of this were happening. We don't expect anything of you except your presence to try to let us get some information through the listening devices and trackers. You're buying us time as much as anything. Don't worry. You'll do fine." She clapped Kitty on the shoulder.

"I'll walk with you part of the way," Joe said. "Like Letitia said, you don't need to do anything but be there. If you can't plant the transmitters, that's fine. Just get rid of them whatever way you can. If you're sure you want to go through with this, we'd better leave now, though."

Kitty walked to the door. "Here goes nothing," she said, snapping Annie a casual salute.

A chorus of "Good luck!" followed them out the door. Kitty heard it click shut with a feeling of dread mixed with a certain surprising level of excitement.

Joe walked with her as far as the Brooklyn Roasting Company. "I'd better leave you here, I think," Joe said. "If I could go in your place, please know I would. And if I thought I should stop you doing what you think is right, I would do that. I love you, Kitty."

"Me, too," Kitty said. "I'll be back as soon as I can." She reached up to put her arms around his neck, and gave him a quick, tender kiss. They held each other for a moment and then separated.

"Don't look for me, but I'll be near," Joe said. "Now go do your hero thing, my darling." His light words were accompanied by a smile that looked genuine. Kitty reminded herself he was an experienced spy—or whatever it was he was.

Walking the rest of the way to the loading dock of CS-Studios, Kitty puzzled over what Joe might mean by saying he would be near. It seemed unlikely he was speaking literally, she supposed. But if not, what was he referring to? She turned it over and over in her mind, finally deciding he must have meant something like "I'll be with you in my thoughts." She shrugged. And then, seeing Dan standing by a delivery truck, she felt all her nerves go on high alert. She made an effort to stride purposefully, willing her hands neither to tremble nor clench into fists.

"Hello, my dear Kitty," Dan said as she approached. "Come on and climb in." He opened the passenger side door, then stepped aside slightly and ran his hand up her right side from hip to armpit under the guise of helping her up to into the cab. His hand lingered momentarily on her breast before he stepped back and shut the door.

Kitty was too preoccupied with pulling a tissue out of her pocket to be more than disgusted by the groping. Having successfully dropped its technological contents on the floor of the truck, she was using the tissue to cover a manufactured cough as Dan climbed into the driver's seat. Noticing how good the disgust felt compared with fear, she considered whether it might be a good strategic stance.

"Well, here we go," Dan said gaily. "I'm sure you would like to know what we're going to be doing this morning."

"No, not especially," Kitty said sarcastically.

"Oops! Got some attitude going here, have we? That's okay! I like a woman with spunk!" He wheeled the truck out of the loading dock parking lot and onto the narrow street. "We have a delivery to make to a film shoot in Lower Manhattan. Then we'll be picking up some packages in Red Hook to bring back to the Navy Yard."

"And why in heaven's name did you want one of us to come along?" Kitty blurted out.

"For the company, of course! Who wouldn't want a lovely lady to ride along with him?"

Dan stretched his arm across the back of the seat and grabbed at Kitty's shoulder.

Crowding the door as closely as she could, Kitty managed to stay just out of reach.

"Very well, be that way," he said with a harsh laugh. "You'll change your tune soon enough."

Disgust, Kitty reminded herself. He's just a disgusting man who tries to use people to get what he wants. I have no reason to be afraid of him. He's disgusting, but not dangerous to me, at least not at the moment.

They rode in silence as the small truck wound its way through the Navy Yards, then out through the Sands Street entrance gate, across Navy Street, and on to join the traffic on the Flatbush Avenue Extension leading to the Manhattan Bridge. A tiny sliver of a crescent moon showed faintly in the sky over downtown Manhattan.

"Now, Kitty, you must admit I'm taking you on a nice sightseeing trip. Manhattan in the early morning is so lovely," Dan cooed, as they approached the bridge over the East River. "I do wish you'd be a little more friendly, though. You're hurting my feelings."

"There's no point my pretending I want to be here," Kitty said. "You are bullying us with this phony story about having some information about Annie's daughter. I don't believe you even know anything about her!"

"Oh, but I do," Dan said, sounding eager. "And wouldn't you like to know what! I'm sure Annie would. Maybe I'll tell you at the end of the day—if you are nice to me, I just might."

"Don't count on it," Kitty muttered under her breath.

Dan had all his attention on the driving now, as the morning traffic into Manhattan was building up. Kitty wondered how the FBI could possibly be keeping track of where they were, much less manage to be close at hand. And if Joe had meant something other than staying spiritually close, he could hardly be keeping his promise in this traffic. Just then, she glimpsed out her window a heavily-bearded man in a beret, driving a truck much like the one she was riding in. That could be Joe, she thought, and then immediately scolded herself for wishful thinking.

# CHAPTER 34

The drop-off at the film shoot near the corner of Wall Street and Washington was actually kind of interesting. Kitty was able to get out of the truck and walk around. The film crew was setting up cameras, reflectors, and screens as quickly as Dan unloaded them. When the actors began arriving, Kitty, behaving with uncharacteristic boldness, struck up a conversation with one of them and learned that they were there to shoot part of a commercial for a painkiller. Before the conversation could go anywhere else, though, Dan came over and touched Kitty's arm. She jerked away and gave him what she hoped was a chilling glare.

"Kitty," Dan said softly, "Come! Now!"

She longed to resist, but didn't. It would serve no purpose.

Back in the truck, Kitty tried to focus on where they were going. Dan had said they were going to pick up packages in Red Hook. Once out of the Battery-Brooklyn Tunnel, he steered the truck on what Kitty realized later must have been a circuitous path, designed to make certain she couldn't find her way back to the anonymous-looking three-story building where he finally parked in an alley. "Stay in the truck," he ordered. She could see no reason to disobey.

A door opened at the back of the building, and Kitty caught a glimpse of a man in an orange and black plaid shirt. Dan disappeared inside, but soon reappeared and came down the two steps to open the back of the truck. The "packages" turned out to be three large boxes wrapped in black plastic. One by one, the man in the outrageous shirt brought them out on a dolly. One was bulky enough Kitty assumed it would require both Dan and the other man to lift it. The others, though smaller, appeared to be very heavy, and the two men took great care levering the dolly down the steps. Kitty could feel the truck shift a little with each one they hoisted, somehow, into the back.

After she heard the back of the truck slam shut, Kitty, peering into the driver's side mirror, saw the two men embrace and then shake hands. Orange-and-Black Man stood on the top step as Dan got into the truck and backed out of the alley. Kitty watched him watching them until Dan had finished backing and started up the street again.

"That went well," he said, as though to himself. "And now," he turned to her brightly, "Kitty, my dear, we have a little time to spare before we're expected back at the Navy Yards. I think we should go to the park!"

A few blocks later, they came to a large open area with ballfields and a swimming pool. Dan parked along a nearly-de serted stretch of street and unlatched his seatbelt. "Might as well get com-for-ta-ble," he said. He prolonged every syllable as he pressed a button on the door and slid across the seat. Kitty grabbed for the door handle, but nothing happened. "Sorry, Kitty. Child locks." Dan smiled and reached out to stroke Kitty's hair. "It's time we got better acquainted."

Disgust, Kitty told herself. Just disgusting. He's not hurting me, he's only trying to scare me.

Dan stroked the back of her neck, and she shivered involuntarily. "What's the matter, Kitty?" he said softly. "You need to relax. We are going to be here awhile. Might as well enjoy it." He slid closer, pressing Kitty against the door. Then he took her face between his two palms and gently but firmly turned her toward him.

I am not my body, Kitty recited to herself. I am not only this body. Hey, I'm the psychologist here! I know how to handle these things. Just don't look at him. She closed her eyes.

"That's a girl, Kitty." Dan's voice sounded thick. He moved his hands over her breasts.

"Starting to enjoy it, are you?"

I am not only this body, Kitty chanted inside. All I have to do is remember I am mind and spirit as well. I have my own will, and this too will pass. She winced as the fingers probing under her shirt got increasing forceful. She gathered herself and used both hands to push him away.

"Hey, girlie! That's no good." He put both arms around her, expertly pinning her arms to her sides. "Go ahead and struggle if you like. I don't mind," he said, and then he lowered his mouth over hers.

At that moment, there was pounding at the driver's side window. A heavily-bearded face appeared at the window. The face was speaking, but Kitty couldn't hear what was being said.

Dan straightened up and reached for the window button. "Hey! What's going on? We're a little busy here." he snarled.

"You need to move on, buddy," the man at the window said. "We've got a parade setting up to start from here, and you're parked right in the middle of it."

Dan snapped the window closed without answering. But he started up the truck. "It's time we were getting on," he tossed to Kitty. Then with an ironic smile, he added, "We can pick up where we left off, later."

"Not if I can help it!" Kitty snapped.

"Ah, but I know you were starting to enjoy it," Dan said smoothly. "And you will again."

# CHAPTER 35

On the way back to the Navy Yards, Kitty sat silent and rigidly erect. They entered the Yards back at the Sands Street gate, Dan showing his CSStudio card to the attendant. Instead of heading straight for the studios, though, he took a left-hand turn where an arrow pointed to the COC Shipyard. Kitty came alert.

Dan pulled alongside a long white two-story building. A battered sign proclaimed that it had once been employee housing for the shipyards. Now, colorful individual logos on the doors suggested small businesses were using the spaces. Dan coasted down the row, obviously looking for a particular one. He pulled out his phone and punched a couple of buttons. "I'm here," he said into the phone.

Almost immediately, a door opened down the way, and a short, stocky man with dark hair stepped out on the stoop. Dan pulled up at the sidewalk leading to that door. The dark-haired man bumped down the step pulling a dolly like the one Kitty had seen earlier, in Red Hook. He headed for the back of the truck. Dan opened the door and turned to Kitty. "You can leave now, my dear," he said. "But if you want to stay, I'll take you back to CSStudios in a few minutes." He didn't wait for her reply, but got out and went to join the man with the dolly.

The two men ferried the awkward packages from Red Hook into the building, as Kitty debated whether to go or stay. It was hard to see what could be gained by staying. She just wanted to go home and take a bath, but she wasn't sure she could walk all that way without collapsing.

A car passed them, heading toward the shipyard. Kitty watched it stop at the iron gate that separated the restricted-access area from the rest of the old Navy Yards. It must not have had the required permission, as she soon saw it backing up to turn around.

Now Dan was back. "Still here, I see," he gloated. "Come on, then, I'll show you the shipyard before we go back. Did you know the *Queen Europa* is in their dock now? She's supposed to be the best little cruise liner ever built, or at least the fanciest, but she has a boo-boo, below the water-line. So she's in dry dock for a few days." He smiled as he started the truck.

Kitty smiled to herself, thinking of the car that had been turned back. Dan apparently didn't know he was heading into a restricted zone. But when they reached the gate, he surprised her by flashing a maroon and green plastic card that caused the armed guard to wave them right on through.

Around the corner of a large brick building, they were suddenly in the shipyard proper. The *Queen Europa*, in her dry dock, loomed over them. Kitty caught her breath! "Looks really big, doesn't she?" Dan remarked. "I thought you'd be impressed. Want to get out and walk around her?"

"No, thanks," Kitty said. "I just want to get back."

"I might need you again in a few days," Dan said, as he turned the truck around.

"I fear I will have to decline the invitation," Kitty said.

"If you don't want to come, I know someone who will. You tell that to Annie; see what she thinks." He chuckled, without smiling.

Back at CSStudios, Dan parked the truck in the loading dock area. He offered no resistance as Kitty opened the door and got out. "Goodbye, Kitty, my dear," he said. "Don't forget what you are supposed to tell Annie. And give her my love." He laughed.

Dan got out of the truck and, turning his back on Kitty, walked up the stairs and into the studio warehouse.

Sighing with relief, Kitty started the walk back to the Cocoa Factory. Soon after she was out of sight of the loading dock, she heard a truck come up behind her. A wave of fear swept over her, and she started to run. But the truck stopped, and then she heard a familiar voice calling her name. "Kitty, don't run. It's me. I've come to take you home."

He came quickly to her and held out his arms. Bushy beard or no, she fell into his welcoming embrace, sobbing with relief.

# CHAPTER 36

After Joe got her back to 5G, Kitty could think about nothing but a shower. She scrubbed every inch of skin and scalp, and let the hot water sweep over her for a long time. When she came out of the bathroom, her face was rosy and she could almost smile. Joe looked up from his computer. "Feeling better now?" he asked.

"Better, but not a hundred percent," she said.

"Come here, dear one," Joe said. "I've just been reading up on your tantric stuff. In ancient times, when warriors came back from battle, specially-skilled tantrikas spent time with them to help cleanse them from the war-spirit and battle scars. I wonder if that might be what you're needing now."

"Well, I don't know that I'm up for any fooling around," Kitty said apologetically.

"No, I just meant, I could give you a massage with some nice lotion, if it sounds like something you'd like. If that leads to other things, fine, but I wasn't counting on that."

He stretched out a hand, and Kitty took it. Together they walked into the bedroom, where Joe made good on his offer. He proved a skillful masseur, and Kitty started to wonder where he'd learned that skill, along with so many others. But part way through the wondering, she fell asleep.

When she woke up, Kitty smelled cooking. She yawned and stretched, and then got up and put on a robe. "What's happening?" she asked Joe, who was standing in the kitchen, a spatula in his hand.

"I took a chance that you'd be in the mood for cheese omelets," Joe said. "If you don't want that, I'll be glad to fix you anything else we have available—or take you out somewhere if you prefer."

"Omelet sounds great. Let's see—he's a master of disguise, does great massage, and best of all, he cooks! What a guy!"

Kitty went to work setting the table. "How did you manage to come up to the truck just when I needed you most? And what was that cockamamie tale about a parade?"

"The *federales* are not the only ones with technology that can track a phone," Joe said, expertly flipping an omelet. "And I was just a little more aggressive about following you than they were, I think. But what do you mean, 'cockamamie'? I thought it was a great idea for the spur of the moment!"

"Well, he bought it, or at least was not willing to risk its being true. I'm so very grateful," Kitty said, giving Joe a kiss on the cheek. "Speaking of federal technology, though, I still have the earrings. How do I return those, and do we have any date with them to debrief and catch up on what they learned?"

"Actually," Joe said, putting the omelet on a plate for Kitty and pulling a second one out of the oven. "Harris called me while you were showering. He wanted to meet right away, but I put him off."

"For which thank you very much," Kitty said. "This is delish, by the way."

"Coffee?" Joe offered.

"Maybe orange juice if we have any," Kitty replied. "But I can get it myself. Sit down before your omelet gets cold."

Joe pulled out one of the old wooden chairs and sat down at Kitty's small oak table. "I think we'd better call Harris back soon and arrange a meeting time and place. I'm expecting he'll want us to come to him again. If you're willing, that is." He poured some milk into his coffee and took a sip.

When Joe called Harris back, his expectation was confirmed. The FBI man requested they come again to the white house near downtown. "As soon as possible," Joe relayed to Kitty.

"I'm ready," Kitty said, pouring some juice for herself. "Want some of this? Did he say anything about who should come?" she asked Joe.

"No, thanks," Joe said. "He seemed to be assuming it would be the same three of us. I don't know how much he'll tell us, but I think we should all go."

When Annie said Gretchen wanted to come along, Kitty nodded vigorously. Joe agreed. "It's always easier to get forgiveness than permission," he said.

So the four of them piled into Annie's car. Annie drove, with Joe giving occasional directions. When they arrived, Gretchen's presence seemed to cause no problem to the Bouncer, who greeted them all with professional courtesy. They were ushered into the same small room, and invited to be seated in the same leather-upholstered chairs.

Mr. Harris came in before they had a chance to sit down. Annie stepped forward to shake his hand and introduce her partner. Harris raised his eyebrows, but only said, "Glad to meet you. Please be seated, won't you all?"

"First," Harris said, when they were seated, "let me thank you all for your help, and especially you, Ms. Toulkes. You have made a big contribution to our investigation, and I anticipate you will give us even more as we talk today. Your city and your country owe you a debt of gratitude."

Joe interrupted what sounded like a rehearsed speech to say, "Harris, no offense intended, but Ms. Toulkes has already had a day that has been stressful beyond what most people would be able to handle."

"No offense taken, sir." Harris looked a bit crestfallen. "I only want to be sure you all understand we are not taking your cooperation lightly."

"So anything you can do to expedite this meeting will be appreciated by all of us," Joe continued. "If you want to debrief Kitty first, that makes sense, and then we'd like to hear what you have learned."

"Very well," Harris said. "Are you ready to tell us what you saw and heard? I'd prefer to have you just unroll it for us, as you experienced it, rather than to start out with questions. If I need to interrupt to get more detail, I will, but only if I feel it is necessary."

Kitty nodded. She began to describe the morning, from the phone call on. As much as possible she focused on what she considered the salient points. "You know I successfully dropped the tracking bugs, on the floor of the truck. At least, I hope it was successful—you did get the signal, right?"

"We did, thank you," Harris said.

"And the sound came through, too?"

"For the most part," Harris confirmed. "We always get some and lose some. That's part of the reason we need your report."

"Then you probably heard Dan tell me he had packages to pick up in Red Hook. There wasn't anything significant until we got there, I think. The delivery to the film shoot, I assume was a legitimate part of the job with CSStudio."

"Yes, we checked it." Harris nodded.

"So, the place he stopped in Red Hook—did your people see it?"

"Tell me about it," Harris said, without answering her question.

Kitty described the building, the orange-and-black-shirted man, and the process of loading, as best she could. Harris seemed especially interested in what she said about the relative weight of the packages. "It felt in the truck as though each of the smaller boxes was very heavy," Kitty said. "The big one was asymmetric and bulky—it took two of them to carry it—but it didn't make the truck, you know, sink, or wiggle, when they loaded it."

"What kind of boxes? Could you see?" Harris asked.

"They were all wrapped up in what looked like heavy black plastic, the kind that some kinds of things loaded on open trucks are wrapped in, if you know what I mean," Kitty said. "I couldn't see the boxes themselves, only that the two smaller ones seemed to be the same, and the other one was, as I said, asymmetric, like, uh, like it had had something sticking up on one side, i guess."

"Okay, thank you. Go on. What next?"

"Well, somewhere in there, Dan kept insisting he did know where Angela is, and teasing that he wasn't going to tell unless I was 'good to him.' So after that pick-up, he drove to some kind of sports field place and parked the truck and proceeded to...to maul me. I couldn't fight him off, so I just closed my eyes and let him—I don't know what I should have done instead." She put her face into her hands as tears began to come. "Joe showed up just in time," she whispered.

"It's okay, Kitty," Joe said. "It's all over, and you can cry all you want, now and later both.  You don't ever have to be near Dan again." He turned to Harris.  "Can we take a little break now? Some water, maybe?"

"Certainly," Harris said.  He lifted a phone and spoke a few words. The Bouncer came in almost immediately with a glass of water, which Kitty sipped gratefully. After an interval during which no one spoke, she looked up at Harris. "I can go on, if you want."

Harris nodded.

"I think he drove straight back to the Navy Yard from there. I assume you know where he went to unload the boxes," Kitty said.

Harris nodded again. "Yes," he said.

"And I suppose you know who he called,"

"We do," Harris conceded.

"So did you see the man who helped him?"

Harris shook his head. Kitty described the man as best she could. "And then, he said he was going to show me the shipyard. I thought he wouldn't be able to get in, because the guard had turned away another vehicle. Was that one of yours?"

"Probably not," Harris said. "But Oponuno got in?"

"He did. He flashed a card. I couldn't see what it said, but it was bright-colored, reddish and bright green." Kitty closed her eyes, trying to remember anything else about that moment. "You know, we weren't close enough to the guard that he could have actually seen what was on the card anyway. It was almost like he was expecting us."

"And you drove into the shipyard. Did you stop? Get out?"

"No. He suggested it, but I just wanted to get back, and away from him," Kitty said, remembering. "And then he said something I thought might be important. He said he might need me again in a few days. And I said I wouldn't do it, and he said 'if you won't, I know someone else who will,' and that I should be sure and tell that to Annie."

"What did you think he meant by that?" Harris asked.

"I have no particular reason to think this, but I thought he might mean Angela," Kitty said. "Mainly because of what he said about telling Annie. Of course, he may have meant you, Annie, but I thought of Angela. I'm sorry." She turned to Joe. "I'm sorry."

"It's not your fault," Joe said.

"Nobody thinks any of this is your fault," Annie echoed. "We've been through so much hell with Angie over the years, we're almost used to it, in a way."

Joe nodded. "Almost," he said softly, as though to himself.

Harris cleared his throat. "What more you can you tell us?" he asked.

"I can't think of anything else," Kitty said after a moment's reflection. "If you have questions, I'll try to answer them."

"Any impressions of the other men, the ones who helped with the loading and unloading?"

"I didn't hear either of them speak, and I really didn't see them that much. Neither of them seemed to have any physical, like, impairment or tattoos or anything I could see. They seemed strong, you know, and capable. But I didn't really notice anything standing out about either one."

"Would you recognize either of them if you saw him again?"

"I doubt it," Kitty said. "Not enough for court or anything like that. It wasn't like I saw them close up."

"What about the places, the pick-up place in particular?" Harris asked. "Any impressions, no matter how trivial they might seem to you?"

"I'm sorry, no." Kitty dropped her head to her chest and closed her eyes.

"How about—" Harris began.

"Okay, that's enough," Joe interrupted. "She's said she doesn't remember anything else. And you can see she's exhausted. Now we'd like to hear what you know."

"Hey, this is an on-going investigation. It's not share-and-share-alike," Harris said, clearly caught off-guard.

Joe looked at him without expression, at the same time patting the air with his palm in a 'calm down' gesture. Finally, he spoke, his voice quiet but firm. "I think some reciprocity is appropriate," he said. "These women have done everything you asked, way beyond what civilians should normally be asked for. None of us is going to feel safe until this man is picked up, and you have plenty on which to book him. But we haven't insisted, and we haven't threatened to make a fuss, or to go public."

Harris started to speak, but Joe raised his hand. "And there's also the significant matter of Angela Treacher's well-being, which is clearly part of this whole situation. Ms. Treacher's and my daughter is being threatened by this man. You owe it to us to tell us what you think is going on here."

Harris nodded, one abbreviated nod. He sighed and seemed to gather himself. "Sir, you know as well as I do that this isn't part of the protocol. But I do appreciate the unusual circumstances, and you have been of immense help, from the beginning." His glance took them all in, but lingered on Joe and Kitty.

"I've told you the electronic traffic has been suggesting a new terrorist threat to the homeland, centered, we think, here in New York City. The pick-up location, I learned just before coming in here this morning, is connected to some people we have been interested in."

Harris clenched his jaw and breathed heavily before turning toward Kitty. "If our current theory is correct, it's possible that the packages you saw being loaded and unloaded contain explosive devices of some kind. The fact that the conspirators moved them close to the shipyard suggests a marine connection.

The presence of the *Queen Europa*, and Oponuno's focus on it, is further suggestive that an incident in the harbor area may be what they have in mind. You can imagine that a major explosion involving a ship of this size, in New York Harbor, would be very serious, not only in terms of direct loss of lives and property but also in terms of disruption of commerce and transportation."

"Any theories as to why he wanted a woman along?" Joe asked.

"I have one," Kitty said, "although I don't like it very much. Apart from his sexual fixation and obvious delight in exerting power over women, it might be that somehow having a woman in the truck with him makes him seem less dangerous to the guards. We've said that. But maybe it's even a signal that an accomplice on the inside has been told to watch for. What any of this could possibly have to do with Angela, though, I can't even speculate." She looked at Joe sympathetically.

"I don't have any better overall theory," Harris said. "If he is to get near the *Europa*, much less bring contraband cargo on board, he'll have to have confederates on the ship or working on the repair crews, or both. We're looking for any connections to any of the crews, but it's a little like the proverbial needle in the haystack. Very likely any necessary communications to arrange things with this hypothetical person or persons took place some time ago, and your idea of the woman companion being a signal is not at all improbable."

"So what can we do from here on?" Annie asked.

"Understanding that any further direct contact between Oponuno and either Kitty or Annie is absolutely out of the question," Joe interjected.

"I don't have a clear picture yet," Harris said. "But I won't ask either of you to get directly involved. That I will guarantee. You can let the professionals take it from here."

"And my daughter?" Annie's voice caught. She cleared her throat, and then continued. "Have you made any progress toward locating her?"

"If the conspirators are actually holding her," Harris

began, "we have only the two locations from this morning. We don't want to raid there prematurely. I hope you can understand why that's critically important. For the rest, we have only the electronic communications, and that tells us nothing about place, so far."

Annie glanced at Joe, who nodded, sighing. Turning to Harris, he asked, "So then what can you tell us about your timetable? Understanding doesn't mean we like it." He forced a smile of sorts.

"If necessary, we'll wait until they actually load the presumed explosives onboard the ship," Harris said. "If any contraband, even any innocent box that is not accounted for, is taken aboard, that will be a violation, and cause to arrest anyone involved in that process."

"So what you're saying is, the timing isn't in your hands," Joe said.

"That's pretty much it, sir," Harris said. "As you know, that is often the case in matters of this sort."

Joe nodded. He straightened, and, Kitty thought, looked again more like the professional colleague Harris was acknowledging him to be, rather than the discouraged father of a few moments ago.

"Well, thank you, Harris," Joe said. "I don't suppose we can count on being kept informed, but any little tidbits you can pass on will certainly be appreciated."

"I'll do my best," Harris said with determination, rising from his chair. "As you said, you've been more than helpful, and especially where your daughter's well-being is concerned, you have a right to be kept advised if we can do so without jeopardizing public safety. Thank you for coming."

He stood at the door of the little room and shook hands with each of the four of them in turn, offering each, including Gretchen, thanks "for all you have done to help your country." When Joe came by, Harris spoke a few additional words, so softly that even Kitty couldn't understand what he said.

The Bouncer saw them out, in his usual grave and courteous fashion. I really should get his name, Kitty thought. I can't keep calling him "The Bouncer."

"What did Harris want, there at the end?" Kitty asked Joe, once they were all in the car and on their way.

"He asked about the listening devices, if it would be okay for Laetitia to call and come by to pick them up from you. I presumptuously said it would be all right with you. Was that okay?"

"Oh, sure," Kitty said. "Just have to figure out what I did with them. I hope I didn't leave them in the bathroom someplace wet!"

# CHAPTER 37

On the way back to the Cocoa Factory, nobody said much, all lost in their own thoughts. Annie wheeled into the grimy parking lot under the BQE. "Anyone hungry?" she asked. "I'm going to take Gretchen to Il Porto for some good pizza, and you two would be welcome to come along."

Joe looked at Kitty, who shook her head. "I'm not hungry right now," she said. "I just need to unlax, I think."

They parted ways, then, Annie and Gretchen heading across the street and Joe and Kitty into the Cocoa Factory, both couples hand in hand.

When Joe and Kitty reached 5G, Kitty stepped back and waited for Joe to unlock the door. "I feel like I just want to sit down on the couch," she said. "Would you sit with me and we could maybe talk about what is going on?"

"Sure," Joe said. Once settled, he put his arm around Kitty and she leaned her head against him.

"So, what do you think?" she asked.

Joe paused before answering. "I see no reason to object to the basic view Harris outlined," he said. "It seems fairly obvious that the job at CSStudios was intended to give Oponuno a truck and an opportunity to drive in close to the shipyard without raising any suspicions."

"So if they think he's part of a conspiracy—which it seems clear even to me that he probably is—what are they waiting for?" Kitty asked.

"Most likely waiting until they have enough of the pieces. Right now, they know where the putative explosives are, and I'm sure they're trying to keep a close eye on them. So long as the boxes don't go on board the ship—"

"Or anywhere else," Kitty interrupted.

"Right. So long as that stuff doesn't go anywhere, I guess Harris feels safe enough waiting a little while to see if his people can connect the dots."

"I don't know anything about explosive devices," Kitty said. "What would it take to blow up an ocean liner?"

"They don't have to blow it up entirely," Joe said. "A smallish explosion or explosions in the right places could sink it, and that may be what they have in mind. Or—and this is the really scary part that Harris didn't mention—they could have one or more of the suitcase nuclear devices. The Russians have said there are more than a hundred of theirs that are missing—lost, stolen, or otherwise unaccounted for. And nobody seems to know whether or how many have made their way into the hands of terrorist organizations."

"Oh, my god!" Kitty was aghast. "That could blow up not only the ship but a good part of New York City—I suppose?"

"Well, put a big hole somewhere, anyway. Create quite a tidal wave, fallout, the whole bit," Joe said. "But there's nothing we can do about that now, so we might as well not focus on it."

"What should we focus on, then?" Kitty wanted to know. She was puzzled by Joe's apparent nonchalance.

"I think right now we should focus on getting you relaxed and comfortable," he said. "Would you like to go for a walk, or maybe go to bed? With or without me, I mean?"

"Maybe a short walk," Kitty said. "I could probably eat something soon. If we walked up to the bagel place, that might be fun."

\*\*\*

After two bagels—cream cheese and lox on poppy seed, ham-egg-and-cheese on an everything bagel—and two coffees, they headed back to the Cocoa Factory and again curled up on the couch together.

"I keep thinking about Dan," Kitty said. "He makes such a strange terrorist, if that's what he is. What do you suppose could have turned him in that direction?"

"I did a little more on-line research," Joe said. "Before the bank robbery, I found involvement with some of the more militant counter-culture groups in the mid and late '60s. Groups that back then were advocating violence to right the wrongs they saw internally in America. It looks like he identified with African-Americans, even though he himself is Hawaiian, and, so far as I know, has no African heritage.

"Then, since the robbery—or alleged robbery, anyway— he's probably been on the run, and maybe some terrorist group got hold of him that way. You didn't say, but what kind of ethnicity would you have thought the men you saw were?"

"Both of them had dark hair, maybe sort of medium darkish skin. I could have guessed Eastern Mediterranean, or maybe Asian subcontinent, possibly. But I really don't know." Kitty frowned with an effort to call up a clearer picture of either man. "No, I couldn't say for sure. Here in New York, one doesn't easily peg people, because all day you are seeing folks of all different colors. You know?"

"That's partly you, my dear," Joe said. "For some people, it's an all-day job of categorizing everyone, by race, by religion, by class. Part of what I love about you is that you tend to just see people as people." He stroked her hair.

Kitty snuggled closer. But when Joe's hand strayed lower to embrace her around the waist, she felt a shudder go through her. She hunched her shoulder under his arm and scooted a little ways away. She turned and stared at Joe, who was looking at her with concern.

"Too soon after?" he asked gently.

"I don't think I can," she said, tears forming in her eyes. "I'm sorry. It's, it's...I can't!" Her face crumpled.

"It's okay," Joe said. "I can wait, as long as necessary."

"I didn't know," Kitty said. "I feel...I don't know what I feel, but...." She began to cry.

"Shall I hold you, or would you rather not?" Joe asked. "Just let me know."

"Yes, hold me," Kitty sobbed. "Just don't touch me!"

For a long time, then, she lay against Joe's side while he held her, one arm carefully wrapped around her shoulder and the other hand alternately caressing her hair or holding her hand. Kitty tried to relax, but found her mind spinning from one fear to another.

Finally, she kissed Joe's arm and wriggled loose. "Thank you," she said shakily. "I think I'll go to bed." She stood up. "There should be some peanut butter in the cupboard, and I know there are hotdogs in the fridge, if you want to bother. I'm sorry. I'm just good for nothing tonight."

"It's okay," Joe said. "You've had a hard day. I'll stay up for a while, and try not to wake you when I come to bed. Unless you'd rather I sleep out here tonight."

"Oh, gosh, no. It'll be okay. I'm sure I'll shake it off. It's nothing to do with you; you know that, don't you?"

"I understand," Joe said. "Just make it easy on yourself. But if you like, I can certainly sleep out here."

"No, please. I'd rather have you....just come to bed when you feel like it." Kitty felt the tears starting again and fled into the bedroom.

Once in bed, she curled up into a ball, and, hugging herself in despair, soon fell into a dreamless sleep.

# CHAPTER 38

The next morning, Kitty was first up, and went down to the Food Friend for fruit and yogurt. She fixed a big bowl of grapes and berries, and set out bowls and spoons, along with coffee mugs. Then she set up her laptop on the end of the table and Googled "sexual assault."

She was still combing through websites when Joe came out to the kitchen. "I'm not finding a whole lot that's helpful here," she said when she realized he was looking over her shoulder. "Most of it is about rape, and there's lots about PTSD, which I don't think is going to be a problem. I think I just need some time to process, and put this all behind me." She turned her face up toward Joe and puckered her lips. He obliged with a quick peck.

"See," she continued, "I don't think I'm in a really bad way. I obviously don't want to be touched in certain ways, but I think I'll get over that. And if I don't, I'll get some help. I'm really sorry, Joe. I want to be with you, but right now I just can't, in that way."

"Kitty," Joe said, touching her arm with his fingertips, "I'm here with you, and I'll do or not do whatever you want, for as long as you want. We can talk, or not talk, cuddle or not cuddle, whatever. I'm not going to take it personally, so just don't you worry about it. Take as much time as you need to heal." Joe looked so earnest, Kitty almost laughed.

"You're an absolute dear," she told him, "and I love you. Now, get me some coffee, if you would please, and help yourself." She smiled as he grabbed both mugs.

"Here you are, m'lady," Joe placed a steaming mug in front of Kitty, as she closed her laptop. "Cream?"

"Yes, please. I forgot to get it out," Kitty said. "And please sit down, if you'd like fruit and yogurt. That's what I felt like, but I can fix you eggs if you want, or even pancakes, I think."

"Fruit looks good," Joe said. "I'll have a little yogurt. And then, I see you got a paper. Do you object to reading at the table?"

"Well, sort of," Kitty demurred. "How about we eat first, and then move to the living room area and we can divide up the paper?"

Joe agreed readily, and they shared a pleasant breakfast, unaccompanied by news, either printed or electronic.

*** 

Later, Kitty took the sofa while Joe settled himself in the recliner, his feet hanging over the end of the footrest. "You know," Kitty said, "if you're going to be a regular fixture here, I'll maybe have to get a bigger recliner."

Joe looked up from the *Times*. "Am I going to become a regular fixture?" he asked. He smiled, but his eyes showed a degree of wariness.

"I guess that sounded kind of presumptuous," Kitty said, "but I do like having you here."

"I thought maybe I was just being tolerated because of the crisis," Joe said. The jocular tone was underlain with something more serious.

"Well, maybe we should say this is a conversation to be continued, then," Kitty said. "I hope you'll stay at least until the present situation is resolved. And then....we may need to talk. You think?"

"Probably so," Joe said dryly, returning to his paper.

A few minutes later, he interrupted the silence. "Here's an odd story," he said. "May I read you a couple of paragraphs?"

"Sure," Kitty said, looking up from her piece of the paper. Joe read:

"A shoot-out in front of historic St. Eleanor Church, in Crown Heights, Brooklyn, resulted in serious injury to a man police said had assaulted an elderly woman. The names of the victim and the alleged perpetrator have not been released, but a police spokeswoman said the victim escaped with only minor injuries. The alleged attacker was taken to the hospital with injuries not thought to be life-threatening. Police on the scene said they were on the scene at the time of the alleged attack because they patrol that block regularly. Asked why that was the case, they could give no answer.

"Further investigation by this reporter revealed that the official locator records used by police and other public safety agencies designated the site of the small 18th century church as "a nuclear submarine." The church is more than 2 miles from any water leading to the open sea.

"No one in city government with whom the reporter has been able to speak has given any clarity to the situation. One clerk, who asked that her name not be used, blamed it on a coding error, saying, "Well, somebody needs to change that code!"

Kitty hooted with laughter. "Well, Dan's conspiracy could just blow up that little old church, then, and they'd have their nuclear explosion!" She laughed again. This time, Joe joined in, and the two of them laughed until they were out of breath.

"Whoo!" Kitty fell back against the couch. "I guess we needed that!"

"Not very nice to laugh," Joe said, wiping his eyes. "The poor man was just trying to mug an old lady, and he gets shot for being too near a nuclear sub." He chuckled again. "I know GPS isn't always very accurate, but I didn't know it could be that far off. I kinda hope they don't change the code. I'll bet the church gets a real shot in the arm out of this."

"Can you imagine? 'Hey, Martha, let's go to that nuclear submarine church, over in Crown Heights.' They may have a real revival!" Kitty giggled. "You want some more coffee?"

And so they passed the morning. Like two old married people, Kitty thought. Lunch was sandwiches from the deli downstairs, and then Joe decided to drive back to his place to check on things, while Kitty did some household chores and took a nap. "The witches are coming around 7:00 tonight," Kitty reminded him as he was leaving. "I don't suppose you want to be here for that, do you?"

"No, I don't," Joe replied. "But I would like to be back to take you to an early dinner somewhere. If that's okay, why don't we ask Gretchen and Annie if I can hang out at their place this evening?"

"I'll ask them," Kitty said. "I'm sure it'll be fine."

Once Joe was gone, Kitty started the dishwasher, then filled her laundry cart with recyclables and made the first of what turned out to be two trips to the recycle bins just off the laundry room. She did a little housework, dusting the window ledges before using the vacuum on the hardwoods in the bedroom and the living room/dining room/office and mopping the linoleum in the kitchen and the tile in the bathroom. Once the dishwasher was done, she put away the clean dishes and then was ready for the promised nap.

Joe came back about 5:30, and they agreed to go to the Turkish place up the street. After chicken shawarma with cucumber salad and hummus on the side, they walked home. Gretchen phoned to ask if she and Annie could come over, and Joe took his laptop and a book over to 5F.

As the sun was setting off to the west, Kitty helped Annie and Gretchen put chairs in a rough circle in the middle of her apartment. Candles were placed on every available horizontal surface, and the small altar Kitty had seen earlier was carried across the hall and set up at what approximated the north end of the circle. By the time the first of the coven members arrived, there was a festive look to the apartment. Gretchen introduced the guests to Kitty as they came in, and she soon felt included in the group.

At 7:30, Annie took her place, standing near the altar, and invited everyone else to stand, also. "You want to call the East?" she said to Gretchen, who was standing three places to Annie's left. Gretchen turned her back to the circle and raised her arms, the filmy lavender sleeves of her dark plum dress floating as she did so. The others all faced the same direction and also raised their arms. Feeling a little awkward, Kitty followed the lead.

"Spirits of the East," Gretchen called out, "of sunrise and butterflies, of Spring and the powers of Mind, the breezes and the fairie folk, we invite you now to join our circle. Be with us now." She paused, as though listening. "The Spirits of East are here," she announced.

"Allison?" Annie prompted softly, turning to face the center.

Directly across the circle from Annie, a tall, thin woman with long straight dark hair turned her back to the circle, her dark red skirt swirling around her ankles. She raised her arms and began to chant: "Spirits of the South, of the Summer and the noontime, the heat of the sun and of Fire, the salamander and the energy of growth, come now and join us in this our work tonight." Again, a pause, and then she said with certainty, "The Spirits of the South are here."

Everyone in the circle made another quarter turn and again raised their arms. A roundish blonde with a white peasant blouse and turquoise bows on her pigtails called the West: "Spirits of the West, of sunset and Autumn, ripeness and completion, the Waters great and small, emotion and the mermaids, we ask you now to join our circle. The Spirits of the West are here."

Another quarter turn, and now Annie's back was to the center of the circle. She raised her arms and called out, "Spirits of the North, of the cold of Winter and the dark of midnight, the elder wisdom and renunciation, the Earth and the Great White Bear, we call on you to join us." After a short pause, she continued: "The Spirits of the North are here."

Everyone turned back to the center of the circle, including Kitty, who was finding it all both a little confusing and quite fascinating. Now Annie continued. "God and Goddess, we ask you to join us in our work tonight." Kitty thought she felt a shift, as though the air had solidified somehow. "The God and Goddess are here," Annie announced.

She sat down, as did the rest of the coven. "This is the night of the Dark of the Moon," Annie continued. "And we need to do a binding. What else does anyone have that needs to be released, or cleansed, or anything else we can do on this night?"

The blonde with the pigtails spoke up. "I have something I'd like to release—I'm losing weight, so I want to release any image I have of myself as fat."

"Okay, Netta," Annie said, encouragingly. "Anyone else?"

Three other women nodded. "Me too," one of them murmured.

"Okay, looks like a general releasing ritual is in order," Annie said. "Anyone else?"

Kitty took a deep breath. "Annie," she said hesitantly, "I think I would like a ritual. Can we do something to clear up what happened yesterday, without my having to talk about it?"

"A cleansing ritual? For sure," Annie said. "We can do that. Is that okay with everyone? Kitty has been through a really frightening experience—may I say just a little bit about it, Kitty?"

Kitty nodded.

"Well, without getting into any details, let's just say a man, a stranger, took extreme liberties with her in a situation where she couldn't defend herself. It didn't go as far as rape," Annie glanced at Kitty, "but the emotional energy was similar. It's good to get that cleaned up, Kitty, and you can be sure you're safe with us here."

Kitty nodded again, trying to look more confident than she felt.

"Let's do the general release first," Annie said to the group as a whole. "If you have something you want to release, I suggest you either write it on a piece of paper and place it in the shell on the altar, or simply shout it out when we release the Cone of Power."

No one moved to write anything, so Annie continued.

Several of the women had brought drums or other

rhythm instruments, and the next step Annie outlined was what she called "raising a Cone of Power." A dark-haired beauty with a large djembe drum started a slow beat, and others joined her, filling in the spaces. As the drumming began to grow in speed and intensity, those without instruments clapped their hands or drummed lightly on their thighs or the sides of their chairs. Kitty imagined she could feel some kind of power building, until suddenly with no overt signal, the drumming stopped. Something like a "whoosh" seemed to happen, as everyone threw their hands into the air, some calling out the specific things they were choosing to release.

"Okay," Annie said after a moment. "Let's take a short break. Glasses in the kitchen if you need a drink of water, and we can take turns with the bathroom. The Circle is temporarily spread out to encompass the whole apartment." Annie smiled, as she swept a large circle with her right hand. She turned to Kitty. "Let's talk a little about what you want to do," she said quietly, as the others began to move toward the kitchen or the bathroom.

"Well, I don't know know what we need to do," Kitty said, "but I can tell you I don't want to relive the experience, or even recall it in any detail. I just want to get rid of the effects, because it has made me not want to be touched by any man." She squeezed her eyes tight shut, with an involuntary shudder.

"I understand," Annie said, nodding. "We can do it without going into the past experience. Here's what I would suggest. I have blessed water on the altar, and sage. I'll get the sage smoking, and do a cleansing with that, which should loosen whatever energy is lurking, and send it on its way back where it came from. And then, if you are okay with it, I'd like to sprinkle all around you with the water on another bunch of sage, to put down a protective barrier. Does all that sound right?"

"It does," Kitty said, relieved that nothing more elaborate was expected of her. "Shall I stay in my seat?"

"You can, if that feels more comfortable, but you could also stand more or less in front of the altar. That would be more convenient, just in terms of the things I'll be using. Either way, as you choose."

"I can come to the altar," Kitty said, and smiled at the turn of phrase. "Did you ever go to a church where they had 'altar calls?'" she asked Annie.

"I did," Annie said, her face crinkling into a grin. "This is rather different."

# CHAPTER 39

The cleansing ritual went just as Annie had described. Kitty hardly listened to the words Annie chanted, as the sweet sage smoke wafted over her. She felt herself relaxing as she breathed deeply. When Annie dipped a loose bundle of sage in the salted water and shook it at Kitty, it did feel like a protective shield going up around her, and when the ceremony was over, she walked back to her chair feeling really clean for the first time since early the previous morning. "Blessed be," Annie said, as Kitty sat down.

The candles glowed brightly as the group sat silently for a few minutes.

Finally, Annie spoke. "Now we need to do a binding. Let me explain a little about binding in general and this situation in particular." She briefly described the personal situation with Dan, focusing on the fact that he was someone she had known years ago and that it seemed he might have some knowledge of the whereabouts of her daughter. It was clear from the re-action around the circle the other women were well aware of the pain Annie had suffered because of her daughter's illness and estrangement. No mention was made of the possible terrorist connection. "He needs to be bound from endangering anyone, not just me or my family," Annie concluded.

"And now about binding in general—given the action of the Three-fold Law, anyone participating in binding someone else will find themselves bound, or prevented, from doing what-ever they have bound that person from. It's really important, then, to keep your mind very clear, creating only what you want to create, and not holding any stray negative thoughts. This is strong magick, and I want only those who freely choose to participate tonight. No hard feelings toward those of you who choose just to watch."

"It seems to me," Kelly, the woman with the djembe, said, "that if you are going to bind him from harming others, that's something I'd be glad to accept on myself."

"Yes, that's the way I see it personally," Annie said. "But I want to leave plenty of room for those who just don't want anything to do with this kind of magick at all."

In the end, after some further discussion, three of the women, including Kitty, chose to pull their chairs outside the circle. The others closed up, making the circle a little smaller. Annie set a large black candle on the altar, and addressed the horn representing the God and the large wine glass that served to represent the Goddess's Chalice. "God and Goddess, bless our work tonight, and keep us safe within our circle. We come to bind one whom you know, my former friend known as 'Dan,' preventing him from causing any further harm or succeeding in any plan to harm any other person, whether by direct action or by neglect or inaction. We wish no ill toward him, but only to prevent his harming others."

She lifted the unlit black candle in her left hand and a tall white candle, already burning, in her right hand. The women in the circle began to sing softly: "We are the flow, we are the ebb; we are the weavers, we are the web."

"As I light this candle," she said, suiting action to her words, "I hereby compel and bind Dan, that he may not cause harm to me and mine, to Kitty, or to any other person. This or something better, with harm to none, and for the highest good of all." She set the white candle down and raised the now-burning black candle, carefully, as high as her head. The chanting continued behind her. "So mote it be," she said firmly, and set the candle down in the middle of the small altar.

Annie sat down in her place, and motioned for Kitty and the other two outliers to come back into the circle. The chanting faded and stopped. "Is there anything else?" Annie asked.

No one spoke. "Then, let's release the God and Goddess and the directions," Annie said, standing up again. She faced the altar. "God and Goddess, thank you for being here tonight. Stay with us for our feast if you will, or go if you must. Merry meet, and merry part, and merry meet again.

"Spirits of the North, thank you for joining us. We release you to your beautiful realms. Stay if you will, go if you must. Merry meet, and merry part, and merry meet again."

Those who had called the other three directions followed in reverse order to that of the beginning, using the same formula as Annie. When the East had been released, Annie announced, "The circle is open but unbroken. Merry meet, and merry part, and merry meet again."

"Now, let's eat!" Gretchen pronounced. The ring disintegrated, as the women rose and moved toward the table where their food offerings had been deposited. Cakes were cut, cookies unwrapped, wine bottles opened, cheese sliced. With Annie's approval, Kitty turned on some lights.

Kitty found she was surprisingly hungry, and said as much to Kelly. "It's always like that," Kelly said. "Working magically is actual work, and it does leave you hungry. And thirsty. I don't drink alcohol, but I find I need a lot of water after an evening of ceremony. Here, have a brownie—these are really good!" She offered the plate to Kitty. "Who brought these? They're delicious," she said to the room in general.

In groups of two or three now, the women chatted noisily as they enjoyed their treats. Kitty could see they seemed to know each other well. "How long have you been working together as a coven?" she asked Gretchen.

"I guess about three years, most of us," Gretchen said. "One or two have come in more recently, but mostly we've been the same group for a while."

"Well, this was really quite interesting," Kitty said thoughtfully.

"I think you would be welcome to join us at some point, if you cared to," Gretchen said. "It would be up to Annie, and the rest, of course."

"I might very well want to," Kitty said, surprised at her own feeling of comfort with the idea. "I'll think about it, for sure."

The evening wound down soon, and people began clearing up the remains of the food and wine. Annie and Gretchen went around putting out candles as the other women were leaving, and by the time everyone else had gone, they were ready to take the altar back to 5F.

"Thank you, Kitty," Annie said.

"No, thank you!" Kitty returned fervently. "I had no idea how powerful this kind of thing could be. I really do feel much better, and I think I'm going to be okay."

"Don't push yourself," Annie warned. "It can take a little while for the full effect to develop, sometimes. And let us know if we can do anything more."

"I will," Kitty said. "And do you need some help getting everything back?"

"If you could help with the door, and then bring the extra chair, that would be great," Gretchen said.

Kitty did that, and also collected Joe from the other apartment.

"Well, how was it?" Joe asked, when they were alone together again.

"Very interesting," Kitty said. "I thought I could actually feel something going on."

"I could almost feel it in the other apartment," Joe said, smiling. "That drumming got a little loud."

"I hope the folks downstairs weren't home," Kitty said.

"Well, it didn't last very long," Joe said. "I don't imagine it bothered anyone very much."

"Was Annie doing Wicca when you were married?" she asked.

"No, or at least if she was she was very quiet about it," Joe said. "In the final years, I was away a lot, so I'm not sure I would have known, anyway."

"We did a 'cleansing' ritual," Kitty said cautiously. "I do feel better. How much better, I'm not sure. But maybe sometime soon we can test it out."

"Whenever you are ready, but no hurry," Joe said.

"Well, not tonight," Kitty said. "But maybe tomorrow. I need to know where I am."

"Okay, just please don't feel under any pressure from me."

"Thank you," Kitty said. "And now, I don't know about you, but I'm about to fall asleep on my feet."

"Bed sounds good to me, too," Joe said.

# CHAPTER 40

The next morning, they both slept in. Coffee and croissants made a late breakfast, and Kitty called in to her office to see whether any true emergencies had cropped up. None had, Alicia reported, and Kitty spent the rest of the morning reading and puttering, while Joe worked on his computer and then went shopping downstairs.

When Joe's phone rang some time later, he was in Kitty's kitchen, up to his wrists in flour and free-range grass-fed minute steaks. ("I learned about chicken-fried steak when I lived in Missouri," he had bragged to Kitty. Challenged to produce this anomalous-sounding dish, he had readily agreed. Hence the current situation.) "Kitty, will you hit answer and then turn on the speaker mode?" he asked her.

The voice coming over the speaker said: "Joe Treacher?"

"Yes," Joe said, raising his voice.

"Joe, this is Albert Trypington."

"Al! I haven't heard from you in a long, long time. I hope this is a social call."

"I wish it were, Joe," said the voice coming from the phone, which Kitty had now placed on a shelf above where Joe was working. "I have something important to talk with you about. Can we talk confidentially?"

"Is this about what I think it's about, Al?" Joe said, frowning as his floury hands hovered over the steaks.

"The situation you've been dealing with Bill Harris about," Al said. "Are you where we can speak confidentially?"

"Actually, Al," Joe said, "I have you on speaker. The only

other person here is Ms. Katherine Toulkes, who is more involved in this situation than I am. Anything you have to say to
me, I'd prefer she hear directly rather than have me repeat it to
her afterward."

"If you can vouch for her reliability. Confidentiality is
vital here," Al said.

"I can, and actually that's the only way I'll be able to talk
at the moment," Joe said. He washed his hands and picked up
the phone. He motioned Kitty to follow him into the living room
area, and set the phone down on the end table.

"All right," the disembodied Al said from the end table.
"First, I have some questions for you. What kind of physical
shape are you in?"

"Pretty good for over 70," Joe said. "I don't run these days,
but I work out regularly, and except for the knees I haven't de-
teriorated much since the last time."

"Keep up your weapons qualifications?"

"Handguns only," Joe said. "But yes. Still good. Eyesight
still good. Hearing, some loss, but not so it bothers me in normal
situations. Anything else?"

"Not at present." Al seemed to hesitate.

"What do you have?" Joe said. Kitty saw on his face the
intensity and narrowed focus she had noticed a few other times
in the past week.

"Our timetable has changed," Al said. "It seems one of the
Bureau's men was careless and has been made. And our custom-
ers have decided to move. We don't think they realize how wide
the surveillance is, but we believe they will try to load and perhaps make use of the packages sooner than we expected."

"You were expecting they would load when the ship repairs were finished?" Joe asked.

"That was our estimate," Al said. "That time is still at least
two-three days away. But a flurry of activity in the ether suggests
they aren't waiting."

"So what do you need from me?" Joe stared at the phone,
as though expecting to pull an answer out by sheer force of his

intent.

"The man you know as Dan Oponuno—does he recognize you?" Al asked.

"He doesn't seem to recognize me as an old schoolmate, if that's what you mean," Joe said. "I assume he would recognize me from our having met here a few days ago. But he has showed no interest whatsoever in me when I've been around him while in makeup."

"We need to get someone on board that ship right away," Al said, "and you are the closest available man."

Kitty clasped her hands over her mouth to stifle a gasp. Joe cocked his head to one side and seemed to be avoiding eye contact with her.

"I don't want to risk using anyone from the teams who have been on surveillance, for fear of alerting the subjects further," Al continued. "We don't know who else they may have noticed. If you agree, I'll send someone over immediately to fix up you up with ID and a badge, in case you need them."

"And swear me into some force or other?" Joe asked.

"Roger that."

"I think with minimal makeup and a hat I can be ready," Joe said.

"You were always good at that," Al commented.

"Will the person you send be able to give me more instructions on just what my task is?"

"Not really. The key here is that we don't know when or exactly how the packages will be loaded, or where they are expecting to stow them. We assume, however, that your man Dan will be the delivery person, and that he will have one or more allies on board. We need to catch them together if possible, or at least identify them for pickup.

"We'll have people waiting to board whenever you say, or sooner if possible without detection. The shipyard security will be expecting you and we'll fix you up with a secure Bluetooth lookalike, so you just need to act like you are coordinating something." Al seemed to chuckle at that thought.

"I assume I'm getting hazardous duty pay for this," Joe said, finally looking at Kitty and winking.

Not having seen the wink, Al answered solemnly. "As always, my friend, and fully insured. We realize we are taking advantage, but that doesn't stop us."

"Never has," Joe said dryly. "Probably never will. Well, I guess we need to quit talking and get to work. Anything else?"

"It will be me on the radio," Al said. "We'll let you know what we are seeing, and ask that you do the same whenever you safely can. Good luck, Joe."

"Good luck to all of us," Joe said. "So long, then, until I get my Bluetooth."

"Thanks, Joe. I'll be in touch." Al clicked off.

Joe reached for the phone and turned it off. He turned to Kitty, who was staring at him in utter bewilderment.

"Do you have to do this? Why would you agree? Shouldn't you leave this to the professionals?" she managed to get out.

"Kitty, honey, I'm sorry, but I am one of those professionals. This is what I do, or did." He stood up and reached his hand out to her. "Come in here with me and we can talk while I get ready. I don't know how quickly Al's man will get here."

"But, but..." Kitty spluttered. Still, she got up and followed him into the bathroom, where he took his kit down from an upper shelf and began pulling out bottles and small plastic envelopes.

Fifteen minutes later, when the doorbell rang, Joe's appearance had been once more transformed, this time with a short gray-brown mustache, wire-rim glasses, a heavy denim jacket, and a stocking cap pulled low over his forehead.

Kitty was no less terrified than she had been during the phone call, but at least she now understood that to Joe this was a matter not only of national security but of the immediate safety of the people he loved, herself included. And that further, as he said, this was his work, and something he felt fully prepared to take on.

The emissary from Al Trypington made short work of outfitting Joe with ID and a badge. He also offered Joe a selection of handguns, one of which Joe hefted familiarly. "I'll keep my own, too," he said, pulling back his jacket to reveal that weapon in a shoulder holster, before tucking the new gun in a second holster at the back of his waistband.

The agent had a few more details for Joe, explaining how he would make himself known at the shipyard and to whom. "We don't want to cause a panic," he added, "and since we don't know who or where the other conspirators are, we can't afford to have you come in openly. And now, you should probably go. It really is considered quite urgent. Do you have a car?"

Joe nodded.

"I suggest you drive, then," the agent said. "I'm leaving. Wait five minutes and then go."

"You'd better have something to eat," Kitty said, as the door closed on the agent. She went to the refrigerator and began taking out food—butter, cheese, lettuce, apples, carrots, milk. "Can I make you some sandwiches? Or will you take some apples with you?" She stood at the open refrigerator door, looking from Joe to the table and back at Joe. "Oh, I don't know what I'm doing!" she wailed. "Do you need...?"

"Hush, Kitty," Joe said. "It's all right, I don't need to eat, but I will take one of your apples. Here, bring me an apple, and a kiss before I have to leave."

Kitty picked up one of the apples and moved numbly into Joe's waiting arms. "I'm sorry, I'm a mess! I will straighten up," she said. She hugged him tight.

He returned the pressure and then used a finger to tilt her head up for a lingering kiss. "And now you can walk me out to the courtyard," he said.

They walked from the elevator to the front door and out into the courtyard hand in hand. When they reached the street, Kitty, seeing nobody else on the sidewalk at the moment, opened her arms for one more hug. Then Joe took off across the street, just before a traffic light change sent two lanes of fast-moving cars whizzing past. Kitty watched him get in his car with a knot of fear in her stomach, but she waved gently as he pulled out of the lot onto Clinton Avenue, ready to head directly toward the Navy Yard.

# CHAPTER 41

Kitty watched as Joe's car disappeared down the street. She was turning to go back into the courtyard when a white delivery truck pulled up into the bus stop. The window flashed down and she heard someone call her name. Reflexively, she stopped to look. The driver was already getting out of the truck, and by the time she realized there was no one else around, Dan Oponuno was beside her.

"Oh, lovely Kitty, oh, Kitty, my love," he misquoted Edward Lear. "What a beautiful Kitty you are, you are! And now you are coming with me, you are!"

"Oh, no, I'm not. No chance," Kitty said, turning to go back into the Cocoa Factory.

"Oh, yes, you are!" Dan said, and suddenly Kitty felt something hard pressed against her low back. "That's a gun, in case you can't tell, my dear!" he said. "Now come along nicely, so I don't have to shatter that pretty spine." He shoved her toward the front of the truck, keeping the gun pressed closely against her. "We'll wait a minute for traffic to clear and then you can get in on my side and scoot across."

"Here, let me open the door for you," he said with pseudo-gallantry, when they reached the driver's side. He used his free hand to open the door, and then grabbed Kitty's arm and boosted her into the seat. "Scoot across," he said, gesturing now with the gun, held just below the level of the windows.

Kitty did as she was told. Dan got in immediately after her, and drove with one hand until he got up to speed. Even then he held the gun, occasionally waving it in Kitty's direction. "We're going on an adventure, my dear Kitty," he said. "You'll be part of history! Isn't that exciting?"

Kitty didn't answer. The truck was going fast enough she was afraid to even consider jumping out, so she simply looked away from Dan and tried not to think about anything.

"We are going to pick up our packages, Kitty, the ones you helped me bring over here. And you are going to get to go on the big ship with me. Oh, it will be exciting! I'm so glad you're going to help. And you'll get to meet Angela, finally. You'll like that, I know. Or, maybe you won't, but that won't matter. The two of you will be just fine together for a little while."

Dan continued his monologue, seeming not to care whether Kitty was listening or not. When he arrived at the building where Kitty had seen the boxes unloaded, he seemed to snap back into the current reality. He pointed the gun directly at Kitty and curtly ordered her out of the truck, on the driver's side again. He motioned in the direction of the door of the building. "Inside," he ordered.

Once inside, Kitty saw two men and a woman, standing in a hallway. The woman was thin, almost emaciated, with long, tangled dark brown curls. A rope dangled from one wrist. "Oh, yes," Dan chortled. "You two are going to become very close." He stepped over to the woman and grasped the rope. "Watch the door," he said gruffly to one of the men, with a nod in Kitty's direction. The man, who could have been the one Kitty had seen there previously, moved behind her, blocking any possible exit she might have thought of.

"Come here, Kitty, my love!" he ordered, again gesturing with the gun. "Kitty, this is Angela. Take her hand. That's it, squeeze it hard." Kitty looked at the younger woman, who turned her face away. "Now, Angela, be nice," Dan teased. "Kitty's going to be your friend."

He turned to the other man, who Kitty guessed to be Orange-and-Black, the one who had helped load up the boxes at Red Hook. "Tie their two wrists together," Dan said. "Not too tight. So they can hold hands. We want them to begin getting better acquainted." Orange-and-Black grunted, but did as he was told, looping the length of rope around Kitty's wrist, tying Kitty's right to Angela's left with several neat knots.

The two men then began ferrying the packages out to the truck, while Dan stood watch over Kitty and Angela, never moving the gun very far from its aim at Kitty's chest. As the third box made its way down the steps and toward the back of the truck, he shooed the two women out of the door and into the cab, Kitty in the middle next to the driver's seat. After a hurried conference with Orange-and-Black Man, Dan climbed into the cab, and, waving the gun under Kitty's nose, started the truck.

He made short work of driving into the shipyard, again using the maroon and green card Kitty had seen before. Pulling up alongside the *Queen Europa*, he backed the truck expertly into place near a gangway leading to a door partway up the hull of the ship. Kitty saw several men in coveralls pushing large wheeled dollies up a ramp and into the ship. "Now, we wait," Dan said.

Shifting the gun to his left hand, he slipped his arm around Kitty. "Might as well be friendly while we can," he crooned, as Kitty squirmed and tried without success to move further away. "You aren't going anywhere for a while, Miss Kitty," he murmured. "Your friend here doesn't like me much, Angela," he said, raising his voice a bit, "but I'm sure she would if she'd just give herself a chance." Putting his face close to Kitty's, he whispered, "Just relax."

Kitty shuddered and closed her eyes, preparing to endure more of his groping. But to her surprise, Dan removed his arm from her shoulder almost immediately. Maybe the magic was working, somehow. Kitty quickly opened her eyes, to see a man in a shipyard security uniform approaching the truck. "Okay, ladies, quiet now. I'll do the talking," Dan said, tucking the gun under his left thigh and rolling down the window.

He pulled a driver's license and what looked like a CSStudio ID card from his pocket, and handed them to the officer. "Mr. Forthright," the security guard said, looking at the ID. "You're going to be doing some filming, I think."

Dan nodded. "And these ladies are special guests of the Studio, as you've already been advised."

"Right," said the guard. "You need someone to help you get unloaded?"

"No, I brought my own mules," Dan laughed. He reached back and pounded on the panel separating the cab of the truck from the cargo compartment. "We'll take care of it from here. Do we need ID to go aboard?"

"Here you go," the guard said, handing Dan three lanyards with official-looking passes hanging on them. "Your guys in back will need them, too. Are they coming out now?"

Dan banged on the panel again, and in the side mirror Kitty could see the two men from Red Hook come around the end of the truck. The guard handed each of them a lanyard. "Just turn them in when you leave," he tossed back to Dan, before walking away.

"All right, ladies," Dan said to his unwilling passengers, "now we go aboard. If you can wait just a minute, I'll come open your door, Angela." He tucked the gun into his pocket, and got out of the truck. He walked around the front of the truck, his gait casual and unhurried, his hand very noticeably on the pocketed gun. He opened the door and stood back while Kitty and Angela awkwardly made their way out of the truck. "Now, I'd like to see you holding hands, like the dear friends I hope you quickly become.

"That's it," he continued, as Kitty took Angela's limp hand in hers. "Now, I'll just pull down your sleeves, so as to cover your bracelets. We are going aboard now, and remember—I have my handy helper right here in my pocket in case either of you should get an urge to speak to anyone!" He motioned them in the direction of a long, steep gangway leading to a deck well up the side of the still-drydocked ship.

Kitty judged the possibility of safely making a run for it to be nil, especially since Angela seemed barely able to walk in a straight line. There's bound to be an opportunity to speak to someone or raise an alarm somehow. He hasn't taken my phone, she thought. Maybe I'll have a chance to call or text. Left handed?

From a phone in my right pants pocket? Not likely.

The three of them proceeded up the gangway, Kitty and Angela first, Dan behind. Looking over her shoulder slightly, Kitty could see that the two other men had set right to work unloading the boxes, in their black plastic wrapping. "Eyes front, Kitty," Dan warned.

Soon those boxes would be going onto the ship, where they might sit unnoticed for days before exploding, causing the deaths of unknown numbers of innocent people—if all went according to the conspirators' plans. Kitty stumbled and almost fell going up the steep gangway. Angela turned and looked at her, but made no attempt to help her. Nor did she say anything. "Keep holding hands, ladies, I insist," Dan said softly. Feeling no response from Angela, Kitty refitted her hand over Angela's.

But the planting of those explosives was what Joe was supposed to be thwarting. She realized suddenly that he was probably already somewhere on the ship. He might even have walked by the truck while she was sitting there. Her heart lightened at the thought that he might be near, and then she felt her chest tighten again. That also meant that he was in harm's way, should the explosives go off prematurely.

And what in the world did Dan want with her and Angela? Were they just distractions, in case anyone got suspicious of Dan's movement? Now that the explosives were here at the dock, wouldn't it be time for the FBI or whoever they were to move in and arrest Dan and his co-conspirators? They could be closing in right now. And...and we—Angela and I—are right in the way!

So what were the police, FBI, Al Trypington's people, going to do? If the terrorists were nervous, suspecting their movements had been noticed, then she and Angela were not so much distractions as—hostages! She gasped audibly, and then tried to cover it with a cough. "Could we stop for a minute, please?" she begged Dan, continuing to cough as though from the stress of the climb.

"Just for a moment," Dan said. "We have work to do."

Kitty leaned into Angela, hoping to provoke a response, any response, from the girl. But Angela only stood passively, neither pushing back nor yielding as Kitty continued to cough, and wobbled back and forth.

"Okay, pick it up now," Dan said, irritably. "We need to get going. Turn to the left when we get to top of the ramp, and look around like you are interested!"

Kitty had no trouble looking interested. She was amazed to see how high above the ground they had climbed; no wonder she felt out of breath. The two men from the truck were just disappearing into the side of the ship lower down, with the boxes on a large dolly. Where were the police? Where was Joe? Why was nobody doing anything?

Dan was right behind them now, prodding Kitty in the back with what she had to presume was his gun. He guided them with softly-spoken directions into an interior staircase, where they passed through a door marked STAFF ONLY.

"Okay, let's stop for a moment," Dan said. "You ladies stand over there, where I can see you." He reached into a vest pocket and pulled out a plastic ID card, similar to the ones the guard had given them. Unclipping the generic VISITOR card from the lanyard around his neck, he replaced it with one that had a photo on it and a colored border that the other lacked. "Now I'm official," he said. "We can go anywhere we want."

On the move again, Kitty soon gave up trying to keep track of where they might be in the almost entirely empty ship, as Dan took them on a path with many turns, but trending downward into smaller, less decorated corridors. Finally, he stopped before a door which he opened with the card around his neck. "Careful stepping over the threshold, ladies," he said, motioning them forward with the gun he now made no effort to hide.

The room they now entered was small and bare, hardly more than a closet. There were pipes of several different diameters, and what appeared to be electrical switch boxes or connective hubs of some kind. And there were the three packages. "Well, here we are," Dan said, with a satisfied air. "Everything we need." The heavy door clicked behind him.

"Cozy, isn't it?" he said, and chuckled. "I hope you like it, because you are going to be here awhile. In fact, you'll be here the rest of your lives. You may get a little hungry. You are certain to get thirsty, if all goes well. But that's all right. It won't last long."

"What do you mean?" Kitty said. "What do you mean is going to happen?"

"Big boom, Kitty, my love, big, big boom," Dan said. "I'm sorry. Haven't you figured it out? Let me explain." He pulled out a small jackknife from his pocket and flipped open a blade. "See this? I could use it on you ladies if I wanted to." Both Angela and Kitty shrank away from him and he laughed heartily. "But that's not what I'm going to do. There isn't time," he said.

Instead, he used the knife to slit open the plastic covering the irregular-shaped package. Reaching in, he pulled out a silverish chain. Something like a bicycle chain, Kitty thought, but more flexible and with slightly bigger links. "So, Kitty, the two of you are staying here. I'm going to be leaving shortly." He took Angela's free hand and began fastening the chain tightly around her wrist, securing it with a small padlock which he also fished from inside the package.

"You may have at least figured out that these packages are going to explode. But not right away." He pulled the two women over to one of the large vertical pipes and wrapped the chain around the pipe, securing it with another padlock. "You see, we want the ship back out in the harbor. If we can, we'll wait until it's full of people. That could take a week or even more. So, that's why I said you will get hungry, and very, very thirsty. It's really a shame, because you may die here before the boom! It's going to be a spectacular boom! Enough to show the racist, fascist world that we are not to be trifled with.

"But no more politics. I'm really sorry, Kitty. I would have liked to take you away with me. But," he continued, now in a singsong voice, "you weren't very nice to me the last time we met." He laughed again, starting deep in his throat and ending at a high pitch, almost a screech.

The man is cracking up right here and now, Kitty thought. What an irony!

As though he had heard her thought, Dan seemed to get a grip on himself. "And of course, I needed to bring Angela—she was the key, the signal, the one our friends knew—and you were really the only person I thought I could trust to join us and come along sensibly. And sadly, I can't take you with me now! Too bad, because..."

Whatever he was going to say was interrupted by a ringtone. He touched his phone and looked at the screen, then turned his back to Kitty and spoke softly. The conversation was very brief. "Ladies, I have to go. Sorry to cut things short. Change of plans." He opened the door. "Have a nice time! As it turns out, it won't be very long at all," he said. And then he was gone. Once more, the heavy door closed slowly, with a threatening click.

Kitty felt her heart pounding. She realized she was breathing fast and shallowly, and feeling a little light-headed. "Well, this is no good, girl," she said aloud. "You need to slow down and concentrate."

She looked at Angela. The younger woman was standing with an utterly blank look, a little way away from the pipe, her arm held at an awkward angle, as though she hadn't moved since Dan chained her there. The arm that was tied to Kitty's was also stretched out, so that, given her gauntness, she really did resemble a scarecrow. Kitty tried unsuccessfully to stifle a giggle, which threatened to turn into hysterical laughter. She looked away and concentrated on breathing, in-2-3-4, out-2-3-4-5-6.

"We have to get out of here," she said. "Angela, we have to get out of here."

Angela stared at her. "I don't know you," she said, in a pleasant, albeit throaty, voice. She sounded a bit like her mother, Kitty thought.

"No, you don't," Kitty replied. "But I'm a friend of both your mother and your father."

Angela's eyes flickered, and then her face went blank again. "I don't have a mother or a father," she said. "They both died." And suddenly, tears began to overflow her eyes and run down her face. "They died when I was in high school, and they never came back," she said. "I needed them, but they never came back."

Kitty felt her own eyes filling with tears as the young woman wept without sound or expression. "But they tried, you know, Angela," she said. "They tried to come to get you. They just couldn't reach you."

Angela looked at Kitty. Her eyes widened. "You think so?" she asked. "You think they wanted to come?"

"I know they did," Kitty said softly, looking directly into the girl-woman's eyes. "They were thinking of you every single day, and trying to come get you, over and over again. They love you very much."

"Well, then, that's good!" Angela said, and she started to slide to the floor, pulling Kitty with her. "I think I can go to sleep now." She leaned against the pole to which her wrist was chained and closed her eyes.

Kitty was now on her knees. Okay, she thought as her knees throbbed, this is not helpful. I'm too old for this. She struggled to get her feet under her, and groaned as she pushed up from the floor. The rope holding their wrists together pulled Angela's hand up as Kitty tried to stand, and also prevented her straightening completely. But as she increased the tension on the rope, she began to form an idea.

"My hands have always been very flexible," she said aloud. She looked at the knots, and decided it was unlikely she could untie herself using only her left hand. But the loop of rope that went around her wrist, unlike the one around Angela's, was actually not very tight. In her mind's ear, she heard Dan telling his confederate, "Don't tie them very tight."

She used her left hand to grasp the loop around her right wrist, and began to roll the rope over her right hand. She folded her hand as narrowly as she could, and pulled. The rope came easily enough over the palm, until it reached her knuckles. At that point, the pressure became painful, but, she told herself, getting blown up would hurt even more. She used her left hand to press the sides of her right hand together, and pulled harder. Got to make it now, she thought, or my hand will swell and I'll never get loose.

And suddenly she was. Loose. She straightened. Shook her hand. Rubbed her aching knees. And remembered her telephone!

Joe was on the ship! If she had a signal, he could come for them. She grabbed the phone out of her pocket, and checked for bars. None at all. Sometimes an emergency call could get through when nothing else could. She dialed 911 and waited. "No signal," the screen told her. Okay, then she had to get herself out of there, before Dan and his fellow—might as well use the term—fellow terrorists, who had apparently been spooked by something or someone, sent a radio signal and detonated what she had to assume were nuclear devices.

But what about Angela? She seemed to have gone to sleep on the floor, still chained to the pipe. And without tools, it was impossible, Kitty saw, to remove or loosen the chain. She pulled on the pipe, but since the rest of the equipment in the room looked electrical, she thought better of trying to rip it loose from either floor or ceiling. There seemed nothing to do but leave Angela sleeping and go for help.

Kitty opened the door and began walking quickly in the direction from which she thought they had come. This time, I'll count turns, she thought. And always go up, whenever I can.

# CHAPTER 42

When Kitty finally reached an open deck—twelve right turns and six staircases later—she rushed to the rail and held up her phone, which now registered full bars. She punched the button for Joe's cell and waited. Looking down, she saw a very different scene from the one she had glimpsed from the gangway not so very long ago. Police cars were pouring into the shipyard from all directions. And uniformed and non-uniformed men with large guns were gathered alongside the *Queen Europa.*

When Joe answered, Kitty almost dropped the phone with surprise and relief. "Are you here?" she asked. "Oh, that doesn't make sense. Are you on the ship?"

"Yes. Where are *you*?"

"On the ship. I don't know where on the ship, but I need you to find me."

"I'm a little busy right now, Kitty." Joe sounded annoyed. "I'm trying to find a couple of bombs."

"I know. I mean, I know where they are!" Kitty was half-shouting in her desperation to make him understand. "I know where the bombs are. I mean, from where I am, I can lead you to them. But I don't know where I am!"

"Kitty, are you okay?"

"I'm fine, but Angela is chained up and the bombs are there and....you have to find me!"

"Okay, calm down. Where are you?" Joe asked, his voice concerned but uncomprehending.

"That's just it. I don't know."

"Let's take it one step at a time. Are you inside, or out?"

"Outside."

"What can you see?"

"I'm looking toward downtown Brooklyn. And I think I'm on the first open deck, whatever that is."

"Okay," Joe said. "Stay where you are. I'm coming. I'm using my locator, too. I'll be there before long. Don't hang up."

Kitty slumped against the rail. She watched a trio of men in what looked like moon suits waddle toward the gangway and begin to climb laboriously up the ramp. Bomb squad, she said to herself. Blast suits, not moon suits. If it's nuclear, those suits aren't going to help much, I shouldn't think.

Joe's voice came over the phone. "Kitty, can you hear me?"

"I hear you fine," Kitty said.

"I have you on the locator app. I'm only one deck away. I'll be there in just a couple of minutes. Did you say Angela is with you?"

"No, Angela is with the bombs. That's why you have to come to me. Because I can take you there. We have to get her." Kitty replayed what she had just said and realized that her frustration and fear were making her sound cross and impatient. "I mean, just please come as fast as you can," she said more gently, "and I'll take you there. You are going to need some kind of heavy chain-cutting equipment, as well as the bomb squad."

And then she saw Joe, still bespectacled, mustachioed and wearing the stocking cap, emerge from a door about 50 feet away. She started to rush toward him, but remembered in time that she needed to stay near the door from which she had come out. So she simply held out her arms in welcome as Joe hurried toward her.

"I have a thousand questions," Joe said, hugging her quickly, "but if you can take me to the bomb, those questions will have to wait. Let's go."

"Will you be able to contact people once we are down into the ship? Because my phone didn't work down there."

"Yes," Joe said. "My equipment works through anything. Let's go."

"Okay," Kitty said. "Don't rush me. It should be twelve left turns, and always down whenever we can."

It took almost fifteen minutes, but Kitty was able to find the little room where she had left Angela sleeping beside the explosive devices. Joe, who had removed the disguise glasses and hat somewhere along the way, was on the radio requesting the bomb squad immediately, seeming unmoved by the sight of his daughter, who appeared to be still asleep.

"Can you cut her loose?" Kitty asked.

"I don't have any equipment," Joe said. "How come you were loose?"

For answer, Kitty held up the loop of rope dangling from Angela's thin wrist. "I was only tied, not chained," she said. "He meant to leave us both here, but he had to go in a hurry."

"Tell me," Joe ordered, all business now. "What did he say when he left?"

Kitty recited as much as she could remember of the last few moments. "I don't think that's much help," she said. "And I'm very disappointed that his phone worked here, and yours works, but mine doesn't!"

"Different company, no doubt," Joe said. "Actually, what I'm using now is radio, not phone, so that makes a difference, too."

Kitty was eager to tell her story, but the first of Joe's colleagues arrived, and Joe turned his attention to the tools and getting Angela loose.

Kitty gently shook Angela and stood by holding her free hand while the men worked at cutting the chain. When the chain was off, they lifted Angela from the floor and stood her on her feet.

"Kitty," Joe said, "will you take Angela outside and wait in the hall? The rest of the bomb disposal squad will be here soon and then we can all leave, but for right now I need to stay here."

"Just tell me this," Kitty said. "Has someone picked up Dan Oponuno?"

Joe shook his head. "We're reasonably sure he's somewhere on the ship. And we have a hundred or so people ready to scour the ship for him as soon as we get this mess here cleared up. We'll find him."

Kitty led Angela out into the hallway, where they waited in silence until the bomb squad showed up in their clumsy suits.

"Now we leave," Joe said as he stepped out into the hallway. "Let's get out of here as fast as we can, which is probably not the way you came."

"I have no clue," Kitty said. "I'm sure we were led here by a very roundabout way. But I have no idea how to get out other than that way."

"I have a schema of the ship on my phone. If I can put it together in my head with the locator, I should be able to get us out quickly." He pushed buttons for a moment or two, and then indicated with a gesture that he was ready to go.

"Angela," Kitty said softly, "can you walk? We need to go now."

Angela nodded. She had not said anything since she was freed from the chain. She held out her hand to Kitty, who took it gently.

"Okay, let's go," Kitty said, starting to follow Joe. Angela stepped out, not briskly, but steadily, and it took only a few minutes for them to reach the main deck.

At the top of the gangway, they were met by two uniformed men—military, Kitty surmised, though she could not have said which branch. Joe lifted his mobile phone, at the same time turning to Kitty. "Give me a minute here," he said. He nodded in the direction of a nearby bench, and Kitty took the hint.

She watched closely as he spoke very briefly with the two young soldiers, and then at length with someone on the phone. She could see Joe was not pleased with what he was hearing. Then, to Kitty's surprise, when at last he came over to where she and Angela were sitting, he sat down between them. "I'm tired," he said. "I might be getting too old for this!"

"What's happening? Why can't we get off the ship?" Kitty asked.

"Oh, we can," Joe assured her. "There are just some procedural things to be worked out. And I need to call Annie." Turning to Angela, he said, "Angie girl, are you doing okay? I'm awfully glad to see you."

Angela looked at him appraisingly. "I'm not sure whether I'm glad to see you here," she said. "But I was glad to see you downstairs." She looked down at her lap.

"Would you mind sitting here if Kitty and I went over by the rail for a minute or two?" Joe asked.

Angela looked at him briefly and then back at her lap. "It's okay," she said finally, without looking up.

Joe stood, and with a look invited Kitty to join him at the rail. "I need to talk to Annie," he said, once they were out of hearing range from Angela, "and it will be easier just to have you listen to this call, rather than explain it all twice." He was dialing as he spoke.

"Gretchen, Joe," he said into the phone. "Is Annie there? Could you put her on?"

"Hello, Chum," he said a few moments later. "News. I've found Angie." He listened, and  glanced at his daughter, who was fiddling with the rope still attached to her left wrist. "As usual, it depends on what you mean by 'all right,'" he said, "but she's safe for the moment, yes. No blood."

There was another pause. "Well, that's the next part of why I called. We can't come to you, because the authorities have it in mind that they need to visit with Angela. I can see—and I'm pretty sure you will agree—that she's in no condition to be interviewed by anyone except a doctor. She probably needs hospitalization, at least to get her stabilized on meds. I can't leave here, so...."

Joe stopped abruptly. "Yes," he continued in a moment. "Exactly.  That's what I hoped you would say. We're on the ship *Queen Europa*, in the COC shipyard inside the Navy Yard. Just come as quickly as you can, and we'll meet you at the bottom of the gangway. I'll get you cleared to come in....yes...okay...good... bye then. Call me if you need anything."

He hung up, and immediately began speaking to someone else via the Bluetooth. He spoke very quickly, briefly outlining the fact that Annie was going to need clearance to come see her daughter. Before he hung up, it was obvious Joe was satisfied the person on the other end—presumably Al Trypington—was able and willing to arrange that.

Finally, he turned to Kitty. "Well, I've done all I can. I'm not able to persuade the powers-that-be to let us take Angela to a doctor first. So, they will simply have to deal with her mother. They'll be sorry, I can almost guarantee." He smiled. "Sometimes it can be an advantage to have a witch in the family."

Kitty's jaw dropped. "You don't mean…." she started.

"That she's going to hex someone? No, probably not. But she's like a mother hen with her chick. And she can be very, very persuasive when she wants to be. It's kind of like the Bene Gesserit Voice in *Dune*, or Obi Wan's 'these aren't the droids you're looking for.' I know from personal experience!" He smiled, and then chuckled shortly.

In a few minutes, they saw Annie's car. Moving back to the bench, Joe reached out a hand to Angela. "Mom is coming, Angie," he said. Angela opened her eyes wide, but said nothing. She took Joe's hand and stood. She and Joe headed toward the gangway.

Kitty stood at the rail as Joe and his daughter walked carefully down the steep gangway, accompanied by the two soldiers, one in front and one behind. Lower down on the side of the ship, she also noticed the bomb squad on the freight ramp, toddling slowly in their cumbersome suits and maneuvering a wheeled dolly holding the three boxes, still partly encased in their black plastic. Most of the police and other gun-toting types had pulled back from the area around the ship. Although if there's a nuclear device, she mused, it won't make any difference whether they are fifty or two hundred yards away. And then she wondered at her own nonchalance, in view of the fact that they still might all get blown to kingdom come at any minute!

By the time Joe and Angela reached the ground, Annie was there to meet them. She put an arm around Angela's shoulder, and stroked her hair. Kitty couldn't hear what was being said, but it seemed clear Annie was treating her daughter with the same restrained, objective compassion Joe had shown. It must be so hard to deal with this kind of illness, year after year, never knowing when another break would come. Never knowing whether your loved one would survive that next one.

Now Annie was speaking to Joe, gesturing emphatically. Joe nodded, and pulled out his phone. He talked to someone and then handed the phone to Annie, who engaged enthusiastically with whoever was on the other end, nodding, then shaking her head "no," gesticulating all the while.

Finally, she handed the phone back to Joe, pointing to him. He spoke briefly, and passed the phone to one of the soldiers who were still standing guard over the little family group. That man put the phone to his ear and seemed to listen intently, then appeared to speak just a few words before handing the phone back to Joe. To Kitty's surprise, she then saw the two young soldiers favor Joe with smart salutes and withdraw.

Joe talked a little more with Annie, then bent down to kiss her cheek (or air-kiss, Kitty couldn't tell for sure). He similarly kissed the top of Angela's head, then turned and started up the ramp without looking back. Annie and Angela got into the car and drove out of the shipyard.

# CHAPTER 43

Waiting for Joe by the rail, Kitty looked around the deck. Suddenly, she caught a flicker of movement on the open stairway at the aft end of the ship. Without knowing quite why, she felt sure she had seen Dan Oponuno. Whether he was moving up or down, she couldn't have said. Should she call out to Joe, she wondered, or simply wait and tell him when he arrived?

Although common sense told her "no," she was strongly tempted to walk down the deck to where she had seen the motion, just to determine whether she'd been hallucinating. Hoping to stymie the impulse, she leaned over the rail and called to Joe, who had paused about halfway up and seemed to be talking on the Bluetooth again.

He waved, and continued with the call, now walking slowly upward as he talked.

Frustrated, Kitty walked back to the bench and sat down. When a door about ten or fifteen feet down the deck opened with a slight pop, she turned, and found herself staring right at Dan.

"Don't try anything," he warned her roughly. "I don't expect to be taken alive. Much as I'd like to fly away with you to some faraway tropical island, I won't hesitate to use this gun if you misbehave."

Kitty looked around desperately for anything she could hide behind or even something she could use as a weapon. Getting further away seemed a good idea, even though Kitty thought it unlikely he would really shoot to kill her. The bench she and Angela had been sitting on was too close, but there was another one down the deck a little ways. Any chance to move was probably now or never, so she turned and made a dash for the next bench. Reaching it without hearing any gunshots, she squatted in the shelter of the heavy wooden end-piece. Peering carefully around the edge, she could see that Dan was still standing in the doorway, looking now not at her but at Joe, who was just reaching the deck.

"Joe!" she shouted. "Look out! Dan, in the doorway!"

Dan ducked back into the interior of the ship, and Kitty stood up, again painfully aware that her knees were seven decades old, just like the rest of her. Joe hurried over to her. "Are you okay?" he barked.

"Fine!" Kitty told him. "But Dan is near, with his gun. Can't we just get out of here?"

"Actually, I think we can," Joe said. "Let's go, quickly!"

They headed for the ramp, Kitty limping a little, but moving as fast as she could.

And then came the gunshots she had been expecting. The first one hit the deck in front of them. The second pinged off the railing, not far from where Kitty had been standing just moments before.

"Don't stop to look," Joe warned. He was behind Kitty now, partially sheltering her and partially pushing. They reached the gangway. "Down," he ordered. "Down on the ramp. Keep your head down." He turned and fired two shots with his own gun, then threw himself down beside Kitty on the gangway. "Try to inch your way down the ramp, without raising your head or any part of your body," he said. "I'm going to cover us." He fired off another shot, which must have hit a window or something, because Kitty heard glass shattering.

She couldn't resist the temptation to look. She raised her head and saw Dan rush out of another doorway and crouch behind a bench to fire again. This time the shot must have zinged right over Kitty's head; she heard its whiz. "Down," Joe shouted.

She turned her face sideways, toward Joe, and laid her cheek on the gangway floor. And it was through the floor that she felt, rather than heard, Dan rushing toward them. Joe raised his gun and lifted only his eyes, or so it seemed from Kitty's angle, above the edge of the deck. He fired two quick shots, and then a third. And then all was quiet.

Joe stood up quickly, and Kitty lifted her head. Dan lay unmoving on the deck, less than 20 feet away. Joe kicked the gun away from Dan's hand, and then reached down to check for a pulse at the throat of the would-be terrorist. When he straightened, he shook his head and re-holstered his gun.

He walked back to the gangway and knelt down next to Kitty. "It's over, Kitty, at least this part of it," he said. "Let's go; the younger people can take it from here!" He helped her sit up, then stood himself and helped her get up the rest of the way.

They were met at the bottom of the gangway by the same two young soldiers who had tried to take custody of Angela. Momentarily, a large black car pulled up, and the soldiers invited Joe and Kitty to get into the back seat. Harris was there, in a facing seat, with another man whom Kitty had never seen. He and Joe were obviously well-acquainted, however.

"I hope we are not inconveniencing you, Ms. Toulkes," Harris said, as Kitty settled herself and the car started to move. "We need to talk, and this seems to be the safest place to do it quickly."

"Inconveniencing? I've been inconvenienced by better than you today!" Kitty laughed. Then turning sober again, she added, "Actually, I think talking about it will be good, for me, at least. I can't speak for Joe."

"It's routine," Joe said. He was unholstering his guns as he spoke, carefully pulling them out by the trigger guard. He dumped the remaining shells from both his own gun and the one he had been issued and handed both guns, with ammunition, to the second man. "At least, I hope it's routine, Al?" he said.

"We'll have to create a report, Joe," Al said. "Since everyone else was pulled back because of the bombs, you two are the only ones who saw everything as it happened. So, we might as well get started." He looked at Harris, who nodded.

"You first, Mr. Treacher, if you please," Harris said. "I'll be recording." He flipped on a device the size of a small mobile phone.

Joe began describing his activities, starting from Al's phone call. Kitty listened as he recounted arriving at the ship, going aboard and—based on the relayed information that movement of the presumed explosives had begun—establishing a post where he could discretely observe both the freight ramp and the pedestrian gangway. "I was not advised that the two civilian women, Dr. Toulkes and Ms. Treacher, were also with the subjects," he said, with a pointed glance at Harris. "That being the case, when the two subjects B and C began to unload the presumed explosives for transfer to the ship, I turned my attention to their movements and left the observation post. I did not see Subject A, Daniel Oponuno, bring the women on board.

"By the time I was advised there might be hostages," Joe continued, "both Oponuno and the two subjects with the explosives were out of sight in the interior of the ship." This time, the glance at Harris was more like a glare, but Joe went on without a pause. "The identity of the hostages was still unknown at that time—or if known, was not conveyed to me!"

Kitty shivered. Of course, she and Angela *had* been hostages. But something about hearing it in Joe's impassive voice was extremely discomforting.

"My instructions at that point," he paused, looking at Al, who nodded, "were to return to the observation point and refocus on surveillance of Subjects B and C upon their exit from the ship via the freight ramp. It was my understanding that at least one additional member of the team was under observation elsewhere, but that pick-up on him, while expected within a short time, was not yet possible. In other words, it was still important not to spook the subjects prematurely.

"I reported when B and C left the ship, and I presume someone else took up that surveillance once they left the shipyard." Al again nodded. "However, shortly thereafter, I observed Oponuno also starting to leave the ship, unaccompanied."

"We assume that was because our fourth man, Subject D, phoned him, telling him agents were moving in on him, D," Al interjected. "We immediately picked up D, C, and B, as well as three previously unknown shipyard employees, texted by D at about this same time. But Oponuno did not leave the ship."

"No," Joe said, "he turned around partway down the gangway and came back up. It was obvious why. Somebody had called the cops. Half the NYPD was headed our way. You can see a long way from up on a dry-docked ship!"

"We're looking into that," Harris said smoothly.

"It was shortly after this that I received a call from Dr. Toulkes. She can tell you what she said." Joe looked at Kitty and winked. "It didn't make a whole lot of sense at the time."

Kitty lowered her brows at him. "Do you want me to tell my side of it now?" she asked.

"Go ahead," Harris said, and Al nodded.

"What I said to him was that I could lead him to where Dan had tied us up, in the compartment with the alleged bombs, but I could only do so from where I currently was phoning from." Kitty paused for breath. "In other words, I couldn't go to him; he had to locate and come to me!" So there.

"Good," Al said. "Now could you go back to how you came to be on the ship in the first place?"

"Weren't you guys watching Dan Oponuno?" Kitty stared, open-mouthed, at Al and then at Harris. "I would have supposed that would be the first thing you'd be doing, if you thought he was going to blow up the ship, not to mention maybe half of New York City if it turned out to be nuclear bombs!"

"We were watching his movements, but we didn't have close, on-the-ground surveillance at that time," Harris said. "So we'd like to hear from your viewpoint what happened, step by step. If you would be so good," he added politely.

"Well, you could have saved me a whole lot of trouble," Kitty began, feeling righteous indignation building, "if you had...."

"Kitty," Joe interrupted her gently. "I want to hear what happened. How did he get hold of you? How did you end up on that ship?"

"Sorry," Kitty said. "It's just that I really didn't want to ever see this guy again, and suddenly, right after you left, there he was! Out in front of the Cocoa Factory! He had a gun, and he...." She stopped, remembering vividly. "He threatened to shoot me in the back if I didn't go with him!"

Joe reached out protectively and drew her closer to him on the leather car seat. "It's okay," he said. "Just skim over the tough parts. They can ask for detail if they think they need it."

"Okay, well, he took me back to the place we had left the packages. Angela was there, and they tied the two of us together by the wrists, so the only way we could walk comfortably was to hold each other's hand. I suppose to make it look natural to anyone glancing at us. All of this was under threat of being shot, you understand." Kitty looked from Al to Harris and then to Joe. "I don't think I really had any choice," she said.

"Of course not," Joe said. "You did the only thing you could. So he took you and Angela on board. Not through the lower door, where they took the packages, but up the longer, steeper gangway?"

"Right," Kitty said, glad to focus on Joe rather than on the two agents. "And then he took us by what must have been a very round-about path, six decks lower, to this little room, with lots of pipes, where they had stored the bombs." She turned to Al. "Are we calling them bombs now? Or are they still 'suspected bombs'?"

"They are bombs," Al confirmed. "I'd appreciate your keeping that to yourselves, though." His glance took in Joe as well.

"And they are disarmed by now?"

"The remotely-triggered detonation mechanisms were easily dismantled," Al said.

"I'm not sure that means the same as disarmed," Kitty said.

Neither Al nor Harris seemed interested in commenting.

"Well, tell me this, then," Kitty said. "Did they have actual nuclear devices? Or not?"

"That's not something we can tell you," Al said, sounding apologetic.

"That's classified!" Harris snapped, at almost the same time.

"Please go ahead with your narrative, if you will," he continued more civilly.

"Okay. Well, you know we were tied up there, Angela chained to a pipe, and me—'I,' I guess I should say—I was tied to Angela. It didn't seem like a good idea to try to pull the pipe loose, because I thought it might be carrying electrical cables." She looked at Joe, hoping for his confirmation that she had done right by leaving Angela.

Joe nodded. "Right," he said.

"So, I slipped out of the rope around my wrist." She glanced at her hand, which was scratched and red, and beginning to turn purple across the knuckles. "And then I counted turns and staircases all the way up to an open deck. And that's where I could call Joe."

"When you were with Oponuno," Al asked, "did he say anything about what he had planned? Or about why?"

"Nothing about why," Kitty said. "Well, I guess he did say something about racist fascists," she recalled, "but nothing else about his motives. It sounded like he was hoping to wait until the ship was out in the main harbor, and blow it up with a whole lot of people on board. He really was acting very disturbed by that time! I thought he was losing it altogether." She shook her head and grimaced.

"And then" she continued, "he got a phone call, probably the one you were talking about, and he left, all of a sudden."

"So," Al said, "you slipped out of the rope, went back upstairs, and that was when your call to Joe's cellphone was able to go through. Right?"

"Right," Kitty said, "and then he came, and we went back down to get Angela."

"Joe?" Al signaled his wish that Joe pick up the story again.

"I found Angela Treacher secured by metal chain and padlocks to a vertical pipe that appeared to be electrical conduit," Joe said neutrally, neither his voice nor his face betraying any emotion as he described his daughter's situation. "As you know, I called for the disposal team, including someone with heavy cutting tools.

The cutting tools arrived first, and we removed the padlocks to release Ms. Treacher. Shortly thereafter, the disposal team arrived, and at that point the three of us—Ms. Treacher, Dr. Toulkes, and I—made our way topside.

"I turned custody of Ms. Angela Treacher over to her mother, Ann Wellington Treacher." Joe looked at Harris, as if expecting some comment. Kitty suppressed with some difficulty a temptation to ask Harris what kind of trouble Annie had caused for him.

When no comment was forthcoming, Joe continued. "As I was coming back up the gangway, Dr. Toulkes alerted me to the presence of Dan Oponuno on the deck. He dodged back into the interior of the ship, but as we moved to disembark, he fired at us, multiple rounds. We took evasive measures, during which time I fired three covering rounds. As soon as I ceased firing, he rushed us, firearm in hand. I fired a total of three additional rounds, all of which I believe hit Oponuno. Once he was down, I checked for a pulse to be certain whether medical assistance was appropriate. Determining it was not, I left the ship, taking Dr. Toulkes with me."

"Do you know how many rounds Oponuno fired at you?" Harris asked.

"Three," Joe said.

"Ms. Toulkes?" Harris inquired.

"Yes, I'd say three," Kitty answered. "But I just remembered something else that might be significant. When Dan first showed up there on the deck, while Joe was still down with Annie and Angela—well, anyway, Dan was some ways away from me, and he was trying to get me to keep quiet—he said he didn't expect to get off the ship alive, implying he'd just as soon shoot me as look at me. I took it he was trying to keep me from warning Joe. Well, it doesn't sound so important now that I say it...." She trailed off.

"We'll be glad for anything the subject said or did," Harris encouraged. "Is there anything else you can add or anything you saw differently from the time you called Mr. Treacher on the phone until you and he left the ship?"

"I don't think so," Kitty said, looking at Joe. "He told you every-thing." Suddenly very tired, she slumped back against the seat. "Can we go now?" she asked, trying not to sound as plaintive as she felt.

Harris and Al exchanged a glance. Harris nodded, and Al knocked on the glass separating the passenger compartment of the limo from the driver. In a few moments, the car pulled up in front of the Cocoa Factory and Kitty heard the locks on the doors snap open. Al opened the curbside door and slid out before offering a hand to Kitty. Harris followed Joe onto the sidewalk, and silently shook hands with both Kitty and Joe before climb-ing back into the car.

"Thank you very much, Kitty," Al said, shaking her hand warmly. "Your role in all this will never be publicly-known, but you have acted with great courage and intelligence. I appreciate what you have done!"

"If I'm right, the public will know as little as possible about the whole affair," Joe said, as Al turned to him.

"That's what the disinformation bureau is for," Al said with a half-smile. He offered his right hand to Joe. "Well done," he said softly, putting his left hand on Joe's forearm. "I'll be in touch soon, and maybe we can have a drink for old time's sake."

"Sounds good, so long as I'm buying," Joe said. "I don't want you thinking you're recruiting me back in."

Al smiled and turned to re-enter the car, which promptly drove away. Kitty and Joe walked together back into the court-yard of the Cocoa Factory. "You wouldn't, would you?" Kitty asked. "Go back in, I mean?"

"Have no plans to," Joe said. He caught Kitty's hand. "Would it make a difference to you if I did?" he said after a pause.

"I guess it would," Kitty said. She didn't say, of course it would, you crazy fool! How could you even consider such a thing? Are you trying to get yourself killed? She only squeezed his hand.

# CHAPTER 44

Once back in 5G, Kitty poured each of them a glass of water. Joe stood by the table and sipped his water, while Kitty curled up in her recliner with an audible sigh. "We should go over and tell Annie and Gretchen what's happened, I guess," Kitty said. "As much as we *can* tell, anyway."

"If they're even there," Joe said. "No telling where Annie ended up taking Angela, or when she will get away."

"You could call her," Kitty suggested.

"I think I'll call Gretchen instead," Joe said. "If Annie is in some kind of doctor meeting, I don't want to interrupt her." He pulled out his phone and sat down at the table. When he reached Gretchen, it became clear from his side of the conversation that she was somewhere other than 5F. Kitty listened, but couldn't figure out much more than that.

On hanging up, Joe explained that Annie was still working to get Angela admitted to a hospital, and Gretchen was with her. Angela was resisting hospitalization, but they had hopes of persuading her to check herself in. "Otherwise, we may have to go through an involuntary commitment procedure," Joe said, shaking his head.

"Oh, I hope not," Kitty said sympathetically. "That adversarial court process—we have to have it to protect individual freedom and all, but it can trash family relationships something awful!"

"And I'm not sure we know enough about where Angela has been recently to even make a good case for 'a danger to self or others.' It would have to be danger to self, of course, and unless she has told her mother how she got into this situation...I don't know. It would all depend on how a judge saw things."

"And on what Angela would say for herself," Kitty said. "I've been in these hearings. If the potential patient is articulate and has a reasonable story of what she's going to do next, most judges won't commit. Angela hardly said a word all the time I was with her. I assume that even when she's unmedicated, she's not usually like this?"

"No. Very down when she's in the depths of the depression phase. But not like this."

"I'd say she's in some kind of shock," Kitty said. "Probably from emotional and physical trauma. No telling how long she'd been —well—captive."

"I hope we can get her into care before she goes into a manic phase.," Joe said. "When she's manic, she can be completely unstoppable. A bit like her mother, only more so!" He smiled, shaking his head.

"Well, if I can help in any way, don't hesitate to say so. I'd be glad to tell a doctor or a judge what I saw, from a professional viewpoint. Just getting mixed up with Dan Oponuno was a danger to herself, no matter how it came about."

"You know, that's an idea," Joe said. "I'm going to call back and make that offer, if you're sure it's okay. It's also possible Angela would trust you enough to take your word about the need for a hospital, when she won't take Annie's. Or mine."

"I don't know that she'll respond to me," Kitty said, "but I'm happy to try."

When Joe broached the idea, Annie was eager for anything that might avoid a court hearing. Joe and Kitty drove directly to the hospital, where they found the three, Annie, Gretchen, and Angela, in a small room off the reception area.

Angela was more alert than she had been earlier. She greeted Kitty and seemed to welcome her presence. "Shall we talk, Angela?" Kitty asked.

Angela nodded.

"Shall we ask your parents to leave us for a little while?"

She nodded again.

Kitty made a discreet shooing motion, and the three others

slipped out without comment.

"So, what's going on, Angela? Why are you here?" Kitty said, pulling a straight chair near where Angela sat in the sort of the overstuffed chair hospital administrators seem to believe patients' families will find comfortable, if not comforting.

"You know how awful that man was."

Kitty nodded. "I do."

"He was awful to me for a long time. I think I'm not doing very well, and my mother thinks I need to be in the hospital."

"And what do you think?"

"I probably could use the rest. But I don't want to be locked up. I get antsy if I'm locked up," Angela said.

"I'm not sure this is the kind of hospital where you'd be locked up," Kitty said. "We can check on that, but I don't think it is."

"Well, if I can get some medicine that will make me feel better, I'd like that. I'm diagnosed bipolar. Do you know about those medicines?" Angela asked.

"No, not much. I know some of them make you feel better, and sometimes you feel worse before you feel better," Kitty said frankly. "Have you seen a doctor since you've been here?"

"No," Angela said. "I have to be admitted first, and I haven't let them do that."

"Would you like me to find out about the locking business? I could at least do that," Kitty offered. "Or, we could ask your dad to check it out, if you are comfortable with that."

"And you stay here with me?" Angela said.

"Right," Kitty said. "I can call your dad from here. I expect he can find out very quickly, if he doesn't already know the answer."

"Okay," Angela said. "Go ahead and call him."

Kitty did, and Joe was back to her in just a few minutes. "On a voluntary commitment to the psych ward here, there are no locked doors unless requested by the patient. And, we have contacted a doctor we trust, and she can be here in half an hour or less. You could tell Angie Dr. Mehra is on call."

Kitty relayed Joe's message.

Angela stood up. She cocked her head and looked at Kitty,

pursing her lips. Then she straightened and sighed. "Let's go, partner," she said, nodding her head and holding out her hand for Kitty to take.

The admittance process went smoothly, with Joe signing for financial responsibility, since Angela had no ID. "She's been on disability and has Medicaid," Annie whispered to Kitty, "but it may take a while to get documentation straightened out. I know the drill all too well."

By the time the hospital staff got Angela into a room, Dr. Mehra was ready to see her. "I think it's better if you all go home," she said. "I'll be in touch after we get her settled, probably this evening. Do I have a phone number?"

Annie gave the doctor her phone number, thanking her profusely.

"Thank me after Angela is doing better," the doctor cautioned. "I'll be in touch."

It was a subdued little group waiting for the elevator to the first floor. "That's the best we can do," Annie said as the door opened. "If anyone can get her straightened out for a while, it's Rashmi Mehra."

When they reached the front door of the hospital, Joe opened it for the women, and then, coming out behind them, offered to buy dinner for everyone. "How about Maggie Brown's?" he suggested. "We could leave the cars at home and walk up, unless someone has a better idea."

"Sounds great to me," Gretchen said.

"Good with me," Annie agreed.

"And you, Kitty? Are you up for this?"

"I'm fine. I'm tired, but it's been a long time, I think, since I had anything to eat. If I fall asleep over my plate, just prop me against the side of the booth until it's time to go home."

Over dinner in the crowded little neighborhood cafe, speaking quietly so as not to be overheard, Joe filled Annie and Gretchen in on what he and Kitty knew of Dan's movements, avoiding any reference to the possibility of nuclear disaster. Minimizing his own heroics and the danger to himself and Kitty, he let them know that Dan had precipitated his own death. "None of this will be on the news," he cautioned. "And we can't say anything outside this little circle."

"Good God!" Gretchen exclaimed. "You two, and Angela, could have been blown to the next borough!"

"I guess our binding worked, in the long run," Annie said. "Dan won't bring harm to anyone ever again, in this lifetime. But I can't believe he really was part of a terrorist organization. What could have made him hook up with people like that?"

"You probably have a better idea of that than anyone else," Joe said. "You talked with him more than any of the rest of us. Kitty said he was ranting about…."

"I think 'ranting' is the operative word," Kitty interrupted. "By the time he picked me up today, he was mostly not speaking very rationally. It's no use trying to figure out why somebody does things most of us would never consider doing. We simply cannot know! He was a very strange and troubled man, and we might as well leave it at that."

"And hope for a better life for him next time around," Gretchen said.

"You're such a good person," Annie said, putting her arm around her partner. "I'd still hex his butt if I had the chance!"

# CHAPTER 45

Back in 5G, Kitty set to work cleaning up the kitchen, where the would-be chicken-fried steaks had been sitting out all afternoon. She filled a plastic grocery bag with the mess, and tied the handles together. "I'm taking this out to the garbage," she told Joe. She walked down the hall to the garbage chute, pressed the bag into the scoop, and shook the handle until she felt the package drop. Heading back, she realized that, for the first time in days, she could feel safe in her own building.

When she came in the door of the apartment, Joe was on the phone. "I need to go now, Al," she heard him say, and he hung up soon after.

"That was Al," Joe said. "He wanted to meet me tomorrow. I put him off till next week. I don't want to think about his kind of work for a while."

"Did you learn any more about Dan and company?" Kitty asked.

"Not much," Joe said. "They did find where several of them had been staying, most recently in that place in Red Hook. And confirmed that Angela had been there, too. I'll pass that on to Dr. Mehra, in case it helps in some way. We have no way to know whether she was there under duress, or why she was with them to begin with. But she may tell a therapist, if they know to ask."

"Did you learn what happened with the bombs? I noticed neither Al nor Mr. Harris wanted to talk to me about that." Kitty moved some newspapers and sat down on the couch next to Joe.

"We are all quite safe now," he said, putting an arm around her. "Apparently disarming them was a relatively simple matter of deactivating radio receivers designed to accept a signal to detonate. Once that was done, they were harmless, or so I'm told."

"And were they nuclear?" Kitty asked.

"He wouldn't tell me, either," Joe said. "No need to know!"

"Well, I suppose since we didn't get blown up, we have no need to know now! But I sure would like to," Kitty said. "I've read that there are lots of nuclear devices unaccounted for, but you always hear that none have made their way into the hands of terrorists. I wonder if that's a bunch of bunk."

"Possibly," Joe said, "but it doesn't do any good to dwell on it."

"Can you tell me why there was the one odd-shaped package and then the two very heavy ones?" Kitty asked.

"No, not really, but the heavy ones had to be the bombs. The other one seemed to be full of just odds and ends."

"Oh, like the chain and padlocks he took out, when he wanted to fasten Angela to the pole," Kitty said. "The security guard at the ship thought we were there to film something, so maybe that package was a sort of decoy. We'll just have to wonder, I guess."

"Yes, because these guys are probably not going to be tried for terrorism. There will be some other charges and a very quiet trial." Joe said.

"That's why the public never knows whether we've had no further big attacks since 9/11 because there are no new terrorist plots or because we are being heroically saved, over and over again, by our brave and clever G-men."

"And women," Joe added. "You were wonderful today, you know."

"I didn't feel very wonderful—just scared almost witless." Kitty turned and looked at Joe. "You were the wonderful one, you know."

"Not too bad for an old guy, I guess," Joe said. "Al seems ready to put me back to work."

"Oh, I hope not," Kitty said. "If there's any chance of his succeeding, I hope you'll give me the opportunity to talk you out of it."

"I'm not sure talk is what would be needed," Joe said. "There might be other, more persuasive means." He nuzzled her hair, and, when she didn't object, went on to nibble on an ear.

Kitty shivered pleasurably.

"Shall I go on?" Joe asked between nibbles.

"I think so, yes," Kitty said.

"Don't feel bad if we need to stop," Joe said, moving down toward her collarbone. "I'm not seventeen."

"No blue balls?" Kitty giggled.

"Ummft," replied Joe, addressing a button on Kitty's shirt with tongue and teeth. After several seconds, he lifted his head. "I used to be able to do that," he said, sounding disgusted.

"They don't make buttonholes like they used to?" Kitty suggested.

"Right," he agreed. "Mind if I use my fingers?"

"Please do," Kitty said. "I'm almost sure I'm good. The magic worked, or something. Or do you suppose—"

Joe cut her off by covering her lips with his. "Less talk, more kissing," he said, coming up for air a few moments later. "Okay?"

"Okay by me," Kitty said, turning sideways for a better angle. "Here, let me help you with those buttons."

Some time later, Kitty, lying on the bed with her head on Joe's chest, stretched and yawned. "You know, I've completely blown my usual routine this week. What with getting attacked and kidnapped and almost blown up, I haven't worked out, I haven't seen any clients since last Friday. I've turned into a real slug!"

"I've got mail piling up at home, my training partners are going to think I've dropped dead, and I'm all out of clean socks," Joe contributed. "So what are we going to do about it?"

"I should call in to work tomorrow morning, or maybe just go in. Probably just go." Kitty propped herself up on an elbow.

"Are you sure you're up to it?" Joe asked. "You certainly have earned some time off." He rolled onto his side to look at Kitty, concern showing on his sun-weathered face.

Kitty ran a finger across his cheekbones, smoothing the wrinkles at the corners of his eyes. "I'm really okay," she said. "You've just proven I have no lasting abuse-related trauma. And

I shouldn't continue to push my share of the work off on my colleagues. It's getting far enough into the semester the kids are starting to really feel the pressure to perform, and some of them will need us."

"Well, then, you go to work and I'll go home, go the gym, and do some laundry," Joe said.

"And then what?" Kitty asked.

"That's the sixty-four dollar question," Joe replied. "Do you want to talk about it now?"

"If not now, then when?" Kitty said.

"Yep."

"You could come back here with your clean socks and we could talk then," Kitty suggested.

"What time will you be home tomorrow?" Joe wanted to know.

"Probably around 4:00, unless something pops up. I could let you know, if that works for you," Kitty said.

"Okay, I'll plan to be here no later than 4:00, with clean socks on," Joe said, reaching for her. "More snuggling now," he said, mock authoritarian, "and then sleep?"

"Yep," Kitty said, wriggling closer.

# CHAPTER 46

Kitty got out of bed carefully the next morning, hoping not to wake Joe, who was snoring quietly. After a quick shower, she breakfasted on fruit and yogurt, leaving half a pot of coffee. She set a mug and plate on the table, along with butter, jam, and bread for toast. She hunted for and found a box of lightly-scented notecards, one of which she propped against the coffee-pot, after writing Joe a note: "Plenty of coffee, and help yourself to anything else you want to eat. Call me if you like, any time, and I will call you back. Love, Kitty."

On the bus on the way downtown, she pondered the "Love" part. If, in fact, the whole thing with Joe had been an artifact of the extreme stress of the past ten days, she might regret that. But, oh, well, she finally decided, if he doesn't feel the same, then he doesn't. It won't be the first time!

Arriving at City Tech, she found herself quickly absorbed back into the routine. Alicia had a full schedule for her, including a couple of calls to return from colleagues, each of whom had taken some of her appointments and wanted to talk over specific situations.

Her last appointment of the day was with Serena Ramirez, who came in with a look more suited to her name than Kitty had seen on the girl's face for a while. "Hello, Serena," Kitty greeted her.

"Hello, Mrs. Toulkes," Serena said, setting down her bookbag and perching on the upholstered bench that was one of several choices of seating for clients in the small office. "How are you? I heard you were sick."

"No, not sick," Kitty said, surprised. "Just had some, uh, personal business. But it's all taken care of now." Thank goodness, it really is! she thought. "And how are you?"

"I'm much better," Serena said. "I'm not sure quite why, because, like, nothing has changed except the study time—which is good, really good. Don't think I am not grateful. It really gives me some good space every day."

"But nothing's changed at home," Kitty said with just the slightest note of question in her voice. She looked at Serena.

"I hooked into an Al-Anon group, like you said," Serena went on. "I've been to a couple of meetings, and I'm bringing Mama next week. It does seem kinda good to hear other people talk about what's going on with them and their families. I think, well, maybe that's why I'm feeling better. It seems like maybe there might be some hope."

"And your mama is willing to come?"

"She says she's game for anything that might help Manuel."

"And do you think this is going to help?" Kitty inquired.

"Too soon to tell," Serena said. "But he is the one who has to want to change. Mama and I can't do it for him."

She's already getting some of the philosophy, then, Kitty thought. So that probably helps explain the greater serenity compared with a week ago.

"Did you have some other things you wanted to talk about today?"

"Well, I've been wondering," Serena started, "am I being awfully selfish, wanting to go to school and everything, when the rest of the family is working so hard? Mama has worn herself out, worn her heart out, really. And maybe if Manny didn't have to work all the time he wouldn't be wanting to take drugs...."

"What do you think, Serena?" Kitty asked. "Does it feel like selfishness, or more like taking care of yourself?"

"Well, I know all the arguments, how if one person gets an education she can help the rest of the family more. And I believe it, I really do, but I also know Mama could sure use me at home. So I guess I just wonder. What do you think?" She looked at Kitty, her big dark eyes full of questions.

"I can't tell you, Serena. You can maybe guess I'd always be on the side of more education, but that's because that was *my* choice. You're the one to decide for you."

"Did your parents want you to go to school?" Serena asked.

"They did," Kitty said. "They didn't have much money, but they always planned for me to go to college. And I know it was hard for them. They had to do without things they could have used so my brother and I could stay in school. And looking back, I know they were very proud of us when we did well."

"Well, I know Mama—and Papa, too—want me staying in school. They always say, 'We came here so you kids could have a better life!' We get tired of hearing it, but I know it's true."

Kitty nodded, sitting silently.

"So I guess I've answered my own question," the girl said finally. "I may not be able to help anybody else now, but I have to try my darnedest to keep my grades up and stay in school.

"And now I better get going, if I want to do that." She stood up. "Thanks, Mrs. T. I always feel better talking to you. I'll make another appointment on my way out!" And she headed for the door.

Kitty stood up. "So long, Serena! Have a good weekend!"

Kitty looked at the clock over the door. Just after 3:00. She had plenty of time to catch the bus and be home before 4:00. As she closed things up in the office, her thoughts were already straying to the discussion she knew was coming

As the bus bumped and swayed over the streets toward the Cocoa Factory, Kitty found herself wishing they didn't need to have "the talk." Of course, Joe couldn't keep staying on a "temporary" basis, comfortable as that had been. The whole purpose of his being in 5G was now gone. But when she imagined trying to sort out with Joe what their relationship might be going forward, she realized her greatest fear was that it would turn into "just friends," or even worse in her view, "friends with benefits." Moreover, talking about such things was never easy, and coming off such a high-tension situation wasn't going to make it any easier.

When the bus passed the Sands Street gate to the Navy Yard, Kitty couldn't resist peering into the Yard. She was mildly surprised to see a couple of police cars parked just inside the gate. Made sense that they would be still processing scenes of crime, she supposed. What would happen with the ship's timetable, now that presumably both the deck and the interior room were locations of serious interest to whoever was in charge of investigating? That might be deduced from the shipping news, eventually, if anyone cared enough to look it up.

But matters of deeper curiosity would probably never be satisfied, neither regarding Daniel Oponuno's real story nor on the final disposition of the presumed co-conspirators. If lucky, she might find out a little more about Angela's involvement with Dan and the rest of the terrorists, but that almost certainly would not be available from Joe's contacts. And it would be confidential from Angela's side, so unless Angela herself chose to share with her parents—and they with Kitty—she'd learn nothing.

Arriving across the street from the Cocoa Factory, Kitty thought she might never look at the building in quite the same way. She walked past the spot where Dan had picked her up at gunpoint, and felt a sizzle of fear up her spine. But Dan was dead, and the whole thing was over, she told herself. Nothing left but the memories, and those would fade with time. Now she needed to get ready for the discussion with Joe.

He was already there when she arrived. The keys to the building and 5G he had been carrying for ten days were on the table, along with cookies from the deli on a plate and an empty mug. "For whatever you like to drink at this time of day," he said. "I'm having tea, and the watert is hot, if you want."

"Did you finish off the coffee this morning?" Kitty asked.

"I think there might be just a little left," Joe said apologetically.

"A little is all I should have this late," Kitty said, pouring the remaining half-cup into her mug and setting it in the microwave.

She got the cream out and lifted a couple of paper napkins from the holder on the counter. When the coffee was hot, she added cream and sat down across the table from Joe.

He took a sip of tea. "Did you have a good day?" he asked.

"Busy. But good," Kitty said. "It felt good to have a normal work day for a change." She smiled across at him. "And you? How was your day?"

"Oh, good, I guess, on balance. The workout was good, although I found I had a few sore spots I hadn't noticed before."

"Derring-do will get you that way, I expect," Kitty commented.

"Missing too many days working out doesn't help, either," Joe said. "And there was nothing in the mail that was too awfully scary."

"Are you like me in recent years—when the only important things that come in the mail are either bills or bad news? I almost hate picking up my mail."

"Exactly," Joe said. "I sometimes wish my social security came in a check, just to have something to look forward to." He chuckled.

Kitty sipped her warmed-over drink. "Not bad for 8-hour coffee," she murmured.

There was a long pause.

Finally, Joe said, "Well, I guess we have to talk."

"I guess we do," Kitty said reluctantly.

"I thought I'd better give you back your keys. That is, unless...." He left it hanging.

"Well, I don't know," Kitty said. "What do you think, going forward?"

"You first," Joe said, a twinkle coming into his voice as he smiled mischievously. "Ladies first, don't you know?"

"Okay," Kitty said, smiling and then taking a deep breath. "Hm...well, I've really enjoyed our time together. I've enjoyed just having you around. I've enjoyed—well, I hope that's obvious —the times in bed."

Joe nodded encouragement.

"But I suppose neither of us knows, really, how much of what has happened between us is due to the extreme situation we've been in." Kitty stopped and looked at her coffee cup, willing Joe to say something, anything.

"We really don't know each other very well," Joe said. "Or, at least, we don't know very much about each other, and we don't know how we would be under more ordinary circumstances." He looked at his own hands, and then abruptly reached across the table to take one of Kitty's. "But I have to say, Kitty, I really don't want to lose we've had, or what I think we might have."

"Neither do I, Joe," Kitty said earnestly. "I'm afraid to say how good I think it could possibly be." She fell silent again, feeling she had probably once again gone too far.

"So how do we move forward from here?" Joe summarized.

"I suppose there is no reason, anymore, for you to have to crash here. I'm sure it's uncomfortable and inconvenient for you," Kitty said.

"Well, and you'd probably like to have your place to yourself again," Joe added.

"Not especially," Kitty acknowledged. "But yes, maybe, in a way."

"So, I should pack up my things, and leave the keys," Joe said.

"About the keys...." Kitty hesitated.

"Yes?"

"Well, I don't necessarily need them back right now."

"It sort of comes down to, how much do you want me to be around, and under what conditions," Joe said. "Your place is bigger than mine, or at least seems roomier, but you'd be welcome to come over there, too."

"It would be maybe kind of weird to go on dates, after what we've been through. But... maybe that's what we need to do?" Kitty said.

"Remember 'going steady'?'" Joe asked.

"Oh, like when you never had to worry about having a date for Saturday night, or for any big event coming up!" Kitty said. "And you hung around together in the halls between classes, making moon eyes."

"Right. I could get into making moon eyes," Joe laughed. "Anyway, so maybe we should go steady for a while. What do you think?"

"We could sort of see what each other's life is like when we aren't saving the world," Kitty said.

Joe raised his eyebrows.

"Oh!"

"Yeah," Joe said, "that was my job for many years. And I am going to meet with Al next week."

"Well, that's just one of the things we have to take into consideration, along with the fact that I have to watch Masterpiece Mystery every single Sunday night," Kitty said, much more lightly than she was feeling.

Joe laughed again. "You're a trooper, my dear! I just feel like I must not let you get away. We'd both have to compromise, but I'm certainly ready to try."

"Me, too, Joe," Kitty said.

"So, will you go steady with me?" he asked, looking very solemn. "I don't have a class ring with me at the moment, for you to wear on a chain around your neck, but I'm sure I can dig one up if you'd like to make it really official.

"I will go steady with you," Kitty said, matching his serious tone. "For a while, at least, until we begin to see how things are working out. And I don't have to have your class ring as a pledge."

"So, what about the keys, then?" Joe asked. "Do I keep them, or give them back?"

"Why don't you keep them for now," Kitty said. "I trust you not to just show up in my apartment without notice, unless it's an emergency—which I think we've had enough of for a while, please God. And it might be convenient from time to time for you to have a set. Does that sound right to you?"

"Does," Joe said. "And now, are we through talking? Because I have something else."

"Typical man!" Kitty snorted. "Just when the talk is getting good, he's off to do something else. But yes, I think we're through talking, for now." She smiled softly at him, hoping he didn't take her outburst seriously.

"Good," Joe said, seeming unfazed. "So, I have a little something for you. Maybe make up for the lack of a class ring." He pulled a jeweler's box out of his pocket and handed it across the table to Kitty.

"What..?" Kitty opened the box and looked down at a pair of delicate silver bangles.

"I noticed you liked the dangly ones the FBI gave you, so I thought maybe you'd like these," Joe said.

"They're beautiful!" Kitty said, lifting one out of the box.

"They aren't diamonds," Joe said, "but maybe one of these days...."

Kitty removed one of the earrings she was wearing and slipped the new one in its place. "You like?" she asked, turning her head and arching her neck to show it off.

"Looks lovely on you," Joe said. "Here, may I help with the other one?" He stood and came around the table. He lifted the other silver earring out of the box while Kitty took off the old one and laid it on the table. Joe gently took Kitty's earlobe and slipped the silver wire through. Then he let his hand slide down Kitty's neck in a caress, and bent to kiss the top of her head.

"Thank you, Joe," Kitty said, "for everything."

"Thank you, dear Kitty," Joe replied. "I'm glad to have you in my life."

## THE END

# ACKNOWLEDGEMENT

I acknowledge with great gratitude all those who have supported and encouraged me in this endeavor:

Lynn and Jay, first readers once again, and lights in my life always;

Cynthia Griffiths Akagi, Cathy Minarik, Jim Lukens, Pat Hyland, and Duane Herrmann, for early reading and critiques;

Rhoda Wiseman for invaluable detailed editing and positive thinking;

Anne Lolley for brave challenges beyond the call of duty;

Jan Stotts for hand-holding at a critical time;

NaNoWriMo, without which this book would never have been written, especially Lissa Staley, Miranda Erickson, and the Topeka Shawnee County Public Library, for hosting the Topeka NaNoWriMo community;

Google Maps and ye olde internet, for saving hundreds of hours of research and travel time by providing quick access to science, history, and geography;

And other friends and family who have kept asking, kindly, about progress. If I've failed to mention anyone else who read and commented, please know I thank you, too.

# ABOUT THE AUTHOR

## M. J. Van Buren

M. J. Van Buren has lived most of her adult life around the edges of the Flint Hills, with intermittent sojourns in more exotic places such as Brooklyn, New York, and Auckland, New Zealand. She now lives in Topeka, Kansas, with her husband and rather too many houseplants.

Made in the USA
Middletown, DE
18 July 2022

69417092R00154